UPON THE SHOULDERS OF VENGEANCE
THE JOURNEY TO ARMAGEDDON

JAMES McCANN

To Sherry Martin, keep your imagination alive in the Spirit!

James McCann

PublishAmerica

Baltimore

First printing

ISBN: 1-59286-681-6
PUBLISHED BY PUBLISHAMERICA, LLLP
www.publishamerica.com
Baltimore

Printed in the United States of America

Dedications

I would like to dedicate this book to
my Uncle Les
who once told me a story about a wizard,
a quest and some very cool creatures.

Prologue

One … two … three … the young boy counted the pebbles at his feet. He loved to count. He had loved it from the day his Master had taught him. "Master." Not "Father," or "Dad," but "Master." He wondered how much life he had missed by not having a family.

Early dawn encased the world, chasing away shadows with shards of yellow, orange and red. Beside the courtyard stood a castle, its eight turrets spanning more than twice the circumference of the city. Walls, so white they reflected the dawn as looking glasses, connected the towers creating an illusion that the city went on for ever. And directly opposite two giant doors that led into the castle, cut into the stone perimeter around the city, two enormous iron gates brandished a shingle made of brass and gold that read, "City Of Gods."

Silence. In a city modeled as Heaven on Earth, all was silence. The boy closed his eyes. Breathed steadily. And only after his heart beat in a rhythmic pattern did he look upon two men who held him captive. They wore cotton breaches, tunics and leather gloves. Black hoods covered their faces. But what identified them was the insignia on their chests, that of a white robed, winged fellow brandishing a flaming sword. Another man stood a few paces away on the edge of a crowd that circled them. He was a large brute with heavy leather armor and a tall pike-ax held by two gloved hands.

One man bound the prisoner's shackles while the other readied a vat of poison. Angels these were not. When their captive was secured to a wooden pole in the center of a courtyard, the man binding him stood by the armored guard as the other took out a whip from the bucket of poison. The captive breathed the fresh morning dew, stifled a sneeze from the humid air that

5

tickled his nose, and accepted this fragrance as that of Death.

A smile broke over his lips as slowly as the light broke over the Earth; in the same fashion that despondence had replaced his soul. A rooster crowed. The boy wondered why it bothered. Hauldine, the City Of Gods, did not need its call to wake. People had gathered for this spectacle long before the moon had descended, and still now they came leaving farms, mines, shops and homes. He wondered if these mortal gods took fascination in his death, or sadistic pleasure in his torture. Never as much as now did he feel blessed to be a foreigner. One who knew the Creation.

Why had he come to this blasted country? He had survived well enough on his own, living hour to hour, day to day, and month to month. Now his life crept minute by minute. He took one final look at the sunrise and prayed this would be the last he ever saw. He had nothing left for Mankind to steal, and now that he had come face to face with Lady Death he did so without regret.

What about....

He tugged on the thick leather straps that bound his wrists to the pole. Clenching his fists he glared at the growing crowd, stared at the products of a world gone insane, and wondered why the Creation had spared him from becoming a product of it. At least he could take pleasure in that. *Maybe they'll write it on my grave marker,* he thought.

Shouts. Cries of judgment. Those were the songs that ended the silence. Like a choir in a theater the people chanted their offering be given to the Life Force. He scanned the crowd for one last taste of compassion before he left this world. But he found none. They stared at him with anger, glad for his punishment. His example.

And then....

An old man stood alone in the crowd. Tall and wiry, he wore a long, grey beard that nearly covered the breast of his flowing white robe. Thin wire-framed spectacles sat upon his flat, red nose, and he walked with the aid of a cane carved from a tree's root. He seemed, by a tear that had escaped an eye only to have been caught within a deep wrinkle, to have pity. Not compassion, but pity. This world, the boy had come to learn, knew nothing of pity.

One ... Two ... The whip's lash descended without warning. Its sting startled him, and when he cried out the crowd cheered with sadistic harmony. Gritting his teeth he vowed that would be their final victory. Listening to the poison-laced whip cut air he recited a prayer to the Creation. But he wondered if It still held Power; for if it did, then It had forsaken him long ago.

Ten ... Twelve ... The horse's whip lashed over his naked back. It made cuts that drank deeply of the venom, a poison that raced through him like a Voice preaching to a zealous following. A sermon that was a prelude to his fall. A summons he wanted to obey. But the crowd's eager faces compelled him to stand. He would die, but in his death those who had come to watch would find no satisfaction.

A rock struck him hard on his calf, and though he buckled he stood. Another struck his arm, his back, and suddenly sharp pains struck throughout his body. He heard, from somewhere in his mind, the executioner yell for them to stop, but that had only made them come faster. He practiced his Master's teaching on pain control to stop himself from falling. He took his mind away from the moment, away from the venomous whip, away from the hurtling rocks, and focused on a young child in the crowd.

She was no more than seven, eight years his junior. Her long black, and rather unkempt hair seemed strange against her light complexion. She wore rough cloth common to Hauldinian peasantry, and as all young gods did she wore them with pride. But it wasn't her outward appearance that attracted his attention, but a light he'd seen deep in her emerald eyes. A sparkle which gave him hope that perhaps the children might repair what their elders were quickly eroding.

Twenty ... Twenty-one ... The poison seeped into his blood. He again looked toward the little girl for strength. Looked in time to witness the rock her parents had coaxed her to throw. It had come nowhere near him, but it still served as a grim reminder that children were what they lived. The girl who had become his sole hope was now one of his condemners. *This whole world is damned,* he thought.

Thirty ... Thirty-four ... The poison seeped through his body as thick as blood, but, unlike blood, the venom made his whole body burn. He remembered the animals he had seen the Umbrians roast alive and felt sorrow for them. Those beasts had succumbed easily to their fate. He looked at the blurry faces and vowed to take away their satisfaction. He stood. He showed them the one thing they had never witnessed: perseverance! Grinding his teeth he prayed for strength. To outlive their condemnation.

But as the executioner's whip reached forty he fell, hearing the crowd cheer.

"Accurse you all!" he whispered

Chapter One

Darkness. An enclosed room with no light, void of sound. In the center an ivory shaft broke through the floor rising to the vast ceiling. It pierced through the blackness, yet emitted no light.

Kimbra could not tell if she was alone. All she could see was the ivory shaft. Then sound; the pound of a drum that was at first faint but intensified until it thundered. It was metallic, like someone slamming chains against a concrete floor though the surface she was on was soft like glass. She listened harder and realized each time the sound thundered it made her sorrowful. A sadness unlike any she had experienced before.

Placing one palm against the floor she crawled toward the sphere. With each step her hands and knees melted slightly into the glass until she slid inside grooves, and with each push her movements brought her farther, not nearer the object.

"What's happening?" she screamed.

A laugh, a low rumble embedded within the pounding metal drum, filled the room.

A cackle that embodied fear.

"Terrell?" Kimbra whispered … and then a face, shrouded within a black cowl, stared at her from within the shard.

Kimbra screamed.

And woke.

A surrounding curtain laced with white silk filtered out the morning sun. Kimbra lay on her large straw bed, sunken into the mattress, with the surrounding curtain as a barrier from that outer world in which she knew she must enter. Roosters called the morning, birds sang welcome to the dawn, but it was the rustle from her caged ferret that drowned out those melodies.

"Damn you Mask," she grumbled, wiping her eyes and breathing hard from the nightmare. She pushed her raven locks away from her face with her fingers. Beside the bed, just outside the curtain, was a wooden bureau carved by Elvin craftsmen. It had three drawers beneath a heavy mirror, the bottom filled with linen, the middle with hosiery and the top held a Oui-ja, Tarot and Lots. She sat up, reaching through the curtain for the drawer where she grabbed the stone-filled leather pouch. The hide was cool, and closing her eyes she whispered a mantra before casting from it Lots. When she peered at the stones, her lips pursed and her heart beat fast. She saw nothing. They foretold nothing. The princess sighed, and brushed a golden lock away from her eyes. The ferret started biting its jail, an attempt to bend the bars that held it captive, but she who reigned over it as a god had her own imprisonment to overcome.

Kimbra took out the Cards, undid their binding, careful not to anger Them, and placed the first face down before her. The second face up to Its right. Death. Just as in her dream, the Life Force warned her of Death. Or was it a promise?

The next she placed above the one that lay face down, and saw Life. Death and Life; End and Beginning; Omega and Alpha. Holding her breath Kimbra overturned the one that lay face down. The Thief. What could that mean? The heiress considered taking out the Board, but didn't like speaking with It unless there was complete silence. And she certainly didn't have that with that damn weasel.

The chamber door opened and closed, followed by the fall of steady footsteps. When they stopped, the metal cage creaked and the ferret quieted. A man said, "Good morning Mask."

Kimbra pulled away the drapes from around her and met Sir Theomund's kind gaze with a smile that said "Good-morning" without words. She stretched, but found that her spiritual barrier still lay untouched. And that meant a day that promised the same old boring routines; the sun shone into the room as usual, the birds sang their same songs. The princess wondered what the point was in being a god if it meant no adventure.

Sunlight burst through the only window, a large concave opal-shape with a cushioned seat on its bottom. The floor was cold stone, save for the foot of her bed where the carcass of a mighty bear lay for eternity. Kimbra rose from her soft mattress and scanned the room for Mask. It sat on the window-seat on the outer side of the curtain, as usual, staring outside at the world it once knew. She slid onto the floor, finding her slippers where her hand maiden had left them, and walked over to them. In practiced routine she drew the drapes and leaned against the seat. As the heiress stroked the animal's sable fur it sighed, glancing at her with opal eyes as she had whenever the Spirits denied what she wanted. If only it paid her attention, Kimbra might have grown to love it as much as she had thought she did when her brother had captured it as a kit. But it was more interested in what it had lost than what it had gained. The princess looked outside to see what it stared at.

Beyond the city walls lay forest-covered rolling hills and a winding river that cut the woodlands in two. That was the freedom her brother had embraced. How long had it been since he ran away? He lived the adventure of which she dreamed. But a cry, a single shriek from the courtyard, brought her attention to the spectacle that her ferret had found so mesmerizing.

A large crowd gathered around the executioner's pole where a prisoner was bound, one with strange skin that shone ebony beneath the cobalt horizon; darker even than when she had accidentally sun-burned last year. He was not old, her age most definitely. Kimbra wondered what circumstance had led to this offender's fate as it was very uncommon to execute such healthy males. Normally soldiers took them as protégé's to enter into the Competition, a brutal sport that pitted one man against another to the death. Her father's idea to rid the country of its growing debt. Prisoners cost too much, executions cost too much. Why simply kill someone when you can charge the populace a fee to watch? His speeches all sounded the same.

The crack from the whip resounded, and her royal highness wondered how the captive could stand the pain. He stood tall, neither flinching nor pleading for mercy. When finally he did cry Mask flinched, but, just as she was about to comfort the animal, Sir Theomund scooped it to the ground and took the ferret's place on the seat.

"What a bloodthirsty crowd. A tragedy," he said, breaking the silence between them.

"That it is. What did he do?"

"I watched his trial yesterday. He stole some bread. For it, he has been sentenced to The Death."

Kimbra smiled, and nearly pirouetted when her prison walls came crashing down. Life. Death. *Thief.* "Sir Theomund?"

"Yea, Kimbra."

"Would you do anything for me?"

The tall knight smiled like a proud father at a new-born. "You know I would."

"Then save him. Take him as your protégé."

Sir Theomund's eyes drew tight and his lips curled in a moustache-hidden smile. He stroked her cheek and focused on the prisoner.

"Please?" she implored with a tone usually reserved for asking her father to buy her something.

"Perhaps this can be my amends."

"Pardon?" she asked, pretending not to have heard the words uttered so lightly they nearly slipped by her.

He hid himself behind his bright smile. "Nothing. As you wish, I shall save him."

The Cards and Lots hadn't lied, nor had they given her bad omens. The Spirits had brought her a thief to end her boredom, and begin a life that would excite her. This day may have begun routinely, but the end looked adventurous!

Kimbra scooped Mask back into his cage, ignoring the weasel as it clawed at its prison.

Forty … Forty-one … after fifty lashes the execution stopped. The prisoner, held against the pole by leather-bound wrists, did not move. His ebony skin appeared milky and he shivered. Tears streamed down swollen cheeks through tightly closed eyes, and a beat like a mighty drum pounded against his temples. The young man's heart thundered as if it might leap from his chest onto the pebbles below. He loosened his clenched fists.

Sweat beaded on the vagabond's fevered brow, blood dripped from his wounds, and Death had whispered a vow that next time He would triumph. The captive wondered what torture his captors planned for him next, and why they had not just let him perish. Perhaps they planned to throw him in a ring with animals, or maybe they had looked at his long, unkempt silver hair and figured him a savage. Or, most likely, they thought their prisoner a demon because of his silvery eyes. Just as the South Umbrians had.

The captive did not open his eyes to see who had rescued him. The deep voice that had ordered the torture to end next told the executioners to depart. The respect borne in the tone was one too polite for a General, and yet the obedience by the guards was of those inferior to a Noble. Footsteps meandered around the pole, like a customer sizing up a slab of meat in a butchery, until they stopped close at his side.

The prisoner forced his eyes to open a crack just in time to see the knight glance toward the castle and sigh. He was a Noble; his bright, colorful, tailored and very expensive garments significant of such a high rank. But, as the executioners gathered the last of their tools, he asked, not ordered, them to disperse the crowd. The people hissed their displeasure as soldiers acted quickly to get them moving.

"To what, indeed, is this world coming?" the nobleman whispered as the spectators departed one by one.

"I could tell you what this world is coming to," the prisoner whispered under his breath.

He opened his eyes wide, tried to brush off the grogginess from the poison, and stared at the blood on the ground that dripped from his naked back. He cringed as feeling returned like nails hammered into a board; first in his wrists, next in his entire being. Blood trickled from his nose, and as his head slowly cleared he realized that The Death was not going to continue. With all the might he had left the vagabond clenched every working muscle taught, grunted loudly, and forced himself to stand. The added pressure against his wrists forced them to bleed more freely, and, as he turned to look at the man who had saved him, his strength faltered. The poison was strong.

The convict leaned on the binding ropes for support and ignored the pain as the leather straps cut deeper. The knight again looked over his shoulder at the castle.

As the sands of defeat washed away in an ocean of victory, the bound boy refused to revel in it. Such victories were small, and when painted on the tapestry of life they hardly showed. He took a good look at the man who had come to change his fate, but mostly he focused on the sword.

"Why'd they stop? That couldn't have been a hundred. They said a hundred," he forced himself to laugh, "and that I'd be dead by twenty."

"It's up to you whether or not the beatings stop, my lad."

"What d'you mean?"

"I 'ave an offer for you. You see, I need a protégé to honor me in the Competition. You, apparently, 'ave a dire need for an 'ome with plenty of food and warmth."

"Competition? I'd be a slave, and nothing more."

"You are in Hauldine. A country where men are gods! Die in the ring for my glory, and in your next life you may be born one of us!"

"From the Creation we came, to the Creation we return."

"I'll give you more time to weigh your options, if you wish." The knight turned to let him be.

The boy spit. The world spun a little, and the sun coated him like coal. He closed his eyes and considered what brought him here, and how it had felt to have been so lost for so long. Perhaps all he needed was time. Time to figure out why he had not died when he had banged, not knocked, on Death's door.

"Sir!" the prisoner called, choking on blood.

"Yea."

"You got your protégé."

"Swell! What are you called?" he said and smiled, walking back to him. A pause. "I know not, Sir."

The knight laughed. "'ow can you not know your own name?"

The vagabond thought it over and realized how foolish he must have sounded. Clearing his throat he said, "I've been on my own for several years. After not being called upon for that long, you don't tend to need a title."

"Then that should be first." He raised an eyebrow and laughed.

"Call me 'Forest.'" He took note of the confused expression given him and at first he thought to ignore it. But he added: "The soldiers caught me in the woods. During the trial, if you could call it that, they called me 'Forest Boy.' I'm not going by 'boy.'"

"All right then. You can call me Sir Theomund … no specific reason."

As the knight untied him they both took note of the small crowd who had refused to leave. Times like this Forest hated the human race. All the undeserved anger they thrust at him was apparent in all … except one. Again he noticed the elder who had watched, smiled, and appeared pleased by the foiled execution.

Chapter Two

A rooster crowed a new day, sending Forest bolt upright in his bed. A pain, as if he had been lying on a bed of nails, shot through his back out his chest. He gasped for air, uncertain if he was still alive. But the heat from a shard of sun that penetrated through a window told him he was. He threw his feet over the bed and climbed from the deep impression his body had cast into the straw mattress. The stone floor was cold, but what had felt strange was that it was a ground which men had made. There was no connection to the Creation in this prison. And what a strange prison this was. The room was round with ceilings higher than two giants standing shoulder to shoulder. There was a straw bed and wooden chest and no room for anything else. It was cool and drafty, the air whistled in through cracks in the stone walls. There were no bars on the window, or any shackles along the walls.

As the vagabond examined his surroundings, the past day's events returned to him. He sighed. It still hurt to move, like his blood was filled with tiny pins. Bending down onto one knee he examined the chest, running a hand along the intricate carving of a winged fellow holding a flaming sword. Forest opened the chest but found nothing inside. He strolled to the window. Below was a courtyard, where young men trained for war. All manners were practiced: sword, javelin, bow, fists and wrestling. All manners, but his.

A knock pounded on his door and he swirled to face it. His knees staggered, feet shoulder width apart, and fists up and tight. He had almost yelled, but instinct was suppressed by reality. He was not in danger. If Hauldine had wanted him dead they would not have forgiven his sentence. Forest approached the door. He reached out for the handle and a second, louder knock sent him back at the ready. He opened the door, prepared for anything, only to find a young man, probably the same age as himself, towering over him. Forest relaxed; his instincts returned to their lair like a lion to its den.

The stranger smiled, though most of his teeth were missing and the rest were yellow or rotted. Someone had shaved his head nearly to its scalp, and Forest moved aside to allow him passage. This fellow wore cotton pumpkin breeches secured to his thin waist by a rope, and a sleeveless tunic crafted from heavy black wool.

"Hey," the stranger said in a high-pitched voice. "I am called Vinn."

Forest's eyes narrowed, and his muscles drew taught. "I am Forest."

"That I know. Sir Theomund asked me to give you these," Vinn handed him a bundle of new clothes, "be it truth that you survived the Death?" he added without pause.

"Aye, it be truth." The vagabond took the bundle and slowly backed away from Vinn. "What be your business with me?"

"Your master asked me to aid you in feeling welcome. 'Tis not as simple a task as I'd thought."

Forest closed his eyes and sighed. "Forgive me, I am a little displaced."

"As was I, but you will learn to love this life. Hauldinians do not consider us as civilized, but should you survive the Training they will honor you as one."

"And who be your people?" Forest started to undress and don the new garments.

"My father be Hauldinian, but me mother was a Protecteurian slave. I have fought in two Competitions."

"This be a strange place."

"And where do you call home?"

Forest tied his breeches and sighed. "I call no place home."

Vinn held out his hand and said, "That part of your life is ended. Call this home, and me your friend."

Forest took the hand and smiled.

"I imagine you be hungry."

"Aye, that I am."

"When was the last meal you had?"

"T'was a loaf of bread ... and ... I did not get the chance to enjoy it."

Kimbra's throne was furnished with a plush velvet cushion, a high back gold-plated with arm rests carved from maple that looked like a snake starting at her left hand and winding its way to her right. The princess sat upon it wearing a long violet dress low-cut with her corset done as tight as it could go. A veil the same color as her dress adorned her face, leaving only her eyes visible. To her left stood Sir Aethelbeorn, head of Military. He was a rather large, orderly fellow who believed in following protocol to the letter. It was his view that in doing so he assured himself the place of prince in his next life. To Kimbra's right stood Sir Theomund leaning against the throne. His world seemed made up of ambiguous morals that assured him the place of popper in his next life.

The training arena below was filled with men and boys of all ages. In its center was a pit 30 feet by 30 feet where challenges were met long before the actual Games, often for the amusement of the trainers. This was a chance for anyone who had broken the law to improve their karma for the next life, though more often than not dying in training and never seeing a Competition. There was but one door below that led to the turret housing the protégés, and a spiral staircase that led to the balcony where she sat. Atop her perch was a door leading into the main castle, the latter two entryways were heavily guarded. Kimbra noticed that Ulger fought especially brutal today, as he did every time she came to watch. His willingness to please her made her happy, and she hoped his karma was strengthened by such respect. But Ulger wasn't the reason why she sat amidst her father's military Generals. She waited for Sir Theomund's new apprentice.

Sir Aethelbeorn had trained Ulger, the top warrior, in a hard wrestling technique. In the pit Ulger eased through every match and displayed his victim to the princess before ending the man's life. Kimbra reveled in such a display of respect.

As Forest followed Vinn into the courtyard, after having feasted like a king, he watched all the boys and men practicing. Some were old, others were just children. But all had that look of empty desire to win at all cost, a look Forest had seen but once in his life. A look that haunted him in his nightmares.

"By our own Divinity!" Vinn exclaimed, though Forest hadn't heard. "Look at the balcony, in the centre with the head military men. The princess be here to watch! This be a real honor."

Forest ignored Vinn as he spied the first sight of the Creation. In the center where a large, brutish man beat another to death, was a pit with a dirt floor. Even from this distance he could feel his god calling to him, beckoning him to fellowship. Vinn was still talking, "Don't be too embarrassed if you don't know nothing. Sir Theomund will teach you..." Vinn noticed Forest staring at the pit, and Ulger staring back. "Are you mad? Ulger has won fifteen Renrock Festivals!"

Forest ignored the warning and walked to the center pit. Kneeling he placed his palms against the dirt and felt a rush of excitement tingle within his veins. Two younger boys scurried past him into the fighting arena and carried out the loser. Ulger ignored the praise that echoed in the courtyard, and walked toward the boy who dared approach the ring. Ulger loomed over Forest, dwarfing him with his incredible bulk. He asked, without breaking his smile, "Have at you?"

Forest ignored the attempt to intimidate him and said, "I just want to fellowship with my god."

Ulger laughed. "He wants to fellowship with his god!" Kneeling he glared at Forest, "You cannot come near this ring unless you are willing to fight me."

Forest fell into the splits, keeping his palms pressed against the dirt. "Any rules?"

Ulger turned and walked to his corner. "None. Except you clean your own blood, if I let you live."

Forest saw a pink silk scarf float down to land at Ulger's feet. The brute bent down and picked it up, both of them looking up at the balcony. All the men were laughing, except Sir Theomund who stood waving his arms that this would not continue. The scarf had come from the princess who, though veiled, smiled with her eyes.

Accurse them all, Forest thought as he breathed steady and concentrated only on his adversary. In his mind the whole world was baked in silence. He saw only Ulger, felt only that presence. Without warning Ulger rose and charged. Forest remained stationary, without so much as blinking an eye. Ulger rushed. The crowd's cheers rose. And, just when they thought it too late for Forest to respond, he flipped to his feet and kicked Ulger in the face. The brute fell back in shock, and the onlookers hushed with surprise.

Ulger staggered from the impact. His nose bled. Forest followed with an axe kick to the forehead, and a foot sweep to bring him down. He turned toward the crowd, smiled, and waited for his praise.

The crowd chanted. Chanted him to finish his opponent. The newcomer reached down and grabbed Ulger by his tunic. The fallen warrior breathed hard and perspiration dripped from his matted hair. Forest raised his open palm in a death-strike, prayed to the Creation to give him honor, but, when he brought his palm down, he did so only in a gesture of friendship.

The large warrior took the friendly hand, and swung the vagabond until he had him in a half-nelson. The spectators switched to cries of, "Ulger! Finish him!"

Ulger whispered, "Nobody makes a fool out of me! Especially in front of the princess!"

Forest gasped. His head pounded from the loss of oxygen, but he refused to panic. He let himself collapse. He let himself lose consciousness. Ulger tasted victory, released his limp victim, and raised his arms in triumph. The brute reveled in the crowd's cheer.

Sir Theomund cursed Vinn for not stopping Forest, but the vagabond rose, threw a back kick into Ulger's unprotected gut, then jumped, spun, and landed another axe kick on his head! This time hard enough to knock him out cold. The masses again cheered for him to finish his opponent, but he did nothing more than say, "Accurse this world." Then to his fallen adversary: "Clean your own blood, remember?"

Vinn ran to his new friend, uncertain what to say. "Can you teach me that?"

"What you need to learn, I have not to teach."

"What's the matter with you? You were victorious!"

"Victorious? This is just more of what's out there!" Forest pointed toward the outside world.

"This will keep you alive."

"We are dead in this prison," Forest said softly, as though he were lost in a trance. Vinn shook his head and walked away.

"He fights like the Renrock clan. The forgotten ways," Sir Theomund whispered as he watched the other young men back away from his protégé.

"That is impossible," said Sir Aethelbeorn.

"'Tis wonderful!" the princess leaned over the rail, adjusting her veil over her face and waving to grab the vagabond's attention.

The Infantry General leaned over to his peer. "What be his name?"

"Forest...."

"Forester? As in the Prophet?"

"Nay. Forest, as in a lot of trees." Sir Theomund smiled and leaned back in his chair.

"He will be our undoing! What should the resident aliens think, should they learn that a man called 'Forest' who fights as a Renrock but is not

Hauldinian...."

"Are you afraid that they will think themselves equal?"

"We are the descendants of the prophet Forester Renrock. We alone have the destiny to become gods! Look at him. Look at him and remember our Holy Book the BOR WA one thirty-eight. 'I'm only five-eight, a fairly slim (but muscular) build, and I have a military-style box cut. No hippie-style, long hair with beads for THIS guy! I also have shining silver hair, and a sort'a grey eyes.'"

"If we are the only gods, then no matter what the commoners think so it will be. You, Sir, should relax."

"And you should have let the boy die." Sir Aethelbeorn narrowed his eyes and pursed his lips. His face turned hard as stone and his gaze colder than a North Umbrian winter. "You will find yourself working in a blacksmithy come your next life."

Forest sighed as, once more, he found himself alone in a strange land. He examined the people around him and looked up at Sir Theomund to see his new master arguing with another General. He wondered foremost if they fought over putting their new champion back to the Whipping, and secondly which, if either, was on his side. It would seem that Sir Theomund was unlike most men, that perhaps he suffered from an acute sense of compassion, but Forest was not a fool. He knew that, probably sooner than later, even this kind knight would have to give up on a vagabond that is damned.

The princess stood against the railing, waving for his attention. When she achieved it, she removed one of her gloves and let it fall to the grass below. Her highness then returned to her seat. Forest walked to the glove and knelt beside it. He knew this was an honor of which other apprentices dreamed, but to him it was the same as shackles. The vagabond sighed and picked up the garment.

There was but one staircase, built separately from the main structure, which wound tightly to the upper level. Positioned at its base was a fully armored guard, who rested his hand easily on the hilt of his sword. As Forest approached the soldier glared from beneath the brim of his helmet.

"I would like very much to speak with Sir Theomund," the vagabond said.

The soldier did not respond.

"I say again, I would like very much to speak with Sir Theomund."

The guard did not even look at him.

Forest walked so that he could meet the man eye to eye. Then he snarled, "Perhaps you would hear better if I kicked this helmet from your head."

The guard, at first, began to draw his weapon, but when he saw attendants escorting Ulger away on a stretcher he chose not to. He turned and hurried up the staircase.

As the soldier rounded the top, his cheeks burned and his temples throbbed. He opened his mouth to speak, but no words came out. Sir Aethelbeorn rose and stood chest to chest with the man.

"You had better have a good reason for leaving your post."

"I ... I have a message for Sir Theomund," to him only: "Sir, your protégé wishes an audience."

The Infantry General pushed against his inferior and growled, "When did you become a messenger? And since when did it become policy for a protégé to summon a master? AND...."

Sir Theomund placed a hand on his comrade's shoulder. To the soldier he said, "Thank you," and to his associate: "Be easy on him. Perhaps in his next life, should he also be a smith, it will be him in charge of crafting your King's armor. You would not wish him to do a poor job should he recall this life during a dream." The bodyguard laughed as he went down the stairwell.

Forest questioned his wisdom, and wondered if he had made a mistake. *Will they send me back to the whipping?* But holding strong to courage, he decided that, whatever happened, even if they did send him back to die, he would accept it all in stride. After a moment or two, a decade it seemed, Sir Theomund finally arrived.

"Indeed a splendid fight." His new master beamed under his thick moustache.

"Thank you, Sir ... I need a favor from you. I don't mean to sound ungrateful. I know you've done lots for me already ... but I need my property that I had before I was ... well...."

"Caught? I'll see that it's in your chambers by the next morning."

"That would be very kind."

Sir Theomund was staring at him, as though mesmerized. Forest chose to ignore the look, and turned to walk away. He could see in his master's eyes a brainstorm, and honestly didn't like it. Then he heard the knight call, "Forest!," and a flush of confusion filled his blood. *This has all been a cruel joke! Damn this world!*

"Aye Sir?" He did not turn around.

"I could get your things now if you'd like, but I would need you to do a small favor for me."

Forest accepted that, this time, his judgment of the knight had been wrong. "Anything Sir."

"Stay with the princess, and wait for me until I return. You have demonstrated that you are capable of keeping her safe, and, for some reason, I trust you."

"Aye. Where is she?"

"Come with me."

Kimbra heard Sir Theomund climbing the stairs, accompanied by someone else. She blushed, and wrapped her veil over her cheeks so that only her eyes showed. Her palms perspired, her heart fluctuated, and she was glad to have covered her smile. The princess hoped everyone would assume she wore the veil to be proper. Sir Theomund introduced the vagabond to her first, then to the others. Kimbra studied him, seeing beneath his silvery gaze the same need of freedom as the Prince had borne. She knew exactly how she'd use the stranger.

Sir Theomund told Forest that, when the princess felt ready, he'd accompany her to her chambers. The Bodyguard smiled and left. Forest kept the silent bond intact by placing his hands behind his back and standing at attention. Not something he did intentionally, but the one named Sir Athelbeorn was staring at him. He looked deep into the girl's eyes and saw in them a smile like that of Tully, his childhood friend, whenever he thought on things certain to land them in trouble. Forest did not wish to stir any more trouble than he already had.

"At ease boy!" Sir Athelbeorn stared relentlessly. "Nothing's going to happen here. Have a seat."

The vagabond reluctantly took a seat, Sir Theomund's chair it was marked, and nodded to the Infantry General. Sir Aethelbeorn stared for what had become an eternity, and Forest hoped his master would hurry back.

Sir Athelbeorn cleared his hoarse throat. "You fought admirably."

"Thank you."

"Where did you learn those techniques? Not even Hauldinians train in Renrock-style combat. How could...."

"I studied under a master in the Coastal Mountains." Forest wondered at what point his trial had resumed.

"Now I remember you." Sir Athelbeorn smiled wide. "I saw your trial. Still sticking to that story, eh? Well let me tell you...."

Without realizing it, Forest rolled his eyes and looked pleadingly at the princess. In no way did he wish to listen to the General's advice on how to "better win popularity."

"Sir Aethelbeorn," the princess whined, "I am afraid that I have suddenly become ill. Please forgive me, but I must steal Forest away." Then to the vagabond: "Would you please escort me back to my chambers?"

The Infantry General crossed his arms and gave a "Humph!"

Forest sighed and said, "Aye. That I gladly would."

As Forest escorted the princess through the drafty maze-like corridors, he knew she wasn't truly sick. He felt strangely grateful toward her for lying; as finding himself stuck listening to Sir Aethelbeorn was the last thing in the world he wanted, or deserved. Forest looked out the corner of his eye, and caught her staring at him. Her majestic blue eyes looked like the sky, reminding him of the Creation. How blessed she must be to live in such beauty with such beauty.

"Don't worry about Sir Aethelbeorn. He's just upset that you beat Ulger."

Forest smiled. "Thank you."

"For what?"

"For getting me out of there. I don't feel comfortable around people in authority."

Her eyes narrowed. Clearing her throat she said, very regally, "I'm in authority. I'm nearly a god."

"Be that the truth, you helped me out."

She smiled, stopped in front of a door, opened it, and entered. Once inside her quarters, Forest saw the caged ferret. The animal leapt from the rags it used as bedding, and scrambled to the bars. Clawing against the metal floor and biting the rods it made tiny grunts that sounded like "Dook! Dook!"

The vagabond walked to the prison and held his palm against the bars. Mask stood on its hind legs, placed its chest against the metal, and slid down as if in defeat. Kimbra sat on her window-ledge and warned, "Mask bites. Well, except my bodyguard."

"You leave him in this prison?"

"Prison? It's just an animal. I found it when it was a kit, and I thought it would be fun to play with. But all it does is stare out the window."

"It stares at its home," Forest whispered as he opened the lid. The weasel

23

leapt onto the vagabond's arm as it was scooped up, and then climbed to sit upon its host's shoulder.

"You are awful," the princess said and smiled.

"Where I come from, man and beast are the same. We are all a part of the Creation."

The princess looked out the window and giggled. "By that idea, eating an animal would be cannibalism."

"That it is."

Kimbra brushed her hand through her hair, and slowly turned to look at him. "What do you eat then?"

The vagabond grabbed a chair and leaned it in a manner that would afford him sight of every possible entrance. One, to be exact. Then, quite by accident, he discreetly eyed her, and even from beneath her veil Forest saw that she blushed. "We eat plants."

"Is it that way with everyone who lives in the Coastal Mountains, or be you unique?"

"Aye. 'Tis that way with us all."

"I heard the Krim 'Tiak laid waste the land. They never leave survivors."

"They didn't have a choice this time." Forest smiled, but his voice resounded with ice.

"Come on. You can tell me the truth."

The young man looked out the window, and recalled a teaching of his Master's. Something constantly reiterated to him. "A world of such deceit, will never know truth."

He took his vision from the window, and again looked at the princess. Her eyes had grown wide, and the corners of her veil widened as if she were smiling. Forest felt like an exhibit for show, and returning his vision back to the outside world he hoped for no more questions.

"'ave you been on many adventures?" she inquired.

He closed his eyes, and thought. His life hardly seemed adventurous, but he supposed to a royal princess that is just what it might have been. He opened his eyes and nodded. "Aye that I have. But..." He wondered if he should continue. "I would not consider them 'adventurous.' I would call them survival, and nothing more."

"Tell me one. A story, I mean."

"All right then. Imagine your whole world destroyed, and your loved ones slain. Picture living alone without shelter in rain and snow and in times when you thought you were going to starve. That, is what adventure is."

The princess shrank from his harsh words.

A knock on the wooden door interrupted their conversation. Sir Theomund entered, looked at them curiously, and handed Forest a wide sheath as well as a large tattered knapsack.

Forest placed it on the chair, and smiled. He grasped the sheath, his muscles pressing out their thin, definitive form, and closed his eyes. Memories swept over him as he slowly drew the item. It was nothing but a flail: two black wooden poles held together by a short chain. A simple farmer's tool used for beating wheat to make flour. Forest chuckled.

"Where I come from it's called nunchuka. My master taught me to use it as a weapon."

"Why?" his new master asked. "Why not a sword?"

"He did teach me swordplay. But in my katas he also taught me to us this because," he paused, and flushed red. When he spoke again, he mumbled, "People get nervous seeing someone walk around with a sword. No one gets nervous of a farm tool."

Forest avoided making eye contact with either of them. "Is there a place where I could go, to be alone? A place with lots of oak trees?"

Sir Theomund cleared his throat before giving directions to City Park. Had the vagabond looked at him, he would have seen genuine pride. Or, had Forest looked at the princess, he might have seen the devious machine in her eyes again at work....

Mask watched the shorter Slave Owner leave, dashing all his hopes that freedom had come at last. But before it left, the man turned, winked, and flashed a devious smile. The ferret wondered what it might mean. Pacing back and forth he waited for the other two Slave Owners to depart. The taller one did at last, and then the woman changed her attire before opening a section in the wall. Lighting a torch she slipped into the hidden passage and ... left the door open!

The perfect escape was right outside his cage, and Mask could do nothing about it. Blood rushed to his head as he paced back and forth, tossing the blanket in his cage with his snout. Then he leapt at the bars, grabbed them in his mouth and squeezed. The bars would not budge, but ... that's when he noticed.

He glanced up and slowly released his grip from the prison. Stretching, he pushed with his nose against the door, and it opened. The latch was never secured! The shorter Slave Owner ... no, the Freedom Giver this one would be named, had left the prison insecure! Mask jumped, grabbed the edge of the cage, and hoisted himself up.

"Dook! Dook!" he shouted for joy, leaping to the floor and scurrying for the door.

The park always seemed brimming with songbirds and tiny scavenging animals, like a mythical miniature woodland. But as the princess walked down the dark, narrow path, she noticed for the first time the shadows. Kimbra stopped, and wondered what it could be that had changed ... what it was that had transformed the grounds into such a terrible place. Why would Sir Theomund have taken her here so often?

As Kimbra meandered through the paths, the heiress reached out with her hand to feel a presence that was not there. Normally she would only walk with her bodyguard, but now she explored ... the world ... alone. Today marked her first excursion into the park without anyone to protect her. This marked her first excursion anywhere alone! Kimbra stopped again to breathe deep, filling her lungs with freedom, and that scent battled her fears into submission. As the princess exhaled the sweet air, she understood her brother's affection for the life he had stolen.

Adrenaline soared throughout her heated veins as Kimbra prayed this would not be her sole chance for adventure. Opening her eyes she strolled until so much time had passed that trees blocked all view of the city. That was when she found the vagabond. Kimbra stared as she quietly hid behind bushes.

He was no longer wearing the uniform required of apprentices: his strange dress looked like battle-fatigue, but not from any war fought by her kingdom. He had a hard, studded leather vest the color of midnight with sleeves that brandished silver metal plates. Black gloves covered his hands up until the second knuckle on each finger, where a single metal spike sparkled. The breaches also looked like soft leather, and hard leather plates held in place by straps protected his thighs and shins. He wore no boots. His feet were brown with milky-shaded soles. They were muddy, but the color, like that on his face, penetrated into his skin.

Kimbra had never seen anyone like him. His strange uniform made her frightful of who he might truly be. She examined him further, finding more intrigue in his helmet. It was bowl shaped with a mail neck-guard that hung loose to his shoulders covering his hair save for the silver strands that fell over his eyes. On its brim was the most dominant figure: a circle cut in half like two tear drops, one crimson the other a shade darker than midnight.

The insignia was not one that Kimbra recognized from her schooling. Nor had she seen it before on her travels. She did recall one similar to it from her theology class, but that was from the Book of Renrock:

"…The headband, my grandfather's, has a yin-yang embroidered on it to symbolize the balance of good and evil…."

Forest knelt beside an oak tree and looked as if he might be praying. She tried to listen … But in the middle of his plea she felt a hand grab her from behind…. Kimbra turned, and screamed!

Once Forest had changed into his own attire, he had set out to venture into the park. Getting out of the castle hadn't been as difficult as he had feared. Those who thought themselves gods rarely took the time to look down upon those over which they ruled. Nor do they pay much attention to what goes on in the shadows, a place where Forest had lived since the destruction of his village.

Blue Jays flew in the trees and sparrows called out to one another. Squirrels busied themselves gathering nuts and hawks busied themselves gathering squirrels. The Creation was alive and powerful here, and pressing his hands over the roots of an ancient Oak he whispered, "From the Creation we were born, to the Creation we shall return.

"I'm lost. Lost in a world where I know nothing. So far every kingdom I've gone to has done the same. Whipped me. I have found a place that wishes to befriend me, but they are so unlike anything I know. Bring me strength, courage, perseverance…"

The woods echoed from a high pitched scream. Forest woke from his meditation, jumped to his feet, drew his nunchuka and sprang headstrong into the shrubbery. After a short run, he found just what he had expected. A large brute trying to take advantage of an innocent girl. *Accurse this world,* he thought.

Forest cleared his throat loudly to let his presence be known.

The man turned and saw the young warrior. He drew a knife and held the lethal blade against the girl's throat. "Back! Or I kill 'er!"

Forest spun his nunchuka in such awe inspiring technique that the vile stranger couldn't help but shake in fear. Neither the man nor the girl had ever seen anyone wield a farm tool with such deadly skill, and they had no doubt how well this warrior might fare in battle. Forest stared beneath his helmet's brim in challenge.

"Go ahead and kill her. It's you I'm after," Forest snarled, not at all certain who was more surprised: the man or the girl.

"What?" the two asked in unison.

"You heard me. I protect the Creation, not its intruders."

The man's eyes darted back and forth, his face beaded with perspiration, and the hand grasping the lethal knife shook visibly. Forest had created a stalemate and needed to think of a way out fast. "I'll cut you a deal," the vagabond regretted his choice of words. He folded his arms and relaxed his weapon. "The woman is a good one. She's clean and healthy. Give her to me for my own pleasure, and I'll let you live."

Kimbra couldn't believe what was happening! Her whole royal life flashed before her eyes as the man's grip grew tighter, and the cold steel against her tender throat made a tiny cut. But her captor threw her to the ground and fled into the woods.

She looked up at Forest. Fear gripped her like a powerful spell, refusing to relinquish its reigns. As he approached she wondered what he intended to do. He extended his hand, and the princess did not know if she should take it. Had this vagabond been serious of trading that man's life in exchange for her virtue, and did he now intend to seize his prize?

Forest kept his hand extended and met her eyes. He bent down onto one knee, turned his hand over to offer only his palm, and smiled as if to tell her she only need take it if she so desired. Closing his eyes he sighed.

He again looked past the luminous trees as if into the ether. When he returned his gaze to her, he did so like Mask. Bound and trapped in a cage. But the vagabond's confinement was the ground and sky. The bars that trapped him, far as she could tell, were the people who damned him.

"You need not fear me," he said. "I am here to offer only my aid. Nothing more."

"But if you are so inclined to aid me, why then 'ave you set that beast free?"

Forest returned his gaze to the sky, and again closed his eyes as though to ward off their eternity. A smile crossed his lips, but no happiness radiated from it. His mind appeared transfixed in another place, perhaps even another time.

"My lady, I gave him my word. If a man cannot be trusted enough to keep his word, then he is not much of a man."

He stood and turned his back to her. His shoulders slumped beneath the bulk of his cumbersome armor, and again he sighed. He walked toward the castle, and Kimbra rose to catch him.

"Please Sir," she said sweetly, noting his surprise. "I have never before met a man of such honor. Please don't leave on my account."

He turned to her, smiled, and reached out to brush her long hair away form her face. "You have yet to meet a man of such honor."

Forest stopped talking. She looked quizzical as he stared into her curious eyes. He again reached out to brush away her long golden locks.

"Perhaps, you would care to sit with me awhile?"

"Indeed I would."

Forest walked toward an open space, past benches that dotted the walkways, to sit in the tall grass. He leaned on his elbows, stretched his limber muscles, and appeared quite comfortable in the wild. Kimbra looked at him strangely, as if she'd never sat in the grass before.

"Where do you live?" she blurted as though his scrutiny was something dangerous.

"The Coastal Mountains."

"'Tis a long way away. You must have had many adventures."

He looked away from her and replied, "Those who have peace, desire adventure. Those with adventure, desire peace." He returned his gaze to her, and watched her lips break into a wide smile.

She asked, "Why do you keep looking at me like that?"

"Forgive me. It's your eyes. I can't determine their color."

As kimbra giggled, a sound of relief emanated from their chimes. "I can tell that your eyes are silver."

"'Tis not only your eyes' color ... you look quite familiar."

Kimbra suddenly rose. "I must depart."

"Don't leave. It's not late."

"I have chores...."

"Do you come here often? Will I see you again?"

Kimbra smiled, and her eyes drew tight until they had become narrow slits. With a voice nearly impassive she asked, "Will you be staying in the city long?"

"I know not."

"Meet me here on the morrow?"

Forest relaxed and let go a laugh. "I don't even know what you be called."

She turned pale, and her eyes darted around. A long pause followed, and then: "Selandria. I am called Selandria." Another long pause: "And you?"

"Forest."

She extended her hand and said, "'Tis nice to meet you, Forest of the Coastal Mountains."

"Thank you," he responded in kind, shaking her hand. "Would you like me to see you home?"

"Yea," she replied. Her mouth dropped and she bit her lower lip. In a voice that sounded fearful she said, "But you can't. My father ... he'd be angry."

"Then I shall say farewell now, and count the moments until next we meet." Forest rose and wandered off, aimlessly at first, but whenever he glanced back she saw by his eyes that he did walk with purpose. But it was not a purpose known to Hauldine, and of what it might be she vowed to learn. Kimbra sighed. Now all she had to do was sneak back into the castle through the secret passages, and hope no one had noticed her missing.

Chapter Three

As night crept over Hauldine, there was nothing peaceful about the calm chill air as, outside the keep, the stars bloomed forth. Forest turned from his window, left that thought to rest, and looked once more at the butterfly knife resting on his mattress. The metal handle was closed around its razor sharp blade, and a leather sheath with an opening to hook onto his waist-rope lay beside it. He could only assume that Sir Theomund had left it for him. Undoubtedly as a prelude to the training ahead. He hadn't touched the weapon since he had arrived back in his room hours ago, nor did he intend to in the hours ahead. His nunchuka lay beside the instrument of death.

Forest returned his gaze back to Nature's map, and saw an emblazoned ruby star shooting across the sky. It made him think about his home; of the freedom the supernal mountains offered, and of what it now felt to have that taken away. But just as bouts of enslavement had displaced freedom, so had friendship displaced loneliness. The Krim 'Tiak had displaced his village's peace with carnage, in turn poisoning his love for life with a distaste for humanity. The thought of the slaughter tainted his heart a murky shade of crimson; displacing his complacency with anger.

He recalled watching the Enemy drag Tully to his death, kicking and screaming. But at least he had fought. Forest felt like his lost honor had taken hope as its traveling companion. He closed his eyes to ward off the thoughts brought on by the black sky, and fondly remembered what it had been to live in a place where everyone knew your name. Where your name meant something. Your given name. Not some made up alias to shield yourself from other's damnation, when the damnation you needed to escape most was that which was created by yourself. Would this peace have to end, in order for his vengeance to be gained?

"My life is cursed," he whispered.

The sound of laughter cawing throughout the stone halls disrupted his warring thoughts. That gaiety led him to believe that it was meant to mock someone, and he wondered whom. He took it as a welcome escape and left his thoughts alone to fight their war without him; hoping they might find a truce. But a truce, so should they find one, would never last.

He didn't walk far when he came upon two boys, neither of whom he recognized. Forest smiled, but his presence ceased their laughter.

"You're the new guy who beat up Ulger?" A taller one inquired.

"Aye."

"Was our noise bothering you?"

"Nay. But it did make me curious." Forest noticed the shorter, unfamiliar boy hiding a letter. "Was it something you were reading?"

The two boys looked at each other in silent conspiracy. Their eyes darted, their faces contorted, and, as the air of fear swept away in a calm tide, an unspoken confidence between the trio was left in its wake.

The unfamiliar one held up the letter. "This 'as been scouring the countryside for someone named, 'Marcus the Avenger'! Can you believe that name?"

Blood that had found complacency in Forest's veins rose, and festered until it boiled so vigorously that his heart thundered. The sound of that name sparked curiosity into raging fires, but the jest these two had found in a title meant for honor had turned that flame into a blaze. Forest grabbed the letter from the messenger, and held it out before them in challenge. Neither boy moved as the lost fear returned to claim triumph. The vagabond stormed back to his room, wielding mastery over that fear.

Forest felt caged like an animal in a holding cell on the brink of execution.

He broke the Krim 'Tiak's familiar seal and shook, for he knew if a letter could have found him so could his enemy. But his conscience reasoned that if they knew his whereabouts, they would have already killed him. No way could they know, and every breath he took gave proof of that.

Every labored, cursed breath.

Forest, I hope you receive this soon after it is written, and that it finds you well. The Krim 'Tiak did not lay waste our land, but have been defeated by our strong spirit! I implore you to return home, we

need your aid in restoring our village to its greatness.
   Your heart is in the Creation,
   Tully.

He walked to his window, again looked to the stars, but now saw them for the brilliance and beauty they endowed. Especially, he thought as he scanned the night sky, the one that would lead him back to his village. Excitement escaped his lungs in a voracious cry as his honor at last knitted its wound closed. He wondered how many years had passed since the letter's original circulation, and knew that his friend must surely think him dead. He rushed to prepare for his journey, glad for having secured a friendship as true as Tully's. He did not even consider why it had been sealed with a symbol of evil.

But what of Sir Theomund? As he packed his few worldly possessions he thought about how much he owed that man. He owed him his life and to turn from that debt would mean his honor's death. Responsibility forbade him from just up and leaving.

Sir Theomund guarded the entrance to the princess's chamber against intruders as he had every night. Normally, strict discipline did not allow his mind to wander, but tonight thoughts of his protégé invaded his discipline. He wondered what plan the Life Force had for their union, and he pondered how much time Fate intended to give them. His thoughts roamed as strict discipline yielded to curiosity. Yet, somewhere in his subconscious, his instincts remained on guard. Another sense, a higher spiritual instinct, heard footsteps. He calmly placed his hand over the hilt of his sword, completely unaware that he had done so. He glanced at the time candle he had lit earlier and saw that the night was mature enough for everyone in this section of the castle to have found sleep. Access was strictly guarded against unauthorized persons.

Who then, could it be?

As the shadow walked into the dimly lit corridor Sir Theomund saw Forest. A smile appeared, but hidden beneath was a curiosity of what was so important that his protégé would sneak in at this late hour. The look on Forest's face, even before he spoke, answered all questions.

"Sir," the protégé spoke freely, even against his master's frown. "I have urgent news. My village has been recovered, and my people need me."

"You know I can't let you go." Sir Theomund wondered how he'd ever stop him.

"I know. But what if I promise to return? I just need time to help my village."

Sir Theomund knew if he let Forest leave, he would never see him again. But could he detain him? Would it not darken his karma to do so? He had heard the promise "I'll return" before, in a dream the night the Prince had run away. Certainly Forest was as crafty as the King's son, and similar treachery would ensue. The vagabond clearly had a higher spiritual path and, perhaps in a life before, he might have been a suitable apprentice to a humble knight. Certainly this was not the case in this life. Sir Theomund made his decision.

"All right. I won't stand in your way. But no one else must know about this! Leave tonight, secretly, and may we meet again in the Last Stages."

The look of gratitude in Forest's eyes was enough to tell the knight he knew the degree of sacrifice this meant. In this life chances were good that Sir Theomund might lose his rank, possibly his life, but what Forest didn't know was the aid this would give his karma. Such a selfless deed might possibly give him the King's position in his next existence.

"I'll be back. Give me two weeks, and I'll return."

"You want me to deem you a liar? Lad, I know you'll never return, and I shan't lie to my lord. Be off with you, and worry not of my repercussion."

"Thank you," Forest whispered.

Sir Theomund watched after the boy as he disappeared into the shadows, glad to have had the chance to know him.

"Take care of yourself. Use your karma intelligently."

Chapter Four

Kimbra, concealed in the darkness by the town gates, pulled her thick cloak tighter around herself to ward off the brisk autumn air. Hard boots clopped against the cobblestone, and praying that the shadows hid her well she held her breath. This was only the first patrol made by the city's guards, and Kimbra didn't want it to be the last she saw. The soldier walked near her, examined the gates, looked about himself, stifled a yawn, and continued his patrol. A heavy sigh escaped her, and a bout of worry replaced the air.

What if she had missed Forest? What if he had taken another route? What if he'd already left? Moments earlier, after hearing the conversation between Sir Theomund and his apprentice, she had changed into her disguise. She thought about that dialogue now, wondering if Forest's claims had been honest when he had said he was going to the Coastal Mountains. The tone in his voice had sounded familiar, and she'd thought back to the conversation that had taken place between her father and brother.

Then a silhouette of a man appeared under the gates. It didn't notice her. Kimbra stepped into the torch-light to make her presence known, and as the shadow turned to her the embers from the fires shone over his face, reflecting brilliantly in his silvery eyes. Kimbra thought hard to recall what name she had given him earlier, knowing she must remember to go by it while with him. She also wondered, only for a moment, if Sir Theomund and her father would miss her as much as they did Terrell.

The shadow spoke, "Why be you here?"

"I was taking a stroll. I saw you departing."

"Kind of late, wouldn't you say?"

"Yea, that it is ... so why are you about?"

"I'm leaving." He looked up into the stars, his eyes looking as a black cat's caught in the light. "I'm going home."

"Let me accompany you!"

A spark flickered in his eyes, not from the torches but from a smile that grew over his spirit. As he slipped out from the darkness into the amber glow, she met his smile with one of her own. He reached out with a gloved hand and gently stroked her cheek.

"I'm going alone."

The princess opened her mouth as if to speak, but chose against it when Forest looked at his feet. He bent onto one knee and said, "And who do we have here?"

A long, slender ferret, one with a mask like a bandit, clung to his leg. The vagabond offered it his forearm and it scurried onto his shoulder. As he stood he met the weasel eye to silvery eye, and it licked his nose. "Do you also wish an escape from entrapment?"

Mask scurried into Forest's hood, curling into a ball and falling asleep.

Kimbra asked, "Would you take a beast with you and not I?"

"The animal flees for freedom, but what of you? What would your father think should I steal you from him?"

"I was leaving anyway." She thought fast, showing him her traveling pack.

"Why?" he asked, his eyes again like a cat's.

"My father ... wishes me to marry ... and I do not wish to."

"Then we best get on our way. If we wait too long, a guard will spot us."

Kimbra took his hand, smiled, and together they fled the city.

Once they had traveled far from the King's prying eyes, Forest stopped to examine the sky. He checked trees and the stream in relation to the flickering lights, curious if his Master had taught him so much in premonition of the future. But, with conscious effort, he forced his attention back to the ether. He needed to choose the best route. The hardest to track. Only a master tracker could follow them in the Forbidden Lands, but he had the girl's safety to consider. With her along, the Forbidden Lands would be suicide. Avoiding townships was a necessity, as was finding a path consisting of woods or streams.

He looked back to the world below and smiled at Selandria. He knew how wrong it was to take her with him, but her friendship, though so new, had come to mean so much.

"I hope you like water," he said.

"Why do you ask?"

Forest stepped into a stream and answered, "Because we have to walk this way awhile. Take off your boots, you'll wish them dry when we resume on land later."

"Why not stick to the roads?"

"Too easy to track. I have a friend who's allowed me to escape, but just in case he decides to track me, he'll never find me."

Selandria suddenly flushed a dark crimson, puffed up her rosy cheeks, and gruffly replied, "I'll have you know..." She stopped. Forest looked at her curiously. Then she calmly finished, "That's a splendid idea."

Forest didn't bother to wait and began walking. Kimbra removed her boots and realized she'd best be more careful with her words. Coming to Sir Theomund's defense was not her best idea, but how could anyone think ill of such a good man? The vagabond especially should not think such things, considering that the one he suspected had saved him from death row! She had known her bodyguard all her life, and not once had he backed from his word. If Sir Theomund had promised not to track him, then they had no cause for worry.

Of course, that was before she had gone missing.

Kimbra stepped barefoot into the knee high stream, clenching her fists tight. The chill water startled her, and a spark of pain shot up her ankles all the way to her thighs. That charge stole most of the feeling from her legs, and what was left took hold of slimy pebbles and algae that grew along the stream's bottom.

She followed him, thankful that at least the water flowed in the same direction in which they traveled. They walked until her feet resembled prunes, and just when she wondered if sensation would ever return to her lower body Forest left the water. She climbed onto the muddy embankment and collapsed onto a patch of soft-looking moss. But the weight of her dainty torso pushed the green vegetation down, and a small pool of water appeared. She jumped back on her feet. Was nothing about adventure to turn out as she had expected?

She looked about the dense woods and found a large, flat rock to use as a seat. The hard stone had not at all felt comfortable, but at least the surface was dry. She stole a deep breath, savored the heavy pine fragrance, and listened to the poplar trees chatter amongst themselves. The autumn air still felt a little brisk to her liking, but trying to enjoy the adventure she reminded herself that she now experienced life as her brother had for the last year.

Forest handed her a stick. "Can you build a fire?"

Oddly enough she could, as Sir Theomund had taught her many wilderness skills. The thought of her bodyguard made her wonder if anyone knew she was missing yet.

"Aye," Kimbra sang, setting out to find bark and twigs to use as kindling. She gathered a handful, and noticed the eastern sun rising into the twilight. From the castle she often watched the sun rise into the waiting sky, but this time it appeared so much more extraordinary. The colors reminded her of a painter's palette, and making it more spectacular they mixed with the stream and tree tips. Kimbra wished for the moment to never end, but when Forest tapped her shoulder she knew it must. As she turned to him he said, "I'm cold, and I'm hungry. Build a fire, or let me do it."

"Nay, I'll do it," she said, a little perturbed by the attitude he had taken with her.

It took her several tries with the flint-rock to finally generate enough spark to start it. She sat again, leaned on her hands, and watched her companion prepare something to eat. He looked into his traveling pack gravely a couple of times, and she wondered what might be wrong. But more so, she hoped for a tale of adventure. She dismissed his look and asked, "Tell me more about your village."

Forest left his task alone and moved closer to her. He positioned himself to feel the fire's warmth, and basked in their growing friendship. His brow grew dark and furrowed, and his eyes sank as though to feed the fire's heart before them. He inhaled a long breath of smoky air, heavily and steadily without choking, and released it in one sudden sigh. The smoke exhaled like an aged dragon's breath as he craned his head to look at her, his eyes begging her to ask a different question.

Kimbra reached out with her hand to stroke his back. She said, "If we're going to travel together, you'll have to learn to confide in me."

Forest returned his vision to the fire. He closed his eyes as if to ward off an unseen pain, and upon opening them he whispered, "My people once lived among the rest of the world, but in desperation to become one with Nalor we took to the mountains. In appreciation, Nature protected us by creating a harsh environment so that no outsider could ever get to us.

"When the Krim 'Tiak invaded my village my people fell into a great shock. We'd never been attacked before, and suddenly skills that we had learned only for exercise and tradition, we had to call upon for murder. Cold, senseless murder. My skills were the most advanced of all my people, but ... my Master commanded that I flee. I would never disobey him so I did what he asked."

As Forest closed his eyes Kimbra felt him slip from her. He said, "My people watched me run, thinking I was a coward."

Kimbra understood what it was that made him so different from anyone else she had met. She helplessly watched his dark complexion turn milky. She wished she could think of some way to express her pity for him, but she could find no words. She reached out and held him.

Dusk's glory woke Kimbra, and she stretched her sore back. The hard ground had not afforded much comfort for sleep, and day's brilliance had, as well, impaired her slumber. But she tasted adventure, and if it was Rough Sleep who acted as her worst encumbrance then the rest of the trip could only prove fantastic. Kimbra wiped away the tiredness from her eyes, looked around for Forest, and found that he had already woken. He was praying into a giant oak tree. How odd, Kimbra thought, for someone to have found such fellowship with Nature.

The princess set up some wood for a fire, and opened Forest's pack to grab a pot and tea leaves. He hadn't packed much food, and she wondered what he intended to do when they ran out. Counting the supplies she realized it wouldn't be long before she found out.

"Have a couple biscuits, and boil some water. We'll have tea." Forest told her, walking away from his holy rite. Then, falling into the splits, he began to stretch.

"Guess I'd best not be gluttonous."

He smiled. "We'll make a stop in the next town for food, after night has fallen. The fewer people who see us the better."

Kimbra breathed easily, knowing that Forest had already devised a plan. She set to work boiling the water, opened his sack again, and took out a few biscuits. He handed her a smaller satchel filled with berries, and she offered him a biscuit. The princess looked at him quizzically. He placed a few on his biscuit and bit down on the hard crust.

After he swallowed he told her, "I woke early and gathered them. Don't worry, I know poison. They're safe."

Kimbra broke her biscuit in half, imitated Forest by placing a few berries on it, and prayed that he was adept in telling good ones from bad. As she tasted the sour seeds she chewed enough to swallow, wondering why Forest had been trained in so many deadly arts. She swallowed so that she might ask, but the dry bread had stuck in her throat. Kimbra wished she'd waited for the tea to boil before eating. She was unable to speak and looked at Forest pleadingly, stifling her desire to gag.

"That's why you eat it with more than a couple berries," he told her. "Put more on next time."

She grabbed a handful of the tiny red fruit this time and did just that, except without the bread. Now her cheeks sucked inward and her eyes squinted at the sour taste but, as the juice dislodged the food from her throat, it helped.

Forest laughed.

"Thanks," she said sarcastically.

"Not a problem. Guess all this discomfort's making you homesick."

Kimbra thought how she could redirect the conversation to get more information from him. "I am homesick for some comforts. How about you?"

Forest stared directly into the flickering fire's blue-base, and his eyes turned as sorrowful as his demeanor. When next he spoke his voice sounded whispered and nearly gibberish, but Kimbra thought she heard him say, "I've been homesick every moment since I left my village. I think the only difference between what I feel and what you feel, is that up until now, I've never been able to turn around and go back." Then he looked her in the eyes and said, "Should you so desire, you can go back."

Kimbra watched him brush his hand through his hair, and return his stare back at the illuminating fire. He had posed the question in such a manner that she only need answer should she so desire. Before the princess took another bite of the dry bread she told him, "Nay, I do not desire to go back. I'm glad I'm here with you ... glad we're friends."

Forest smiled and said, "Finish eating. We'd best keep moving."

They entered a small town as darkness fell, just as Forest had anticipated. Very few passers-by walked about the barren roads, and the few villagers who had wandered out all scurried into a building brandishing a shingle with a picture carved into it of an eagle drinking ale. Forest chose that place as their destination and Kimbra clung close to him for protection.

This had marked the second time he had come to this village. The first had been quite the learning experience. He had come in search of work, desiring a means for paying for food as opposed to stealing. He had found plenty, all requiring an assassin's skills, and had departed quite unemployed. This village was a vile, evil place to which he had vowed never to return. But because it was situated between two warring trading towns it enjoyed an infamy known by humanity's seedier lot; a place where those of warrant could venture without fearing recognition. Everyone was wanted for something, and anyone who met the other's gaze by anything other than accident would find a knife in his back.

Forest and Kimbra strolled into the tavern before night completely devoured the nourishing light. He found an empty table encased in a dark nook and after lighting a candle Forest sat with his back to the wall and Selandria with hers to the clientele. She was far too inquisitive of her surroundings, a curiosity that could get them killed if challenged by the wrong person. Forest hadn't been as excited as his companion about being in a place so full of drunken adventurers, but the prospect of food, however, had excited him.

He looked across the room and tried to catch the barmaid's attention by meeting her gaze. She was about the only one with whom one could take such a liberty, and after several failed tries he wondered what more he could do. Then, as he watched the large woman meander her way around the crowded tavern, he noticed an aged man watching him. He was leaning back in a chair, smoking a long wooden pipe. He donned his grey hair long, matted together at his chin where a beard had grown to the bottom of his skinny chest. Underneath wire framed spectacles his skin wrinkled and smoothed, indicating pensive thought. He had a familiar quality, and through those spectacles the old man stared intensely at Forest. Quite a risk for a man of such advanced years.

The barmaid took his attention away from the gent. "What kin ah git ya'?" Her wide smile brandished several rotting teeth and Forest reminded himself of the food's quality. Although, it had been several years since he had last eaten in this tavern.

"We'll have..."

"Two plates of haggis and a bowl of your finest stone soup for the Gent!" the elder interjected, welcoming himself to their table.

"Can I help you, old man?" Forest placed much emphasis on the word 'old'.

"Perhaps." He smiled, and sat between the two youths. "I seek someone traveling to the Coastal Mountains."

Forest glared at him suspiciously, still uncertain from where he knew him. "And I am to believe that our meeting is coincidence?"

"So cynical for a man of such youth. Am I to believe that I have found two such travelers?"

"You have not found those whom you seek."

"My concern is only in the destination, I assure you. I take no other particulars. I am getting on in age, and need the companionship to assure me of my journey."

"We have no need for burdens."

The barmaid brought them their food, and Forest felt a swift kick from beneath the table. He met Selandria's gaze, and knew she wanted to help. He didn't want, nor did he need, anyone else further encumbering him.

"You can journey with us," Selandria said as she smelled the meal in front of her. She chewed, swallowed quite forcibly, and reached out to her mug of water. Drinking a hefty swig of the liquid to wash out the foul taste she paused as she picked at the meal. She asked, "What is this?"

The old man chuckled. "There are things in this world, my young friends, which are best not told by us who know." In his eyes remained a look stern and serious. "Be careful with your questions. Ask only those things you truly want answered."

Forest sipped at his hot soup, raising the bowl to his mouth with care. He asked, "Why do you wish to travel to the Coastal Mountains?"

"Such an odd thing for us to know so much about one another ... yet so little of our names."

"I am called Selandria, he is Forest."

The gent smiled, and trailed off into a world all his own. No happiness emanated from his expression as he repeated in a whisper, "Forest and Selandria."

"And what is your title, Sir?" she asked.

He smiled and the wrinkles on his face seemed, for an instant, to have disappeared. When next he spoke his voice was hushed and filled with despair. "At my years a name is no more than a formality. I am called many things, several I like but many I don't. Aren't people odd, all particular with titles and such. As if a label can change what resides in the hearts of men! I'm certain whatever name you choose for me, I will like it the best of all."

Forest spoke before Selandria could, "And what if I chose to call you, 'Old Man'?"

"Then you will learn just how unoriginal you are."

Chapter Five

Trapped. Trapped inside a shell as fragile as an egg, yet as impenetrable as the chastity belt on a virgin. Young Alviss, Protecteur's only wizard apprentice, felt entangled in an eternity of casting the same spell over and over again. Casting and failing. Casting and … such was his lot in life; one that would not have seemed so terrible, had this been the only incantation at which he had flopped. But it seemed that all the magic he tried failed. And because of it, no matter how zealously he worked, Alviss felt doomed to a life of ridicule. That was his destiny in life. Being a wizard in Protecteur meant he was the thorn on a rosebud. The oddball. He again tried the spell only to fail his umpteenth-millionth try. A failure that meant he would never earn respect. Never have the chance for a friendship that consisted without fear of being shunned.

One such as Andras had shown him.

It seemed to the youth that barriers surrounded all good things in life. His was "Wyborn," an older boy who had been his arch-rival since the first day they met. Although, if it had not been him it would have been someone else. All the squires were the same: finding comfort in numbers and ego boosts in beating anyone weaker. And because of that prejudice he feared going to town and for that reason he infuriatingly tried to master this new spell.

Only to find he'd failed. Again.

"Alviss! What are you doing now?" His teacher always arrived at the most inopportune moments.

The small room was in shambles. Windows ripped, vials smashed, potions spilt, and scorch marks everywhere. Damage always followed a blundered spell, and a severe reprimand always followed several mistakes. Alviss slowly turned to meet his teacher's angry gaze. He tried to think of a good lie, but that failed too.

"I'm practicing," Alviss replied in a voice so weak that it cracked.

Master Eistein tried hiding a smile. He was going to grab a nearby broom and start sweeping, but he frowned, smiled ... and frowned. "Alviss, Alviss, Alviss," he mumbled and sighed.

Alviss knew what it meant when his instructor sighed. Though a rare occurrence (be it a common one for him to expel air), it did happen. And when it did it meant a story. The apprentice took a seat to make himself comfortable.

"Alviss, you must learn to start at the bottom. Simple spells. Don't try to fly ... before you can walk the astral plane!" Master Eistein burst into a fit of unchecked chuckles, making the youth wonder if he'd ever get so old that he might also lose his sense of humor.

"I want to be great," Alviss said, daring to interrupt the laughter. "The other boys in town are all learning to fight and...."

The elder gave him that look. His eyes drooped like suns unable to set, and they became misty like a waterfall damned at its roots. He used his long, bony index finger to force his pupil to look up into those eyes that said *I know*. Sitting on the edge of the bed he said, "They beat you each time you go into the township?"

"Aye. That they do. You ... you knew?"

"I had thought they might ease up as they got older," he chuckled, "that, I thought, of warriors! Squires once beat me, too, sometimes nearly to death. And I had, as well, wanted to become a powerhouse to teach them respect."

"What did you do?"

"I did nothing. My master taught me incantations to protect myself. Every wizard who has learned to survive has done so only because he accepts fear in place of respect." Eistein paused before whispering, "I am sorry that I have neglected to teach you this protection ... just as my master had neglected to teach me." Then he added, more to himself, "I am getting on in years."

Time elapsed ever so slowly as Alviss listened to his instructor speak. Master Eistein seemed to go on for hours, telling of ways to fight without violence; depressing his pupil with more promises of magical power. Power that Alviss knew he'd just never achieve.

"But Master," the youth interrupted again. He paused, to see if he would be allowed to continue. When Eistein gave no more than a frown, Alviss said, "Have you never taught your apprentices power?"

The elder's frown slowly turned to a grin. He sighed, and his eyes turned empty. A candle that burned beside a stack of papyrus seized the master's attention. He whispered, "There has been another, as I am sure you have heard."

"The townsfolk have said."

Eistein raised a finger and silenced the boy. "You will not interrupt again! I said there has been another, and I will tell you that I did teach him power beyond trickery. I gave him what I thought I wished at his age, power through savagery. I enabled him not to defend, but to offend. Is that what you wish?"

Alviss at first said nothing. His upper lip trembled and then he, too, looked at the candle. The wax melted from its top but spilled over only one side. The pupil did not look away when he said, "Aye. That is what I seek."

A laugh escaped the teacher. Not one imbued with joy, or one with frivolity, but a laugh that comes when one man has seen the truth in another. Even when that other has not seen it in himself.

"You seek it. But do you want it? Ask yourself what it is in yourself that you love the most, that others love the most, and ensure that whatever you seek it does not destroy that thing." Again the candle became his focus. "Seek not what will destroy you."

Alviss watched as his master rose from the mattress, and shuffled out of the room. Looking at the mess that awaited him, the youth grabbed a broom and began to clean. He considered what it was that he loved about himself and thought, *Nothing*. But Andras liked him, if not loved him. What did she see? Perhaps when he went into the township next week for the ritual of Manhood, he would ask her. Provided Wyborn didn't kill him first.

Alviss was too afraid to open his eyes. He stood in the center of his room with his palms up, and his arm stretched away from his body. When he'd spoken the chant he'd done so without thinking on the words, and without tripping over the accent one took with such speech. He was still alive so he knew he had not overdone the ingredients, so that left only two options: either the spell failed, or it ... Alviss forced one eye to open a crack, and then slowly he opened both. They grew wide and long, nearly as much as his mouth had dropped. A sensation erupted from his heart as if a prison of ice had suddenly melted.

Success! Alviss thought as he stared upon the six-inch flame that hovered above his hand.

Clapping at the entryway stole his attention, and he turned to see his teacher looking over the skin that was the door between the pupil's quarters and the common area. The elder was smiling, and had made no attempt to suppress it. Alviss took a step toward him. "I did it!"

"Aye, that you did. What a difficult time you have with this power, and how proud I am that you do not give up."

Alviss closed his palm and the magic disappeared. "P-proud? Truly you are? Of me?"

Master Eistein took hold of the skin. He bit his lower lip and walked inside to sit on the bed with his pupil. "Dear child, I have cherished every moment spent raising you. It is uncommon for wizards to have that joy. Our apprentices are usually those who fail Manhood, but you were left on my stoop as an infant."

"Why? You never told me. Why did you not Choose a woman and have a boy of your own?"

Master Eistein looked away. "That is unimportant," he said. Looking back to the youth he added, "What does matter is that you know how much I have cherished your need of my praise."

"I will always need...."

"Nay, that you will not. Today, you will become a Man."

"Man or boy I shall always seek your praise!" Alviss stood and walked to the entrance, but before he departed he added, "You're my master."

Eistein waited until his pupil had left and was well onto the road to town before whispering, "And I fear that I will do you as much wrong, nay, more so, than my master did me. After today, you will never wish for my approval again. But I have known since your birth that I would have to lose you, in order to have you."

Chapter Six

Alviss donned his worn beige tunic and old cotton hose. His boots had a few holes in them, his apprentice cap drooped, but he walked the dirt path that led from his home to the village straight and tall. He strode with his pack slung lazily over one shoulder, and took nearly an hour to trek through the wild countryside. He stopped to smell the flowers, even to pick a purple bloom, and thought nothing of the test which awaited him in town. Even his worries of Wyborn were at rest.

The cold nip in the air, one that intensified as he neared civilization, overcame Alviss' carefree attitude. The sun had risen over them in full bloom, but it offered no heat from the merciless summer chill. But even if it had borne warmth it could not have won a war with this frigid air, as this nip did not come from the weather. Merchants lined the streets with their wares; few in the outskirts but more clustered in the bazaar. Alviss scanned the many tents erected by the various guilds, and at first he wondered how he'd ever pick out the one for him. But he knew. A gang grouped themselves before a small canopy in the village centre. Alviss looked about for an escape then decided not to even try. Once they spotted him they would give chase until he was caught. Today he vowed that things would be different. The wizard concealed a few ingredients to a spell in his palm, gained confidence in his magic, and pressed on.

It didn't take long for the warriors to spot him. With practiced unison they circled him and stilted his movement. Wyborn moved from the circle's edge, and stared as he towered over his much smaller victim. The adults kept on with their duties, and the young women ran to watch. Again the wizard was reminded of just how alone he was in this society.

"Yer back?" Wyborn pushed him. "'Sided to put another dent in me fist?"

"I'm to meet my master here," Alviss replied, ignoring the threat.

"Ooooo, what d'ya think? Yer master'll save you? My sword is mightier than yer magic."

"Move out of my way. I am to have the Ritual of Manhood," the wizard paused, wishing his voice didn't quake. Then he said: "'Tis a lot more painful than the warrior's."

The insult landed right where Alviss had hoped. Wyborn puffed his lips, frowned, and narrowed his eyes. His face looked like clouds before a thunderstorm as he grabbed his adversary by his tunic. "You sayin' you'll be more a Man than me?"

"No more!" a feminine voice shouted from outside the circle. A young woman with long blonde hair and beautiful green eyes forced a break in the ring as she stepped between the two. Alviss used the diversion to begin his chant. Wyborn let his opponent go and turned to look into the girl's eyes, his desire shown by the way he brushed her cheek.

"I do this for you, Andras," Wyborn said sweetly.

"I don't want you to hurt him anymore!"

The storm returned to Wyborn's soul. His powerful form shook from rage, worsened only by the smile on Alviss' face. Wyborn pushed the girl out of his way, charged his victim with fists flared and ready.

And found himself stopped by a three foot flame leaping from the wizard's palm!

The arcane fire scorched the warrior's face, sending him fleeing in pain. With his followers close behind.

Alviss closed his eyes, breathed deeply to savor the scent of smoke that trailed his would-be assailant, and spoke a few words to dismiss his chant. When he again looked upon the world, Andras embraced him and shrieked. The young magician trembled, not from his triumph but from the grin on his friend's face. It was only slightly larger than his own.

"You were legendary," she said.

"Aye ... I mean, thank you, for standing up for me. Again."

"Not that you needed it," her tender caress on his cheek made him blush. "I had come this day with a troubled heart, but your bravery has chased it away."

"Why would your heart be troubled?" Alviss realized he was still holding her, and feeling his cheeks burn he let her go.

"Do you love me Alviss? I mean truly, with your heart and soul?"

"Andras, you speak so plainly. I-I don't know what to say," his cheeks lost their color, but handing her the purple bloom he whispered, "Aye, that I do. Truly, with all my heart and soul."

The girl reached out and hugged him. Taking the flower she placed it in her hair, without letting the wizard go. Alviss could feel her cold tears on the nape of his neck, and she said, "I am here for the Choosing. I will be given to the Man who wins me."

"Wins you? I have no desire to own you. I want to love you equally, as a man should a woman."

"You are so odd." She tried to meet his gaze, but he stared at his feet. With tenderness she cupped his chin in her hand and brought him eye to eye. "And that is why I love you. Be wise, Alviss. Be wise, be strong, and be brave."

Andras kissed him, but Alviss did not return the gesture. "I cannot be in the Choosing. I am a wizard, after all."

Again she held him close to her, this time so tight that each could feel the pounding of the other's heart. Alviss said, "I will make them let me win you. I will become a Man, and then I shall challenge them all. For you Andras, that I vow!"

This time when she kissed him he did so back, and though neither wished to let go slowly they did. And, as Andras walked away, neither spoke another word. Alviss raised his hand and bid her farewell, oblivious even to the chill in the autumn breeze. I love you, he mouthed.

Oblivious even that Master Eistein, as he held a tear at bay, watched from outside the tent where his pupil would become a Man or die.

Alviss lifted the skin-flap and poked his head inside. There were benches covered in dust, and a stage large enough for only three. His teacher stood upon the platform, holding no tools, no herbs, not even so much as a magic book. The pupil could not hold back his elation, and as he rushed inside he shouted, "Master! I did it! I defeated Wyborn!"

Master Eistein grinned, and looked at his apprentice. Alviss saw the tears welling in the elder's eyes, and for a brief moment he wished not to call this man "Master." He blushed as he realized that he thought of him more as a father than a teacher.

"Enter Alviss. Sit upon this stool," Master Eistein said. His voice sounded flat, unmoved. His eyes even appeared cold, like an underground river frozen by witchery. As the pupil approached the stage he picked up a stool along the way, and started on the first of three stairs. Each step seemed like a mountain, and each time he lifted his foot it was as if he lifted the entire world. When he finally sat upon the stool, and stared upon the dust that had settled where an audience should have been, his energy felt spent.

Master Eistein circled the boy several times before kneeling before him. Alviss stared into cold eyes that had turned ebony, but before he could speak his instructor grabbed his forehead.

First he saw nothing. Then it was....

Color.

A myriad of shades beamed around him like a hurricane.

Red was like an earthquake. A giant movement of his body that made him no longer aware if he was still whole.

When Orange came upon him it did so not unlike a volcanic eruption. Alviss screamed.

Yellow and green made him nearly beg for the Ritual to stop.

But he didn't.

It continued until Blue had turned Indigo, and past a myriad of all hues as they crashed about him; not in a caress but as thunder.

The worst had been the violets.

Black made the boy open his eyes, and in the absence of color he fell to the ground shaking.

His entire test had been color.

Alviss collapsed to his knees, uncertain if he was still alive. Blood that had poured down his naked back during the Ritual now dried in rivulets, leaving the pupil uncertain which wounds remained fresh. Unable to rise past his knees he tried breathing steadily to regain his strength. At least he had enough energy to open his eyes. Enough, anyway, to see master Eistein place a bucket filled with water down beside him. In that bucket was a rag and lard. Smiling at his teacher, though no kindness radiated from his gesture, he wondered if his Ritual had not been too harsh. In an effort to forget all that had just happened, Alviss took the heavy rag and began wiping down his sore body. Water seeped into his wounds, and the lard cut like acid. This pain the pupil accepted. This he controlled. That self-determination made pain feel welcome.

It was, at least, colorless.

The water was now as crimson as the blood in his veins. No matter. He'd cleaned himself as much as he could. As his numb body slowly regained its senses, one thought took predominance over all others: the Choosing would soon be at hand. Ignoring the bloodstained liquid he dunked his head, and, taking out his submersed head, Alviss noticed that blood still trickled from his nose. He disregarded it and braided his hair like a true wizard. But had he become a Man?

Alviss took his apprentice clothes from the table where he had laid them, and began to dress. He still waited for his master to speak, to say something, *anything!*, and, as the apprentice pulled the rope in his pants snug, he wondered if mere survival constituted a pass. Perhaps he failed and his teacher was too ashamed to tell him.

Alviss opened the curtain-doorway halfway. As a barrage of warm rays from the Sun poured over him, his sore body welcomed the heat They possessed. The Sun held much Power, and slowly it replenished some of the magic he had spent during the Ritual. His master still hadn't spoken a word, and opening the curtain Alviss started out.

"Alviss," Master Eistein said.

"Aye?" the boy answered quietly, trying to hide the hope in his voice.

"You will need this robe so that all might know you are now a Man." The teacher held out his arms with unconcealed pride, offering his pupil a red robe with black astrology symbols sewn all over it.

Alviss fell back a step, astonished by the pleasure he took in his first step in becoming a Wizard. Taking the robe he pulled it over his trembling body, drowned by pride that swelled from within his heart. And again he turned to leave, wishing to hurry so he could participate in the Choosing. He heard his master clear his throat and say, "Would have been shameful."

"What would have been?"

"For you to have left without proof of your Manhood. They may not have allowed you to take part in The Choosing."

"You mean ... I can?"

Alviss's excitement blinded him to the tremble on his Master's upper lip. His teacher nodded in affirmation and his pupil rushed from the tent. At long last, so Alviss thought, he had a chance for Andras!

Until now, Alviss had never known the joy of being a wizard. He strutted about the streets in his new garb like a rooster cocked for a fight. He met people eye to eye, refused to look to the ground, and gained courage from their whispers. No one met his gaze for long, no one blocked his way, and no one conspired to ridicule him. As an apprentice they had borne him no respect, but as a Man the warriors feared him. And, as his Master had said, wizards in Protecteur had to learn to accept fear in place of respect.

And Alviss took to it like a child to sugar.

But the bravado didn't last. Ahead there was a raised platform, where the town leader refereed fights for brides and their dowry. To the left a tent had been raised to house eligible women, and to the right fathers of both girls and Men watched. Before the stage a crowd of males waited hungrily for a challenge they could win.

Alviss stood at the back of the audience, where he had to stand on the tips of his toes to see. The Choosing had begun long ago, but whether Andras had been auctioned off he had no way of knowing. The wizard prayed to the Sun that she had not.

Time was not unlike Alviss's spirit; as disparity took dominance over hope it grew darker and darker. The leader's voice sounded grating from a long auction, and, as most of the Men had been paired (or killed) the wizard knew there couldn't be many brides left. Someone, undoubtedly Wyborn, must have chosen Andras while he was in Ritual.

Alviss turned away, the last of his hope expelled with a sigh. Until he heard: "Who will combat for Andras, daughter to Sebastian?"

The wizard fought his way through the crowd, wishing he could quell the lust-filled warriors with his magic. When he reached the stage he met her eye to eye, and their love vanquished his despair like a magical charm. She smiled, as did he, their vows unspoken. A young warrior stepped onto the stage, stopped only by his father who asked, "What is her dowry?" and gave a glare to warn his successor of marrying out of their station.

But Wyborn took the stage, dressed in the tanned leather attire common to noble Men. He paced, glared at all who might challenge him, and came to stand before Andras. He brushed her cheek and said, "She be mine."

"Do we have a challenger?" the leader said quietly. The other who'd taken the stage now stepped down.

Alviss tried to answer, but his voice failed. Andras looked at him again and mouthed "Please." A tear left her eye. The wizard tried to speak again but fear entangled his voice. It made his body feel weak, and dissolve his will. It didn't help any that the Sun, his deity, deserted him for its slumber.

Alviss breathed deeply and forced himself onto the stage. His heart pounded beneath his robe a thousand beats a second. The entire town, drowned in silence for ten thousand of those beats, burst into an uproar. The chieftain raised his arms and the village again fell into silence. He paused, looking first at the wizard and then at the burn across Wyborn's face.

"My people, what fear is this I hear uttered from your lips? Are you afraid this boy's magic is greater than this Man's might? What would you do should the elfin women attack, would you flee their spells and cower in your homes? Perhaps it is the women who should be competing for the males." He looked at the frightened warrior on-stage, "Wyborn, if you fear this challenge I will consider it a victory to this wizard and a defeat for every one of your ancestors who has competed in the Choosing."

Wyborn puffed out his chest. "I will accept the Challenge."

The crowd cheered. As the orator lead Andras offstage she smiled and whispered to Alviss, "Fare well, my one true hero." She scowled at Wyborn.

That gave Alviss the confidence to begin his chant.

The two adversaries stepped closer to one another. Alviss spoke loudly so that Wyborn would hear his arcane speech, taking in heart the fear he sensed. As his final words left his lips Alviss courageously threw the spell. Wyborn screamed, flailing his hands, but as the magic ignited in a blue flame it ... extinguished. Nothing but ashes struck the warrior in the chest.

The spell ... failed.

Wyborn uncovered his eyes. Alviss sensed his adversary's fear die. The warrior walked up to his opponent, grabbed him by the scruff of his robe, glared into his eyes, and smiled.

Alviss turned his gaze to the crowd, scanning it until he found the one he loved. She looked back at him, tears running down her cheek, and blew him a kiss. Alviss then turned back to Wyborn and tried to fight back.

The crowd cheered, knowing the outcome of this battle.

And Master Eistein, as Alviss caught a glimpse of him in the crowd, walked away. The apprentice's only hope for safety was crushed by the reality of what it meant to be a wizard in Protecteur.

Failure.

Chapter Seven

Master Eistein peeked over the curtain at Alviss who lay face down on his straw mattress. The pupil did not flinch when the cold tears rolled over his burning cheeks, nor when they fell from his swollen chin to meet in a pool of sorrow on his feather pillow. They must sting: his bruises, cuts, and scrapes; but the elder knew the pain that truly poisoned his apprentice. The pain of wanting something, someone, so terribly that he would endure anything to have it. Or in this case her. Master Eistein sighed, knowing this pain well.

"...But you were left on my stoop as an infant."

Why? You never told me. Why did you not Choose a woman and have a son of your blood?

The elder knew now that he should have been honest with the boy from the start. But would he have understood? Could Alviss, at such a young age, accept the place from where he had come? Could he accept the blasphemy that his Master had practiced? Eistein shuddered as he recalled.

The night was exceptionally dark, yet blessed with the full moon. A tent erected on Sacrifice Hill sounded with the screams of a woman in labor, those wails reaching the ears of even the Master Wizard. But Eistein ignored them, as he always did whenever they sounded. He buried himself inside a book, flipping from one page to the next. Perusing the titles, but not the incantations themselves.

Whether it was from the book itself, or from a Power that does not come from the voice of man, he did not know. From a flash of light a woman appeared, clad in a brilliant gown and a ring of sun which haloed her golden hair. Eistein leapt from his seat and began to chant for protection. The Being laughed.

"You need not fear me. I have been sent to you, from the One True All."

The elder fell to his knees and could not look upon the face of the messenger. He knew this All, as did all men. This was the Nameless God, the One who sent the Prophet Renrock astray, the One forbidden to be worshiped. *"You are not my god, why do you come to me?"*

"I am no one's god. But the All is. He has sent me to grant your greatest desire."

"You do not know my..."

"There is on this night born a child, he shall be left to die on the Altar. You will save him, raise him as your own, and then give him to the All when he is a man."

"You would give me a son, then take him from me?"

"The All would give to you, what you would give back. Then He will give the boy back to you with a truth of which you can only dream."

That was fifteen long autumns ago. The old master had made a deal with this Nameless God, a blasphemous and scornful act, and now he must see it to completion. Through an open window dawn encased the boy, and outside birds chirped melodies to the coming morn. The Sun rose an inch higher as the elder entered softly. Night still staved off the dawn within these walls, but the teacher chased it away with a burning candle. Alviss muttered a curse before rising from his mattress. He wiped away the free flowing tears from his bruised cheeks and refused to meet the elder's gaze.

It had taken the entire night for Master Eistein to work up the courage to come to his pupil. Now that he had, he considered turning to leave. At least if he kept the boy as his own, he might repair this unjust deed. The sorrow sensed in his pupil was met with his own, though in him there also lived a touch of haunting shame. The admiration once offered so freely by this pupil was now spent. Washed away by reality. A tide that had stolen away the boy's innocence, as well.

The light in the youth's heart was now extinguished.

Alviss finally found his teacher's dead gaze. "You walked away. You let them beat me."

The old man said nothing.

"Didn't you!?" Alviss rose, his hard features a sign that he no longer feared his instructor's wrath.

Master Eistein could find no more in himself other than to nod. He considered praying to this All, begging Him not to take away his pupil, but, even though dawn now ignited much of the tiny room, all he could think to do was light candles.

Alviss sat back on his mattress and buried his teary face deep in his palms. "Why didn't you aid me?" These words, spat through grinding teeth, dashed the old man's hopes for reconciliation. He wanted to tell Alviss that he had done what he had thought best. What his master had done before him, and his before that. But he knew they who came before him, and himself, were wrong. But he was the most wrong, as this was no pupil given from a failure of warriorhood. But from a Nameless god. Eistein wished he had treated Alviss more like a father than a mentor.

The master ruffled a scroll that he had considered keeping hidden. But he followed through with his deal and threw it beside Alviss; where he saw the patch of dampness on the pillow. He yearned that he'd spared the boy this painful lesson. He departed.

Dashing his dreams of hearing the name "father" spoken just once from the boy's lips.

Alviss mumbled a curse. He shirked away from the scroll, and at first rejected it. He wanted nothing more to do with that old man's teachings. But losing his battle with curiosity, he finally picked it up and examined the seal. It was designed with a wolf, one who bayed with teeth bared. Alviss broke the seal and unrolled the papyrus:

> *Herald Alviss the Wizard,*
> *Your presence is requested at a meeting of the Select Eight. That is, those people favored to aid the Chosen One in his destiny to make mankind a god. You will journey to Peaceland, where you will be given instructions for your destiny.*
> *The Wise.*

Alviss was speechless. Was this true? Did he at last have a Destiny that would lead him out of Protecteur? The pupil scrambled off his bed and started to pack the things he would need for travel. Even if it was a hoax, he would take the chance. The chance to at last find the peace of his dreams.

Alviss walked the wrong way. He held the scroll tightly in one hand, and slung a knapsack over his shoulder to keep his other hand free. He wore his wizard garb and a belt-purse filled with the only spell he had mastered.

He walked in the wrong direction for many miles and beneath dawn's fiery light he crept into the township. Only when he had come to a house did he stop, and as he searched the ground beneath him he hoped no one would discover him. He found a pebble and held it. He did so as if the two were the keys that held life, and, as he sighed, he cast the rock against wooden shutters.

A moment passed. Nothing happened.

Alviss searched the ground for another.

The shutters opened.

"Hello?" Andras called out.

"'Tis ... 'Tis I." Alviss wondered what he should say. After his humiliation, did she still love him?

"Alviss!" she reached out, barely able to caress his cheek. "Look what he did to you! I'm so sorry."

"The apology should be mine. I am not much of a Man."

"You are a human-being."

Alviss smiled, and a tear left his swollen eye. "I've come to say farewell."

"Farewell? Where are you going?"

Alviss handed her the scroll. "I have been called upon by the Ancient Wise. They need me to aid the Chosen One."

Andras took the scroll from him and unrolled it. After reading it she handed it back. "You mean ... the Prophecy is not false?"

"Nay. The New Age is upon us."

A tear left her eye, and landed on Alviss's bruised cheek. He left that tear alone to mix with his own, and said, "When I return, I will be a leader. I will be a ruler for the Chosen One."

"I will be long wedded to Wyborn."

"You can come with me now."

"I cannot. Should I go they would track me and kill you. I would impede your quest."

"Then I will return for you. Wedded, or not."

Andras reached down to brush her fingers through his braids. "Would you still want me, even after Wyborn has taken my virtue?"

Alviss took her hand into his. "'Tis not your virtue that I love."

And as the two lovers embraced a moment of stillness, each knew that this farewell was undoubtedly their last. Alviss destined to die at the hands of some warrior, and Andras destined to wish she shared his fate. The wizard started on his way, stalwart in that whatever he might face it would not be as horrific as that which awaited his true love. Desperate in his belief that he might beat the odds, escape his doom, and free her from hers.

Chapter Eight

A low, steady laugh echoed through the castle's dank hallway. After which a second bout of laughter, louder than the first, followed closely behind. The cackles echoed like madness, creating an air of fear nearly as thick as Death's heavy aroma. Amidst the chortle a cluster of soldiers escorted two prisoners, only one of which, so it seemed, felt the chill of fear in that wail.

"Me name is Stoke. You ever meet Death before?" the not-so-brave man asked.

The hooded man turned his head to stare at Stoke. He brought a chill nearly as awful as that given by the ailing chuckle. Then he turned away, and quietly followed the soldiers who escorted them.

"I only ask 'cause you don't look afraid."

Again the low, steady laugh echoed through the hallway. This time the hooded man cackled quietly with it and spoke in a voice as dark as a starving wolf: "Death does not scare me, boy."

Stoke did not look at the hooded figure again, but faced the double iron doors at which the armed troupe had stopped. His face flushed white and beads of sweat drenched his clothes. As two iron doors parted like shadows of the night, a glow cast by torches held to walls by iron sconces banished the darkness. A long, narrow crimson carpet led from the entrance down the center of the room until it reached the base of a giant throne. Soldiers stood alongside the carpet, and where on the throne's one side a stoutly man stood stoic a voluptuous woman lay on the other. On the throne itself sat a man who looked more like an apparition than a man made of flesh.

That phantom bellowed laughter.

"Welcome to Judgment, boys," it said.

Stoke couldn't move. In what manner of madness had he found himself? A hard push on his back made him stumble forward, his Judgment was first. He stole one final look at the hooded man, but still sensed no fear. He wished he could find that courage in himself. But is that courage, or madness?

Stoke got back on his feet and walked to the end of the crimson trail. His knees weakened, and his eyes fell to the floor. Stoke was unable to meet Death eye to eye.

Again, It laughed.

"And what manner of man do we have here?"

"I – I be from Mount Groth." Stoke spread his arms wide to display a thin, wing-like blanket of skin that reached from his pinkie to his ankles.

A low chuckle erupted from Death's throat. "And what do you have to say, for your defense?"

Stoke sweated from the dank heat. "I committed no wrong. My people committed no wrong. Why have you laid waste my land?"

"Not all is dead. Your people, most anyway, are now slaves. They make weapons for a Great War to come."

"But your people continued to slaughter us. Even after our surrender."

"Zealous lot, aren't they?"

"You act as though you are a god," Stoke shrank from the apparition.

"A god? Does this look like Heaven, boy?"

"I've been a good person..." Stoke felt the tip from a serrated blade touch his spine.

"Come, Stoke. Join my Life-Force!"

The hooded man watched the Grothian die, smiling as if the screams brought him great pleasure. He walked the crimson strip, without waiting for permission, and met the apparition's gaze from beneath his cowl. He stopped only to make way for attendants to drag away the dead Grothian and then continued until he stood but a few feet from the apparition. The hooded man started to laugh in unison with Death.

"And what manner of man are you?"

"The kind unafraid to meet Death, face to face."

"Ahhh, yes. The kind who makes Judgment so easy."

Death waived, and a guard, the same that killed the Grothian, raised his bloodstained sword. But the prisoner raised his shackled hands, spoke strange arcane words, and a brilliant green flash enveloped the soldier. When the flash ended, the guard clutched his chest and fell to the floor.

The apparition clapped.

"Does this mean you have come to challenge me?"

The hooded man lowered his cowl and let his long cobalt hair fall over his shoulders. "I am called Kol the mad. I am here to choose sides, and to offer you my life. I know you cannot be killed for you are not flesh. Nor do I have enough magic to destroy your army, should you choose to destroy me."

"A brave confession. I see why you are called 'the mad.' Now that I have seen your power, tell me what it is you wish to offer."

"I will deliver to you, the Chosen One."

"You would bring me the man who would make even the likes of you a god?"

Kol chuckled. "That I would. I will deliver this person in chains."

"How would you do this?"

"If I told you that, you wouldn't need me."

"I do not need you now."

"Then kill me! Kill me and lose your Chosen One forever!"

The apparition glared at him. "What reward do you seek?"

Kol's face hardened. His eyes narrowed. He breathed with difficulty, and sweat beaded on his furrowed brow. "Revenge."

When the howling stopped every creature in the Forbidden Lands shuddered. Lore told of a beast shaped like a wolverine, one as ferocious as a Kodiak bear and as cunning as a man. One that bayed to the moon in anguish. Many a would-be hero sought the pelt of the beast, following as their map the despondent sounds. And so, when silence wept over the wasteland, all knew that Death was near.

Peter had died in the time it took him to cry in anguish. The embers from the fire where the camp had dined only hours earlier glowed as ruby as the eyes of the prize which had come to the hunters. A score of tents, where more than two dozen men had slumbered, were now empty. Yet only two men had not abandoned their mission when legend became reality.

As in the tales the creature bore the same features as the wolverine, but its bulk dwarfed even the largest Kodiak bear. White fur, ruffled and soft like the Umbrian wolf, covered limbs muscular like a man's. It stood over its victim, blood dripping from its lips and onto the corpse's broken neck. A whip cracked from behind and it spun. Tasting only air.

And fear.

Drust, who had struck the beast, stumbled backward. Garon fell back with him. The creature growled low, and its lips curled as if in a smile. Stepping onto the corpse's chest the beast pushed through. Then, as it held the men's gazes with its own, it crushed Peter's head with its powerful jaw. The demon tore the head off and tossed it behind to Drust.

"By the word! It attacks for pleasure, not for food."

"Did you see the joy in its eyes?" Garon said, holding his sword tight.

The over-sized wolverine barked, the sounds coming out like laughter.

Garon leapt to the offensive, lashing out with his heavy blade. But the beast ducked, pounced, and pinned him to the ground. Garon cried as the beast dug its claws deep into his flesh, ripping out his heart.

The beast spun to face Drust, the only one left alive. It growled, narrowing its icy-blue gaze. Its next victim's jaw gaped as he asked, "What manner of beast are you?"

The animal bared its incisors. "Beast? Is that what you consider me?"

"Aye. What else could you be?"

"You invade my home to kill me, to take my skin for a reputation, and I am the beast?"

"I will have your pelt! To avenge my friends, not for my name." The hunter carefully picked up Garon's sword.

"Please don't make me kill you. Return home, and tell the others that I am not worth the hunt." It turned, slumped its head and whispered, "Let me live in peace."

Drust cried out and attacked. The creature whirled, leapt, and hit the man hard in the chest. They rolled onto the ground. Drust struck with hands and feet. But the beast ripped out the man's throat and threw it into the air.

It stopped only when it heard clapping. There was no need to turn to know who had come.

"Bravo, Didzyn. Bravo!"

Didzyn bared his bloodstained teeth and growled without the intent of play.

The man asked, "Is this how you treat your creator?"

"Damn you Kol! When I agreed to take this body you promised me untold respect!"

Kol laughed. He walked to the headless body, reached down, and took a pipe and some tobacco from its pack. He packed the pipe and after lighting it Kol breathed deeply. "Ahhh. They have been to Peaceland."

"Answer me!" Didzyn advanced with fiery eyes and saliva dripping from the corner of his mouth. The beast stopped only when his creator, standing straight with crossed arms, narrowed his eyes.

"Didzyn, you were a man of hatred when I found you. What did you think? I would turn you into a tiny rabbit to frolic about in the grass? Nay. I gave you what you thought you wished. Look around you. You have respect."

"I have madness." A hushed breath escaped the wolverine's lungs. He left his carnage and turned his back on Kol. "All I have is madness."

Kol puffed on the pipe while keeping one foot on a corpse as the scarlet moon stared upon them. The mad ignored it. "And soon … you will have more."

"What could you possibly have to offer?"

Kol said, as smoke blew from his nose and mouth, "Aid me and I will make you a man again."

Not even the empty howl at the moon could impede the Wizard's duty. Master Eistein drew a circle on the floor of his home, ensuring that the line was an exact three-hundred and sixty degrees. Perfection was not so much a virtue this night as it was pure survival. Sweat beaded on his forehead as he made certain that when the two ends of his circle met they did so as one. When at last they connected, the old magi rose and wiped away the perspiration from his brow. The air in his cabin was strangely chilled, and his soaked robe made him shiver.

But once again, as he heard the howl of madness from beneath the full moon, he dared not stop in his task. With the careful grace of a dancer he stepped inside the five pointed star that he had drawn the circle around. And again he heard the baying.

Master Eistein spoke concisely as he sang out the spell's magical words. He did so at first as though he raced for time, but nearing the end of his long chant the grip of fear no longer held him. He knew he would finish in time.

The door of his home burst open, the howl followed, and as he uttered the final word to his chant ... he slipped. He pronounced the arcane word wrong. The spell failed.

The only way to undo his mistake would be to start from scratch. Circle and all. "Blast!" he muttered.

The wizard looked up from his failed task and saw Kol sitting atop a giant wolverine. The man lowered his cowl and laughed.

"My dear Master Eistein. How long has it been?"

"Not long enough. Not nearly long enough."

"You did not truly expect that I would never return?"

"How could you have found your way out? I embedded you centuries ago beneath Mount Groth!"

"And still the Krim 'Tiak's mining parties found me. Amazing what you'll discover, should you dig deep enough."

Master Eistein looked at Kol with keen eyes. "The Grothians would not allow anyone to dig beneath their mountains. They are too afraid of disrupting whatever might be evolving."

The evil sorcerer smiled, and the beast beneath him laughed. The hooded man dismounted and wandered around the cabin walls. He absently knocked vials from their shelves, but stopped at one marked with a scarlet triangle and three amber dots. He left it alone, and came to face his host.

"Slaves do not have much choice where their owners want them to dig."

The old magi's eyes grew wide, and he exhaled. As silent as the intake of breath he said: "The Grothians are enslaved?"

Kol turned to signal his beast to enter. The giant wolverine lumbered toward the older mage. Eistein stayed relaxed. "How have you been, Didzyn?"

The wolverine's eyes narrowed and it bared yellow teeth, growling as saliva dripped from its jaw. "Regretful."

"Such pleasantries, brings back so many memories." Kol reached into his belt-purse and took out a pipe. He reached for the vial he had spared only moments earlier, uncapped it, and poured a small amount of the liquid into the pipe. Dropping the glass container onto the floor he lit the liquid and puffed generously. Kol smiled.

"You always did make the best magical tobacco."

"What do you want?"

Kol walked to a wooden chair where he sat, but not before cleaning it of dust. "For now, a spot of tea would be nice."

"Not even if I had the leaf to spare."

As Kol's eyes grew dangerously narrow, he rose from the chair and walked to face the elder. Didzyn growled louder.

"I want the baby you spared from Sacrifice Hill fifteen autumns ago."

Now, the magi felt his heart skip a beat. "I know not of what you speak."

"Oh, please. Let's not go through this charade, I know you turned to the Nameless God in hopes of a son."

"You have come in vain. I have done no such thing."

"Didzyn, rip out his throat."

The beast approached. "I am sorry, I do not wish this life of mine."

Eistein whispered, "Then turn from it. You can…."

64

Kol laughed. "You have changed, old master. What happened to the vengeance you sought on warriors?"

"You happened."

The evil sorcerer laughed, lashed out and grabbed the master by the neck. "You will tell me where the boy is."

The magi struggled for air, but offered no words.

"Fine." Kol released the old man and walked to the door. Once outside, he puffed generously on the pipe and said: "Didzyn, find out where the apprentice has gone."

The wolverine started to shake, and a tear left his eye. "Forgive me," he whispered, "but the madness...."

"You are forgiven," the magi said as the beast leapt onto him.

Outside, the night became overcast. Clouds rushed in and it rained upon the Earth as if to drench away evil. Kol the mad, though it extinguished his pipe to do so, walked out into the downpour. He relished in the screams from within the hut, and those he heard from Sacrifice Hill.

"It's good to be home," he said.

Chapter Nine

Forest curled into a ball, squeezing himself tightly against a corner of the hut. Tears rolled from his eyes, fell from his chin and landed on the sod. His body trembled, sweat soaked his toga and a strange coldness consumed him. Outside he could hear screaming, metal clashing on metal, and cries of both mercy and victory. Forest closed his eyes, covered his hands over his face, but could not shake the vision of what he had fled.

Huts had been set ablaze so that the once friendly village now resembled Hell. Women who tried to run were defiled then killed. Men who fought were slaughtered. Children were rounded up and imprisoned. All wondered what they had done to deserve such abandonment by their god.

All but Forest.

"I cannot," he whispered.

The skin over the entryway burst open, but it did not startle Forest. Tears blurred his vision, and he hoped that Death had come. But when two wrinkled hands grasped his biceps, he knew it was his Master. Forest looked up, wiped away his sorrow, and saw his teacher for the elder he was. Old and frail, a man with no more joy or pride. A stone weathered gaze conquered eyes once filled with pride.

"You will fight."

Forest shook his head from side to side and whispered, "I cannot."

"You are the only warrior skilled enough. You must champion for your people!"

Forest cried no more. He trembled no more. Numbness took hold over him, beginning with his head and ending in his toes. Again he whispered, "I cannot."

"So be it then. But if you will not fight, you will flee."

"I beg of you … let me die with my people."

The elder picked his pupil off the ground, and faced him to the window. Ripping the skin from it he forced Forest to see as he said, "Your people die, but they do so with honor. They do so in defiance of those who do not worship the Creation! Do you see the women? Do you see the children? Do you see the men?"

A hard sun beat down as women fled. A wind rose when the enemy caught them, dust drew into the air as they were thrown to the sod. Blood covered the dirt, running under the feet of men who came to rescue only to be stuck with swords and spears. Cries carried over the air's howl as children were bound with ropes. Forest nodded as his master met him eye to eye. Then his teacher said, "Champion your people or damn them."

Forest grabbed his nunchuka and satchel. He turned to his master who added, "I gave you an honorable name, Marcus."

Never before had the elder seemed so cold, his eyes so dark and his jaw so stern. Forest … no, he realized. His name is that which means the Avenger! He looked one last time at the only man he had known as a father and knew that he had never known a father. Between broken sobs he pleaded, "I cannot."

"Then what you see is the end of your people. What you see is blood on your hands."

The Krim 'Tiak were merciless in their carnage. Each time they killed they cried a triumphant victory of their god over the Creation. Marcus ran from the tent, met their evil eyes, eyes tucked deep beneath steel helmets that bore a statuette of a wolf howling. A wolf that bayed with teeth bared, an idol that protected their glowing, hate-filled crimson eyes. Marcus stared long at them, seeing the demons for the first time outside his nightmares. These beasts' hearts were blacker than any evil, darker even than the blood that dripped from their jagged-edged swords.

Nausea swept into Marcus' throat. The world around him, as the wind carried smoke from rooftops to the sky, seemed surreal. This could not be happening, not when their god had protected them for so long. Marcus trembled. He sweated. Tears threatened to return. The Avenger vowed there would be no need for them. Not if he championed his people.

A scream caught his attention. Marcus turned and saw Tully fighting a hopeless battle. The Krim 'Tiak had him outnumbered three to one. Marcus froze as he watched a devil slice Tully across the knees and another kick him in the chest. Tully turned and saw him. Marcus gaped as his friend fell. Tully yelled, "FLEE!" before hitting the ground.

Did no one believe in him?

One of the knights continued to kick and pummel Tully. The others turned to pursue the Avenger, but still he did not know what to do.

He screamed.

Screamed… and Forest woke from his affright.

Forest gasped, bolted upright, and scanned where he was. Trees surrounded him like sentries, with branches raised out to each other. They did well to hide the trio. The vagabond leaned against a trunk and looked at Selandria who lay curled in the dirt. Her raven hair cast like a blanket beneath her head and the dress she wore was muddied by the journey. Silent, steady breaths given away only by the movement of her bosoms were the only indication that she was alive. That, and her gentle smile. Whatever dream in which the girl was engaged must be wonderful, and of that Forest was jealous.

Even the elder who now joined them snored from a deep slumber. Forest peeked inside his cowl and found Mask snoozing away the night. Peace be with you, they had all said to one another before succumbing to shut-eye … but peace was not a part of the vagabond's life. He closed his eyes, shuddered and muttered, "Accurse this world. I want these nightmares to stop."

"They will, but only if you do not re-enact them."

"I thought you were asleep," Forest did not look at Old Man.

"Tell me why you travel to the Coastal Mountains."

"To see new sights."

"Odd. I thought it would be to aid your village."

Forest's eyes narrowed and the senior smiled as if sensing the young man's uneasiness. Then he said, "The Krim 'Tiak's conquests are widespread, the village in the Coastal Mountains who suffered their carnage is no exception. I go there to offer my services."

"And what service could a man of such age offer?"

Old Man paused, stared off into the dark ether, past the stars and long past the world itself, and no longer looked so wise when, sounding ashamed he answered, "That of magic. I possess the service of magic."

"You offer them magic. I offer them my life! The village we speak of is my home."

"The lone survivor of a peoples lost to genocide. You must desire retribution."

Forest glared at him. "My people defeated the Krim 'Tiak."

"You are very knowledgeable for someone who has not seen his village in many years."

"A friend of mine, Tully, sent me a letter. Why are you so curious?"

A hint of sorrow filled the senior's eyes as he stared back into the black. When next he spoke his voice sounded as if he revealed something he wished was not so: "Such a wonderful gift. To write."

"Aye, that it is…" Forest cut himself off. He closed his eyes tight, and realized the trap for which he headed. *How could I be so foolish?* He turned red, clenched his fists, and recalled that only his Master had borne the knowledge of literacy. And he had been his only pupil. Opening his eyes he glared at his new companion. "How is it you know me so well? Have we met?"

Old Man smiled when he met the youth's gaze. "My knowledge comes from reading you. After living so long, I've come to learn that it's the light in a fool's eyes that always burns brightest."

"Your presence was neither wanted nor requested. Especially by me! If you think me a fool, then you must be twice that to travel with me!"

Forest's glare did not make Old Man flinch nor did he back down. A stern quality of its own accord lived inside his eyes. As his aged features drew taught a confidence was portrayed in them that only experience could produce. "A candle will burn out when held under a glass. Take away that glass, and that same candle can burn into an inferno."

"No more riddles." Forest glanced at Selandria to ensure she slept soundly. "What are you trying to say?"

"Many want vengeance on the Krim 'Tiak. Countrysides are littered with the graves of heroes. But I can teach you to defeat them."

Forest wondered what the stranger had implied.

"First," Old Man answered the youth's thoughts, "you must learn to fight from beneath your glass."

Forest said nothing. Then: "Can you teach me to break my glass?"

Old Man removed his spectacles. With a clean portion of his long white robe, he began wiping the dust from them. "There is so much death in this world. Why do you wish to bring it more?"

"To avenge my people."

"Your people or yourself?" He put his spectacles back on. "Is it an eye for an eye? Have you seen so deeply into the hearts of these beasts that you know their darkness?"

"You dare defend them?"

"'I'm not judging you. I am asking you to consider *with what you are saving the world, and how different it is from what you mean to save it.'"*

"I know the Holy Book. I do not need that lesson from you."

"Do you? Then why do you seek to destroy evil if you must join their ranks to do so?"

"Because I cannot defeat them otherwise."

Old Man leaned onto his elbow to bring himself nearer, and stared into Forest's eyes. Then: "Come on a quest with me."

"I am already on a quest. One that cannot be delayed … for any reason."

"The quest I offer would be invaluable. After, you may continue yours. It will not matter when you dig your grave, Forest. Be in no hurry."

Forest did not like the liberty with which this elder took. But he could not ignore that the letter may be a forgery, and if it was … he looked at Selandria who slept soundly as though under a spell. If the Krim 'Tiak did await him in his village he might still escape alive, but never with her along.

"I'll go on your quest. Under one condition: after its completion, you will see the girl home."

"We are agreed."

Mask sat perched upon Forest's shoulder as they watched from atop a hill Selandria and Old Man walking in council. Clouds crawled over the sky, and a Southern wind had risen carrying with it the scent of blossoms. The woods had ended long ago, and the hills were not only tiring but also dangerous. Yet it was neither the weather nor the terrain that occupied Forest's thoughts, but his companions. When dawn had broken and he'd told Selandria they would not be going to the Coastal Mountains straight away, she did not seem all that disappointed. She seemed rather excited.

Forest relaxed onto one knee, and Mask scurried to sit on his other shoulder. His companions bobbed in and out of sight as they ascended and descended hills, but neither had noticed that they walked minus one. Their conversation, a boring tirade of morality, had begun soon after they'd woken and continued on even now. Forest chuckled and looked at his furry companion.

"How strange it is, that people who can eat other living beasts, can dare speak on what is principled."

Mask licked his human-friend's nose and scampered inside the hood.

"You can't tell me that it is because of the people's immorality that the Forbidden Lands is a desert."

71

Old Man licked his lips and stroked his beard. As he walked he leaned heavily on a cane, but did not appear out of breath for the journey. "It is because of the men who worship Death that this land has been cursed. At one time it was lush and bountiful."

Kimbra laughed. This elder was truly more amusing than any court jester that had come to humor her. He spoke in riddles set out like mind traps, but none that had yet to capture her. And when she rebutted with a trap of her own, he dodged and parried as well as the smartest of tutors. But this time she had him! "That is but a legend! And again you call something 'evil,' without defining what it means to you. 'ow can you win a debate if you speak so ambiguously?"

"You are well-schooled for a commoner," Old Man never looked at the princess who blushed. Sometimes he seemed to know much more than he let on, and this time he seemed to know the impossible. He continued, "But if you desire an explanation, then I would venture to say that an evil person is one who does not honor his brother."

"Honor? Are you so daft as to think you can honor in every action?"

"I am so daft as to believe that I can."

Kimbra rolled her eyes. This was almost too easy, but it was good to give lessons to the less scholarly. "You only know what lay in your own self-interest, and thus can only serve another by serving yourself. You would 'ave to be very powerful person to know the 'earts of others."

"I only know my heart."

"Then you can only do what you desire! See, I'm right. You can only act selfishly."

"But the All knows the hearts of all men. It is through Him that I can do what is right. Thus if I honor the All, I honor my brother."

"The All?" She knew who that was. It was not unheard of, although it was banished in Hauldine. A group of people who worshipped a "god" that wished to have a friendship with humankind. It was hypocritical, ludicrous and unbelievable.

Old Man smiled. "Aye. He is my god."

Kimbra laughed so hard that she had to stop walking. "God? Surely you must be joking. Renrock gave us the paths to be our own gods."

"Then you must know the hearts of men, and have no excuse to act selfishly. Or, you are not much of a god."

As they descended the last hill, Kimbra gave her senior a smirk. She had no idea what to say to that, for he had scored a point and snapped his final mind-trap shut. Through riddles he had created a labyrinth of words that had lost her, but when she saw the Forbidden lands she forgot their conversation. A great tide of sand, as if they were two hands pushing each other away, rose against lush vegetation. On their side the breeze was gentle, flowery and sweet, but over the boundary it howled dust bitter and cold. The sun that had risen beautiful amber in the East now set a bloodstained red in the West, casting a crimson blanket over the desert.

Old Man did not look at Kimbra when he said, "I will feel much safer knowing that I am with a god."

Kimbra ignored the shot as the elder climbed to the top of the dune and waited. Forest came up behind her, frowned, and hopped over the border. The princess shook, and an eerie fright petrified her legs. Nightmares from childhood, affrights long forgotten, returned all at once. The monsters that lived in shadows, the goblins perched upon her windowsill, phantasms chanting her name from barren hallways. Old Man reached down and offered his hand. "Come young god," he whispered. "Gain strength from something other than yourself."

The princess looked up into his eyes and felt the fear leave her body. The reassurances of apparitions being just that, apparitions, and the knowing of adulthood that the ghosts are not the dangers of the world filled her thoughts. The sensation was not unlike when she was cold and servants drowned her in blankets. Reaching up she took the elder's hand and let him lift her to the top.

Chapter Ten

A dozen wild mustangs grazed in a dell cut in half by an ageless brook. Surrounding mountains reached as high as the stars, covered by Douglas Firs which bled down the slopes into the valley. Above, Night bid adieu to its ruler Moon, while simultaneously Day greeted the master Sun.

The trickling brook, uncaring which star governed the sky, gave life to that which came to this land. The grass, woods, steeds ... and a young teen who cooked rabbit over a burning fire. Life went on in this dell by the strong killing the weak; the stream cut through rock, the steeds devoured grass, and the man ate beasts. Nature was harsh, bitter and often unkind. But as for the human, separated from the horses by the water, he knew the cruelty that was Mother Earth and he loved everything about her. It seemed that Nature had taken an equal fascination with him as well. The wild had sculpted his body into the shape of heroes. His matted black hair had grown long, his face bearded and bushy. He stood tall and wide with muscles rippling like the brook over rock.

He leaned back in the long, waving grass, breathed the scent of cooking flesh, and watched the sun drive off the chill night air. The heat was welcome, and this wild human wondered what might give recourse when the cool breeze completely left. He considered that he would do well to befriend the uncaring brook.

As the horses grazed in the field across the stream, a smile captured the stranger. His attraction to them did not go unnoticed, but although their unbroken spirits formed a strange kinship with him a scout studied him as if to show that the bond was not mutual. They were much like him, so much so that they, too, possessed the same mistrust of humans. But they made no distinction between mankind and him. It was determined that although their spectator posed no threat, they would do well to keep watch over him. Just as they would with any other man.

Every one but a yearling.

He stood apart from his brethren, boasting broad shoulders and a strong chest in challenge of his thrall. Under the emblazoning sunlight the steed's dark coat gave a shadowy aura, crowned by a bright white mane. As the beast drifted apart from the pack's safety toward their watcher, the boy rose, cocked his head to one side and met the piercing gaze. But whenever the animal drifted too close its elders whinnied and called the youth back, demanding its return. Stealing freedom.

This went on until the Sun had left Its highest throne and began the journey toward slumber. The boy lay back in the field, closed his eyes and sighed. A pain in his chest, a strange, unyielding ache, kept him from finding total peace. He did not understand this hurt, but it was as real as any sword wound.

A shout, not from nature's beast but from hunters, sent the boy bolt upright. Strangers emerged from the dense forest brandishing nets and whips. Their shouts startled the horses, and before the white-maned steed rushed to its brethren's aid it shot its watcher a look as if it thought him in cahoots with the attackers.

The boy stood by his fire, his face long and muscles frozen, as six hunters skillfully threw a net around one of the younger mares. Without heed of its own peril, the white-maned yearling rushed into the fray, but in anticipation of such an attack the other two hunters threw a net over the brave stallion. Their watcher boiled in tempest, his muscles quivering and the blood pumping a crimson hellfire to his face.

A battle cry that could have shattered the war in Heaven echoed as he leapt over the brook, drew his sword, and charged the would-be tamers. He stopped only a few feet from those who held the steed, shocking them into ceasing their actions. Saliva dripped from his lips and he breathed heavily, tasting the bile that had formed in his mouth.

He liked that taste.

The larger of the two, a lumbering bearded fellow who looked as if he might be more comfortable at sea than on land, drew his sword. He gave the stranger a once over before he approached, then he asked, "What are you thinking boy? Do you mean to do us all in?"

He said naught a word.

"We thought these horses free, not tame. Where is your Master?"

The boy held his ground, and flexed his mighty muscles to show that he was no boy. "I 'ave no Master. And why should any beast that is not tame be man's property? Would you mean to tame me as well?"

"Boy, you need a lesson in manners." The bearded hunter's voice sounded cold and harsh. As his otherwise dark complexion burned, he left alone the sword he wore and readied a whip. Without a word he reared it and struck the boy's face. The whip cut.

He felt the sting but ignored the sharp pain. Yet another scar. Another of many. But a tool meant for beast, not man, had made this one.

"I am no boy. I am Terrell the Wild!"

As the battle fever rose in his veins an intense ring in his ears peaked until he thought it might make him mad. The enemy grew a bright crimson, and no longer did Terrell feel the whip's sting as it bore repeatedly. He succumbed to his madness and attacked. A fray that ended as quickly as it had begun.

Terrell turned from his fallen foe. Blood dripped from his sword. His gaze, saturated with crimson, met with the other men. They all stared back, helpless, unable to overcome their astonishment. These were farm hands, not warriors, so it was no surprise when they never joined the melee. The surprise was that they had stayed.

Terrell's battle fever subsided, and, calming himself, he shouted, "Leave now, or learn the wrath of my steel!"

Dropping their nets and whips the men fled.

And so also did the pack of horses. They wished to stay around no man, not even if he was as wild as they were. For that Terrell did not blame them; and, sighing, he walked back toward his burning dinner. The pain in his heart returning.

But a loud whinny from behind stopped him. His brow fell on him hard, and looking over his shoulder he saw the shadow-like stallion that bore the white mane. The elders in his pack beckoned it to follow, but the horse ignored them. Terrell turned and ran to meet the steed.

"Why do you come to me? Can you not see that I am human?"

But meeting its gaze he understood. They both shared kindred spirits, one and the same. They were not man's tools, nor were they creations of their societies. They were wild beasts of freedom, independent and untamed. Both wanted to explore the world without boundaries, without ordinance from their elders, and neither wished to do it alone.

Chapter Eleven

Marcus rubbed his biceps and smiled at the emergence of a third muscle. "'Tis the tenth Welcome the Creation has granted me. What do you think I should do in thanks?"

"What does it matter what you do?" Tully shouted from his perch on the first branch of the tree he was climbing. "You are already more blessed than any of us."

Marcus squatted and picked up a stone. Tossing it into the air and catching it again he said, "It was not my wish to be Created like this."

"But you were and you've no need to be ashamed." Tully scaled down the tree and walked to his friend. "If I am to be jealous of anyone, I am glad it be you."

"There is nothing to be jealous of!"

The two boys stared at each other, each friend wishing they'd never have to part. As a cool breeze weaved through the trees, disturbing shrubbery and berry bushes, Tully rushed toward the crag. Marcus overtook him and blocked the way. "You know we are not to go there!"

"I so wish to see the Outer world. I heard tales that they eat animals below the mountain."

"And next you'll be telling me they have horns, or eyes as blue as the sky! We are too old for such tales."

Tully said, "What do you need of tales anyway? Come three more Welcomes and you will see it for real. I am stuck in this land."

"You sound like it is a prison."

"Aye, that is how I feel. Let's go to the crag."

"Nay!"

"Be you afraid?" Tully goaded.

"I fear nothing."

Tully side-stepped Marcus and laughed. "Come on then! If you be so brave, then let us go to the crag and see the Outer World."

"We were told not to."

Tully danced around making clucking noises until his friend grabbed him. They tumbled to the ground, their frolic only half-play.

"I am not afraid!" Then he whispered: "I will go."

Marcus approached the crag slowly with Tully close behind. It was narrow and jetted out far, and at its edge they peeked over. People of the Outer World, like a million tiny specs, surrounded the Creation. Tents were raised that could house several villages, and fires burned in such a multitude that it appeared as if the land were ablaze. Behind the troops there was no sign of Creation, only a barren desert where Death howled in triumph.

"What is going on? Do they mean to climb our god?" Tully leaned over the edge, and a rock beneath his hand broke away. He tumbled, but Marcus caught him by the wrist. He pulled, but was unable to bring his friend back onto the ledge. Tully cried, "Run!" and Marcus looked about himself.

They were not on the crag. The village surrounded them. The Krim 'Tiak were everywhere. As one devil sliced Tully across the legs, Marcus screamed....

Forest sat bolt upright and gasped. His heart pounded, and his lungs thundered with shallow breaths. A tear fell from his eye and Mask crawled from the hood where it had been sleeping. The ferret scampered onto Forest's shoulder, and licked his human's ear.

"Thank you friend," the vagabond whispered as it scampered back into the hood. Dawn was breaking over Nalor, and Forest sighed. He had not expected to see as many sunrises as this when he'd agreed to journey to this cursed land. It would not have seemed so terrible had the Red Star not beamed its power so ruthlessly, changing from a night of uncomfortable heat to a day of incineration. Far off in the horizon, where a town dotted the barren landscape, Forest hoped the trek would end. As his companions woke he wondered how much more of this hellish land he could take.

Suddenly the weasel began wheezing, and Forest took it from the hood. Mask looked into its companion's eyes, its own gaze glossy and pleading. "Get water!" the vagabond shouted at Old Man.

"Give the animal to me."

Forest surrendered the ferret. "You will use magic?"

"Nay. I will use Faith."

"Use magic! You said you were a man of sorcery!"

"Do you know me by what I have said, or by what I have done?"

Forest glared, unable to speak.

"Hand me your helmet."

Forest did so, and the elder placed Mask inside. Old Man whispered, "I knew a man who owned a hat like this once."

"Mask had better not die," Forest growled, snatching back the helmet and beginning to walk.

Groups of men all marched along different roads that led into one which would take them to civilization. Those groups who met at the fork fought, and those wishing not to fight made new paths off the highway. Forest's group was one among those who chose to walk in the sand, to create a new path into the town.

Long before they came this close to civilization Mask had recuperated from the heat. The vagabond ignored the smile on Old Man, and refused to question him. He'd had enough riddles for one lifetime. Not even when the elder tugged on his shoulder to direct him into a tavern did he meet the senior's gaze. Inside, they found tables and tables of adventurers, all telling incredible tales. Old Man led them from the dark smoky room into the back, where a small group sat along a table. The high noise level inside the private area fell into a dead silence. Old Man rushed to a keg of ale and quickly poured himself a mug, drinking the liquid thirstily. Before he sat he poured himself another, stopping only when he had realized that the room had fallen silent.

Old Man rose, sat, rose, and chuckled. "My apologies for being so rude. I thought I could have an ale or three before the bickering begins."

A tall, thin man stood. He donned a hooded cloak with the cowl down as if to show off a narrow, pointed face with tanned skin and crimson eyes. His hair, worn short on his head like a crown, had the appearance of a raging fire. "You have an audacity beyond your wisdom."

"Sit, Dedrik. Sit, and I shall introduce you. When my audacious wisdom feels it fit to do so."

With the elder's insistence Dedrik sat. Old Man continued, "May I save Dedrik for last, and first introduce the largest of our trio. Borysko, Chieftain of North Umbria."

The largest of the three stood, spilling the liquid from a giant mug that his

81

large hand dwarfed. A fallen bear whose empty skull made use as a helmet lay on his back, and beside him, resting casually against the table, was a war hammer. The man nodded, let out a grunt and sat.

"Next, I shall introduce the lovely Kasmira the betrayed."

A woman, not much shorter than Forest but with a much slender build, stood. The candlelight shone brightly against her fair complexion, and beneath dark eyelashes danced eyes more emerald than any gemstone. Her long scarlet hair, as if it were a mane stolen from a goddess of lore, reached the middle of her back and draped casually off her shoulders to the bottom of her bosom.

"Now, introduce me," Dedrik said as he stood.

Old Man sighed. "This is Dedrik the fallen. He was the last to come to the group, yet the first to lead."

"Old Man, when you requested we postpone our quest you promised me a prophet! What you bring me are children!"

"I bring you Forest the vagabond, of the Coastal Mountains. And Selandria..." the wizard paused, and looked into her eyes. He said, "Selandria, the Adventuress."

Dedrik slammed his fists onto the wooden table before him. A mug of ale fell, spilling over the table's surface. "Damn it! This Movement is not a joke!"

"Nor am I here to make it one," Forest said.

"Child, aren't you a little young to be out adventuring?"

"And Dedrik the fallen, are you not a little old to be out so late?" Forest took a seat and crossed his arms over his chest.

Dedrik placed his open palms onto the table and leaned on them hard. He glared at the youth with bared teeth as white as porcelain. "Would you care to see just how old I am?"

Forest first looked at Old Man, and then he stood, noting Kasmira and Borysko's interest. Mask climbed out from the hood and perched upon the vagabond's shoulder. It puffed out its chest and jabbed its snout into the air as if sensing the challenge between the human it rode and the one across from them. Forest scratched its belly as he met Dedrik's fiery eyes with a stern glare of his own. "Where I come from we fight our enemies, not our companions."

Old Man rose before Dedrik could answer, and placed a comforting hand on his shoulder. "Dedrik. 'Tis not the way of the All to fight. Do not test the Laws."

"I mean no challenge on the Laws, only on him. If he is not worthy of my testing, perhaps he should find a child's game to play. And stay away from a man's world."

The elder seemed flustered for words. All eyes in the room turned on Forest. He turned beat red and decided he would damn himself before turning down such a blunt insult. He ignored the disapproving look from Old Man and said, "I'll meet your challenge."

Forest followed the party outside. He placed the ferret on the ground and whispered, "This be not your battle. Wait for me." The animal responded with a firm "Dook!" before scampering to the tiny group. The night air felt warm to the young warrior, and looking up into the heavens he noticed that several eyes watched through many scattered windows along the lane. The cowardly derelicts in the alleyway ran for safety, as Forest took his vision away from the barren sky. He looked at his opponent, and wished for more light than what the few burning street lamps provided. Dedrik stood several paces away, drew his sword, and embraced the naked blade with crimson eyes of fury. As he broke into a frenzy of swordplay Forest heard his foe whisper, "Bring me honor, Koontah."

Still uncertain just how he'd found himself in this predicament, Forest fell into the splits.

Dedrik's eyes widened as they fell on his adversary. With teeth brandishing the terror of battle he yelled and charged. The razor sharp blade raced toward Forest, yet he did nothing to retaliate. Then, as the blade swung inches above his skull, a glimmer of confusion tarnished Dedrik's battle fever. Forest took that opportunity. He drew his nunchuka, used the chain to block the menacing blade, spun onto his side and kicked his opponent hard in the gut. As the air from his foe's lungs expressed itself, Forest spun to foot sweep him to the hard desert ground. Flipping to his feet he twirled the farm tool in a frenzy that equaled Dedrik's swordsmanship and watched the fury in his opponent's spirit give way to amazement.

Forest offered his hand and asked, "Well enough?"

"Well enough," Dedrik took the hand and shook it. He blushed, rose and spoke; his voice cracking as he struggled to say, "I pray you might forgive my weakness. I had no right to test you."

Forest's smile was only half filled with sincerity, "You are forgiven."

"Old Man," Dedrik shouted, "please accompany me in prayer."

The elder lead the Fallen inside, and when Forest turned back to the tavern, he saw Selandria with Borysko. They walked off together, hand in hand, without saying so much as a single word to him. A lightly accented voice sang sweetly from behind, "A very valiant display, warrior."

The vagabond looked over his shoulder, and turned completely around. When he met Kasmira's eyes he became spellbound. Mask sat perched on her shoulder, and Forest held his arm out to it. The ferret crawled up his sleeve and into its cowl. He smiled at the red-haired beauty and turned away. He wished he'd stayed on his course to the Coastal Mountains.

And that he'd gone alone.

The group retired to a private room in the inn, but neither Old Man nor Dedrik had joined them. To pass the time Kasmira and Selandria listened to Borysko boast wild stories of adventure. Forest, so it seemed to Kasmira, didn't care about tales. That made her curious. His animal lay obediently by his side, as he sat before the fire, poking the flames with a metal rod intent on heating a room void of cold. She thought it odd that a warrior would try so hard to avoid a conversation that he could certainly dominate.

Borysko raised his voice an octave when he noticed he might be losing his audience. The North Umbrian swelled with pride from his tales, swelled from a pride common to those of his stock. Kasmira turned her attention back to him, but kept glancing at Forest.

"Eh!" Borysko grunted, again securing her attention, but the Umbrian had not spoken to her.

The young warrior by the fire turned as the large Umbrian asked, "How many adventures have you seen? You're a good warrior."

Forest grew a deep shade of scarlet, turned himself back to the fire, and whispered something about the world being accursed. Mask licked his ear and snubbed his chest at the Umbrian. Kasmira was intrigued. She bit her bottom lip tenderly and rose, walked to the young warrior, thinking she might like to sit with him awhile. But the door to the tiny room opened as if to intentionally thwart her decision. Old Man and Dedrik entered. Kasmira looked at Forest again, who was now looking at her, as if in relief of her foiled decision. He sighed.

"Good evening, my companions. My friends." Dedrik strode to a small table. Old Man began arranging chairs in a semicircle around the table, and motioned for them all to come sit. Dedrik continued: "For the benefit of our two new, and much welcome, companions, I feel an obligation to explain our quest."

Forest took the blunt hint and left the fire alone, moving to take a seat on the semicircle's edge. Kasmira did the same, sitting between the young warrior and Borysko. Beside the Umbrian sat Selandria, and Old Man stood beside her, nodding for Dedrik to continue.

"I am called Dedrik the fallen. I am called that for deserting my people. For twenty-seven years I served under Death, unconscionably, until a single word brought me from my darkness. This single word, spoken by a mother protecting her child from my carnage, was 'Please.' My darkness was replaced with guilt and hatred for myself. In secret I left my people."

Forest's brow furrowed, he shifted, and he cleared his throat. "Who are these evil people you escaped from?"

Dedrik's eyes grew sullen, and, as he answered, Kasmira kept an eye on the vagabond. "'Tis a difficult thing for me to admit. Especially to you, Forest. You claim to come from the Coastal Mountains, a land ravaged by the people of my birth. I was born, raised, and educated as a Krim 'Tiak. As you saw earlier, it is still difficult for me to forsake a way of thinking that I had believed right for twenty-seven years. I should have recalled the Holy Book, 'Losing your temper is something anyone can do. Be unique.' But then, who amongst us can cast the first stone?"

"I can!" Forest stood, drew his nunchuka, and let his shaking voice ring with his desire for retribution. Mask leapt to the floor and scampered to sit on Kasmira's shoulder. "I did not come here to follow a god that I do not know, nor One who accepts a race of Death!"

Dedrik quickly drew his sword, and Kasmira gasped when she saw the battle-fury saturate his eyes. Dedrik walked to Forest and Kasmira moved. But the Fallen stood before Forest, fell to his knees, and offered his sword by the hilt.

"If you are so free of sin that you know my Judgment, then I ask that you deliver it."

Forest was stunned.

Dedrik rose, the shame in his eyes, Kasmira knew, mistaken by all for battle fury. "Or you can aid us, and your people, by forgiving someone whose dark heart has found the Light. I do not follow a god who accepts Death, I follow a god of Life, Who accepts repentance."

The Movement stared at Forest. They waited for his response. The young warrior turned red, his body trembled, and his muscles drew tight and oily. The vagabond put away his weapon.

Forest said, "Perhaps it is better that we accept one another, then it is to die fighting. At least, until it is time for us to part ways."

Dedrik returned Koontah into her sheath and smiled. "You can avoid conflict with me easy enough, but don't fool yourself into believing that you can run from the war in yourself. I have been there also." He chuckled. "I am there, also."

Forest started to speak, but Old Man stood and bellowed, "Can we get on with this? I have ale in the tavern, and she's getting warm."

"Aye," Forest replied, taking his seat.

Dedrik continued: "When I left the Krim 'Tiak, I took to living with the elves. In exchange for my battle prowess they offered me shelter and food. I owe those people much, and regret deeply having had to leave them. But, for many years I sought repentance for my acts as a Krim 'Tiak, and the elves could offer me none. It was not until I found Old Man, or perhaps it is more accurately said that he found me, that I saw my path to redemption. Old Man showed me the All, and in return the All showed me forgiveness."

Dedrik paused. He took out a small wooden pipe from his belt purse, filled it with tobacco, walked to a lamp, used its flame to light the drug, and breathed the heavy smoke deeply before returning to stand before the group. He took a few more puffs, and gazed into the eyes of each and every one. Then he spoke with a hushed tone.

"The Krim 'Tiak await their Leader. The world awaits a new messianic figure, one who will make them all gods. This 'Chosen One' the world awaits to unite them will be the body for the Evil Leader. The Chosen One of this New Age will damn the world, not save it. For the love that the All has shown us, we must warn the world that the End is near."

"How will we do that?" Forest asked.

"First, we must find the Tools. Without the Tools, the Chosen One will be powerless."

"And what are these things?"

"The sword, Koontah, which we have. Only the Eyes, the two keys to Hell, are left to find. One is hidden in the Other World, where none of us can get it. But the other is hidden on our world."

Forest asked, "Do I want to know where this 'Other World' is?"

Dedrik took a puff on his pipe, and held the heavy tobacco smoke to savor its rich flavor. He stared at Forest, deeply into his eyes, and shook his head from side to side as smoke spewed from his nostrils.

"Then tell me what this quest of yours is."

"The Chosen One is clouded with the illusion that he is working to destroy Evil. When he learns we have the tools he needs, he will come to us. We will implore the elves to give us sanctuary while we wait."

"Then I wish you the best of luck. After I aid you in finding this Eye, I will be continuing to the Coastal Mountains."

"Then perhaps," Dedrik's words rode solemnly on the tails of his puffs of grey smoke, "it is the rest of us who should wish you the best of luck."

Dawn was several hours away when the Movement began their quest. Each member rode a brown Clydesdale raised by Dedrik who rode lead with Old Man and Kasmira. Selandria and Borysko followed closely behind with Forest and Mask in the flank, far from the others. The vagabond whispered his thanks to the beast whom he rode, and took special note of the respect it paid the ex-Krim 'Tiak. The vagabond, as he watched Selandria flirt with Borysko, whispered, "At least I am absolved of one burden," and brushed his nose against Mask who then crawled inside the cowl.

Kasmira broke riding formation and came beside the vagabond. Forest faced forward and ignored her. But she stared, rode closer and said, "Such silence for a man so filled with opinions."

Forest glanced at her. He said nothing.

"Tell me your hidden truths," she asked.

He shot her a piercing glare, closed his eyes, opened them and breathed hard. "How can anyone find truth in a world so bent on deception?"

Borysko broke riding formation to come beside them. "There's a party ahead. From the dust I'd say it's a large group. Dedrik wants us to wait here, except Forest; he wants you and him to approach them alone. You don't have to...."

"I'll go," Forest answered, taking Borysko's words as a challenge.

As Forest rode with Dedrik toward the oncoming party, he glanced over his shoulder and saw the group disappear into the desert. Oddly, he felt sorrow for Old Man having had to use his magic. Dedrik halted, and Forest fell in beside him. They waited for the party to draw near, both hoping the strangers would not attack when they saw a Krim 'Tiak riding without his army of Death. The group stopped. The dust cloud cleared. One man stepped from the ranks and advanced near. Forest whispered, "Damn you," and thought, *They've hunted me like a beast!*

When the man rode within earshot Dedrik called, "Be you friend or foe?"

"That depends on your companion."

Forest answered, "Why have you come? I thought we had an understanding."

"You betrayed my trust. You know why I 'ave come!"

Dedrik asked, "You know this man?"

"His name is Sir Theomund. I am his slave, and he has come to bring me back to bondage."

Sir Theomund rode a few steps nearer. "I did not come because of your desertion. I came because you kidnapped the princess."

"Of what do you speak?"

"You know well of what I speak. I find it all too coincidental that you disappeared the same day as she."

"Very … but I never kidnapped her."

"Then why make your trail so 'ard to track?"

"Habit," Forest paused. He tried to think of an explanation. "I'm not the one you're after. The only person I've been traveling with is..." The girl he had come to know as Selandria, Forest realized, was the princess in disguise! He smiled and said without pause, "...Dedrik. Look around us. There is no one else."

"Then you must be hiding 'er!"

"Where? You show me where! This is the desert!"

Sir Theomund could no longer look at his apprentice. He sighed, opened his mouth to speak and cursed. Forest said, "I understand your plight, and I wish you luck. But please, trust me."

"I don't know what to say."

"Wish me luck."

Without a word, Sir Theomund signaled his men to depart. Once a large cloud of dust again replaced their presence, Forest and Dedrik turned to ride back to their companions.

Forest laughed. "Dedrik, let's keep this between us. We'll say they were only adventurers."

Dedrik looked curiously into his companion's mischievous eyes, but, seeing in this an opportunity to form a bond of trust, he agreed.

Chapter Twelve

Terrell and Lightning stood high atop a crag on mount D'or Nak. They stared at the valley below, once a land of Eden for any man or beast. A verdant tarp split only by a navy thread, life for all beasts that came. Memories told of birds that flew in the skies, fish that swam in the rivers, and caribou that ran from hunting wolves. Yet no animal or fowl enjoyed the brisk North Umbrian wind that rippled both grass and stream. The sky was empty, the stream nearly dry, and vegetation had turned brown. Terrell breathed deep when that wind howled by him, catching his long mane and mixing it with his stallion's, for he knew what it was that had driven the wilderness from this freedom. As the Wild looked into the setting sun, he bid it a kind farewell and waited for Night. The Elementals were gods in these parts, and while in them he would respect that. Even if he did not believe it.

Fires began to ignite the valley below, their numbers in this part of North Umbria surprising the two friends. They did not expect to still find life, let alone in such multitudes. The man brushed his hand down Lightning's white mane; he needn't speak, for between them thoughts were as one. North Umbria was once a desolate place, but the camp told that humanity had come to live in these parts. And where humans settled, freedom was always lost.

But never without a fight, Terrell thought.

"K'on Grommat!" a voice shouted from behind.

Terrell did not respond. He stared into the dell, his muscles tense as he and Lightning prepared for war. He thought on the proper Umbrian words, and hoped his speech was not too rusty.

"You need not know my name, or my companions." They turned and faced an Umbrian horde, one that was ready for full-scale war.

The one who had spoken was crowned with a helmet made from a strange beast. Its hide was thick and orange, with a circle of hair from ear to ear that stuck out like flames. Two ivory tusks covered the man's cheekbones, and where eyes had once been two ruby gems now sparkled. The rest of the skin lay upon the huge Umbrian, as though the animal rode the man's back. The stranger carried a large war hammer and flexed his muscular form.

"You speak Umbrian. That good."

"Do you speak Hauldinian?"

"Nay. Are you that breed?"

Terrell considered. Then: "Nay, I be not. I am a beast as untamed as the stallion with me."

"If that be, we welcome you to sit and drink by our fire."

Terrell turned his back on the Umbrian horde. "I did not come for your welcome. I have come to find my peace."

"Then you have come to the wrong place, friend. By morning you will be standing on war ground."

Terrell turned to face him. "North Umbria is at war?"

"As surely as Mount Groth fell. Soon, South Umbria be at war also. Elves would be at war too, had they not sold their souls."

Terrell stared hard into the Umbrian's eyes. "And who, I beseech you, is this predator?"

The Umbrian laughed heartily. "Kor 'Dak must send you! The god of jest!"

"I be no jest, nor be I one afraid of your numbers! I am Terrell the Wild, and I will fight for my freedom. No matter how terrible the death!" He drew his sword. "I beseech you again, who are the predators!"

"Keep your sword arm easy, the predator is not us. It be the Krim 'Tiak! You must be sent by Fri 'lah, god of freedom."

Terrell looked at Lightning. Again thoughts passed between them. He looked back at the Umbrian, and relaxed. "If my companion is also welcome by your fires I will join you this night. What are you called, friend?"

"Karel. Come then, there is much to do."

After the sun had set and the moon had risen Terrell and Lightning found themselves sitting by the horde's fire, amidst the camps they had thought it best to avoid. Beside them was a great statue, and for a long while the Wild stared; his mind digesting every carved angle. He only relaxed his scrutiny when Karel, coming to him with a meal, sat to eat his own. Karel stopped, noticing his guest's curiosity.

"The god of freedom, we carved the idol from our finest gold. When dawn breaks, we will bathe it in lamb's blood. Already, we are blessed with a warrior of freedom!"

"The statue ... it, it looks just like me."

"As if you are an omen from Fri 'lah. You must be the leader we await."

The Wild filled his mouth with meat and chewed. After he swallowed he replied, "What of you?"

"I am no leader. A man called Borysko is our Chieftain, but a Nameless God sent him on sojourn. That is why the Krim 'Tiak chose now to attack."

The Umbrian horde all turned to Terrell. The Wild's brow furrowed and grew dark. He met their gazes with one thought emanating in his mind: *I am a man.* Terrell put his plate of food onto the ground, stood, and flexed his stiff, almost sore, muscles. He had spent such a long time in freedom.

"I am no god," he said at last. "I am a man, made from flesh like all of you. I bleed when cut. I die when stabbed. If it is a god who you seek, perhaps you should have accompanied Borysko on his sojourn."

When he met Karel's eyes, his stern demeanor weakened. Neither man spoke, and Terrell realized that his welcome had come to an end. He turned with Lightning to leave.

"We would follow a man!" Karel called out.

Terrell paused, looked at Lightning and wondered how right it would be for a boy to lead an army. Certainly he possessed a man's physical stature, but in many respects his mind grasped to the child within. *Am I ready to be a man?*

Freedom, Terrell remembered, at any cost.

"We fight at dawn!" Terrell cried as Lightning whinnied, incensing the Umbrian horde into a fervor that echoed in the valley.

Long before dawn's advent Terrell climbed high atop the idol of Fri 'lah. The sun had now peeked half its body over the horizon, and the Wild looked upon the army he intended to march against the Krim 'Tiak. He wondered when he'd become so arrogant as to think it right for him to take command of a people who did not belong to him. People who belonged to someone else. To gods he didn't know. Terrell raised a horn crafted of bone to his lips, and pondered at the wisdom of his next actions. But he could not lead these people into battle if they thought him a manifestation of their god. *I am only a man*, he thought.

He could not go into battle unless they followed him as a man and not a false idea of what they needed him to be. But his actions, Terrell knew, would either incense them to victory or fell them into damnation. Perhaps, it might be best to give them false hope?

The dim scarlet sun had little more than peeked over the horizon, and it told Terrell to make up his mind. He considered his words, hoping he knew all he needed to say. The North Umbrian tongue was not a complex one, and was lost to many universal expressions, but if he could communicate with Lightning so well without words, surely he could communicate with his own kind with very few. His own kind. Terrell wondered how much truth existed in such a bold statement. He stared at the sleeping people of North Umbria, thinking how odd they were. How odd they made himself seem. Without a leader they would find themselves broken slaves by afternoon with no more lives to call their own. But without honesty, Terrell could be no leader to them at all. Terrell made his choice. He blew his horn loudly, until every North Umbrian woke from their slumber.

One by one they gathered around the towering statue of Fri 'lah. They stared up at him, upon Terrell the Wild, shocked by what they saw. Terrell balanced himself with one foot on the statue's left shoulder, his other on the statue's head. He rose to his full height and held his arms outstretched. Terrell hoped he had the custom right.

"Look at me, North Umbria! Look at my naked body and see I be man! I be not a god, and I promise you no victory! But I lead you, so should you desire. I lead you and together we wage war on Krim 'Tiak and send them back to Hell! Raise your arms, North Umbria. Raise them and fight!"

All the tribe stared blankly at him. No one yelled. No one raised an arm. No one looked upon him anymore as a god.

"He be only man!" one yelled.

"They slaughter us we follow man," yelled another.

And systematically, North Umbria turned their backs on Terrell the Wild.

The Wild did not have to look to know that Lightning stood by him at the statue's base. Nor did he have to look to acknowledge that Lightning had never wished to be a part of these humans. Why his heart ached at the sight of their backs, and why that ache had left at their praise by last night's fire was a mystery to him.

Terrell looked upon them to see a young child drag a heavy war hammer out from the crowd. *Is this the army of Terrell the Wild?* he wondered. The child tried lifting the heavy war hammer, but was quite unable to do so.

Karel, the man who had welcomed him by last night's fire, walked to the boy and raised the hammer for him. Then Karel turned to his people.

"Are our spirits so broken that only this child dares war on Krim 'Tiak? Our gods forsook us! Our leader follows a god no one knows! But Terrell the Wild is here to aid us, and I will stand by him!" Karel hoisted the child onto his strong shoulders and turned to Terrell. They held the hammer high. "If you won't, then shackle yourselves now and begin your march to the slave camps."

Terrell smiled. He had thought Karel's efforts in vain, but one by one every North Umbrian turned with raised weapons until the valley echoed with cries of: "Terrell! Terrell!"

And raising his own sword high Terrell yelled back, "To war!"

Terrell the Wild stood stoically on the edge of war. Lightning stood on his right, and Karel as his advisor on his left. Behind them, North Umbria stood in wait to spill the Krim 'Tiak's blood. Strange westerly winds had risen form the Forbidden Lands, carrying with it the stench of the Dead. Terrell stared down from his vantage point high upon the mountain's ledge, and saw the smoke from the Krim 'Tiak's army advancing nearer. Sweat beaded on his tense muscles, and he hoped the North Umbrians might think it from the burning sun.

Soon the smoke from the advancing army changed into silhouettes, which in turn changed into a mass of warriors. Never before had Terrell seen such an incredible number. His own army, though impressive, would never withstand such a force, and with Krim 'Tiak war would end in either death or slavery.

And war with Terrell the Wild would have freedom at any cost!

A man donning a red cape and silver plated breastplate stepped away from the massive Krim 'Tiak army. He lumbered until no more then a score of feet remained between him and the Umbrian leader. The captain drew his sword, grinned beneath a helmet adorned with a tiny statuette of a howling wolf's head, and drew a line with his blade's tip in the muddy ground. Then he returned the weapon to its sheath.

"I seek the man who calls himself 'Borysko, Chieftain of North Umbria.'"

"I am called Terrell the Wild. I am Chieftain of these people."

"Go home, boy." The captain's smile turned to a snarl.

"Not before I send you to yours." Terrell drew his sword.

"I came seeking slaves or sacrifice. To my deity, it matters not which."

"Then you and your deity have come in vain!"

Terrell flew into action across the mark drawn by the Krim 'Tiak with sword in hand. Behind, he heard Lightning and Karel follow, and after a call to war all of North Umbria met their enemy on the battle field. Terrell knew his own duty. To meet this army captain head on. To take down the first domino, so that all the others would follow in succession.

Metal met metal in a whirlwind of confusion. Terrell's sword sparked when it struck its enemy's, but when it stabbed flesh he felt strong. Karel and Lightning did the same with other warriors.

"No one can save you!" The Wild yelled, knocking his opponent to the ground. "The only sacrifice to your deity on this day, will be Its own people." With that Terrell pushed his sword through the captain's armor, and into his heart.

Then Terrell cut off his head and ran to the cliff's top with Lightning and Karel by his side. The Wild blew his horn and threw down the Krim 'Tiak's head!

"North Umbria! To victory!" Terrell cried, incensing the North Umbrians into a fervor.

Beside him, Karel crossed his arms in pride of his people. "You did good for a man. North Umbria will owe you Her life."

Terrell the Wild stared down at the battle below, watching as the tide of battle swept the Krim 'Tiak into an ocean of blood. He waited for the smoke to settle.

Soon, the battle of North Umbria would end, and these people would beg him to reign as their Chief. But he had given that up long ago when he had chosen to live his life for freedom. *I am no god*, Terrell thought. He closed his eyes tight, and wondered what Power had wished to test him so. Again he opened his eyes to oversee the battle, knelt onto one knee, and refused to look at neither Lightning on his right nor Karel on his left. He refused to answer Karel's unspoken question, and stared at the battle below. The Wild felt sickened by humanity's carnage.

"Will you stay to lead us?" Karel asked.

The strong winds carried the Wild's long hair like a banner. Through the corner of one eye he looked at the Umbrian. "I come from a race of people who think themselves gods. They rule because they have divine wisdom, as all gods do."

"Then be our god!"

Terrell stared into the heavens, and closed his eyes from its mystery. "I am not a god! I am Terrell the Wild and nothing more!"

He rose and did not look at Karel again. He did not because he could not. Lightning stayed by his side when he started down the mountain, when he walked away from the battle, and even as he wondered how he could have tried to live among his brothers. But more, Terrell wondered why he desired to stay. Karel threw a pouch to him.

"May the gods be with you, Terrell the Wild. Should you ever find yourself in need, remember that North Umbria is indebted to you."

Chapter Thirteen

Dusk had only begun to settle when the assorted party of adventurers faced the caverns. The opening jettisoned out from the ground like a snake's head yawning a jaw full of jagged teeth. The scorching desert air had cooled, but come to life in a hissing wind. A blood-red moon, full it always was in these lands, hung low over the western horizon turning the pink haze a shade of amber. Then, as the party stared at the humble-looking entrance, a beast of prey far in the distance howled in anticipation of coming night. Forest braced himself once more for the cool breeze that gained strength with every blast. Mask hid inside his cowl, and Forest hoped the nippy gusts that had been strong enough to find their way through the openings in his armor, carrying tiny grains of sand, hadn't found their way to it. He had become used to the discomfort of adventure long ago, but wished he was home, in his village, and sneaking a glance at the princess he held fast to the anger he felt for her obvious enjoyment of adventure. To her this was a frivolous novelty, a game that would end whenever she wished.

To him adventure was a poison. A venom without an antidote.

Kimbra met his gaze and smiled, all the while staying close to Borysko. She brushed her long, raven locks from her eyes and Borysko, too, met Forest's stare. He caressed her back and puffed out his chest until the vagabond looked away. And Forest did, holding himself stoic with obvious disgust for both of them.

Dedrik stood before the brink of his destiny. The double doors that lead into the caverns were crafted of a rotted maple, and barred shut with a rusted lock and chain. Old Man grasped his shoulder to comfort him, whispering that they best continue. Every moment he spent basking in the astonishment

97

of the unfolding prophecy was one more moment gained to the Krim 'Tiak.

Dedrik leaned to grasp the long doors by their base and gave a solid tug. When the rusted hinges gave way and cracked, he cast the doors open, heedless of what damage he might cause them. The Fallen raised a portion of his cloak to his nose to brace himself against the sickly stench of past adventurers, those who were now nothing more than corpses. As Old Man passed around ignited torches Dedrik peered inside the dark cavern. A steep marble stairwell lead downward, just as his maps indicated there would be, and the walls, Dedrik noticed while stepping onto the first stair, were cut and honed to a mirror shine. There were no webs made by dangerous arachnids.

He stepped outside, turned from the entrance, and walked back to his mount. He braced himself against a stronger, cooler breeze, and again a howl from a hunting beast rose in the advancing dusk. Then another joined that howl, and another. The bays came ever nearer. Dedrik rubbed his prized steed's long nose fondly, and wondered how wise he was to leave them outside. Alone.

Dedrik turned to his party and said: "We must choose who will lead. Though I wish nothing more than to gallantly brave the unknown terrors for you, my kind will invoke battle on any strangers we might happen upon. I will be the flank." Dedrik began to gather his supplies.

"I will lead." Forest volunteered, checking his own supplies. Mask climbed onto his shoulder as if to say, "And I shall be your second."

"And I shall be next," Kasmira offered.

"That's not a good idea," Borysko grunted, more to Forest than anyone else.

"But Borysko," Kasmira sang sweetly while batting her long, dark eyelashes. "Doesn't it make perfect sense to have a warrior up front and the adventuress second?" Then to Forest: "That way we can send brawn and brains into battle."

Dedrik watched Forest grimace, let loose a long sigh, and turn to the woman. His silvery eyes and rigid jaw brandished his exasperation. "Are you implying that I don't have both?"

"Your kind never do." She smiled.

Forest turned from her. He walked a few feet, and, though no one in the group except Dedrik had heard him do so, he whispered, "Accurse this world."

"So be it then," said the vagabond as he stepped inside the cavern, with his torch held further in to light the way. But Borysko left the raven-haired beauty who had attached herself to him and grabbed the leader by the shoulder.

Spinning the much smaller warrior to meet him face to face, both looked undaunted by the incredulous gust of wind that had blown out their torch light.

"I am a better warrior! I'll be first!" Borysko shouted.

In the advancing night the two warriors glared at one another. They positioned themselves to square off. The beasts howled in the near distance as Dedrik stepped forward, but Old Man stopped him with a reassuring hand. Kasmira, as well, had stepped forward but stopped when Forest stepped aside to offer the leadership to the Umbrian.

"So be it then. You may go first. And for her protection, I'll walk with Selandria." He winked at her, making certain Borysko noticed.

Dedrik watched as Borysko stood perplexed. He stepped one foot inside the cavern, and kept his other out. He frowned as if a great war raged in his mind. He looked at Forest and shook his head.

"No! No! No!" the Umbrian said, waving his hands out in front of him like a child. "Selandria shall be up here for me to protect!"

"Borysko," Kasmira sang sweetly, ignoring the howling beasts who drew ever closer. "What talent does she possess to earn her above me? I, at least, have experience."

Borysko looked even more confused. Dedrik considered making this decision for them, but Old Man had given him that look. That look that said he knew. The Umbrian slowly took his foot out from the cavern and walked back to Selandria. He then made a gesture to Forest, quite an obscene one that told him he could have the lead.

Dedrik smiled, but not as much as when Forest had stepped back into the cavern and said to Kasmira, "Once my Master told me, 'Never judge a man by what you have learnt from others'."

With that, he entered the cavern.

"Touché," Kasmira replied under the whistling winds. She followed, a glint in her eyes as if the vagabond and not the cavern were her adventure.

Selandria followed Kasmira, and Borysko after her. Dedrik next, but not before taking one last look at his beasts. Another terrible gust of air had risen, blowing sand all around them, and the night creatures wailed above the bluster's whistle.

"They served me well," Dedrik whispered to Old Man. Again he felt the elder's hand on his shoulder.

"And they will serve you again. Just have Faith."

Dedrik turned from his mounts. As he entered the dimly lit cavern the horses whinnied, and the Fallen hoped he did well to trust Old Man. Truth was, he knew very little of him; only that he had been Kasmira's tutor in the All. But Dedrik knew Old Man's loyalty, kindness, and trust in the All. That, for him, was enough. As for why the elder had kept so much of himself secret, Dedrik never dared ask. He knew that everyone in the group had pasts they'd rather not reveal. Himself not an exception. He recalled his own life as a Krim 'Tiak and felt ashamed. He had the right to question no one.

Forest reached the stairwell's bottom, holding his torch out as far as he could inside the tunnel he had just descended. The darkness, which not even his torch cut through, covered a long, narrow corridor. Unlike the stairwell the walls appeared as though Mother Nature were the mason, and a few paces down a strange green moss, an aspect of the Creation Forest had never seen before, lived deep within the imperfect structure's cracks. An eerie bluish-green glow emitted from that strange foliage.

Forest entered cautiously. The eerie moss became thicker the farther they traveled until it gave off enough light so they no longer needed torches. He extinguished his and took out his nunchuka, placing the torch inside his scabbard. He walked cautiously, listening to skeletons crunch beneath his feet. He wondered what manner of creature might have taken their souls; more so if it lay in wait for them.

Forest came upon a corner. He readied his weapon; kept his muscles alert, tense, and ready. He listened for any sounds he might hear, suddenly realizing how strangely quiet the caverns were. He rounded the corner and saw a pig-like man covered only at his waist kneeling in the dirt, munching on the remains of a human. Mask leapt from his perch onto the ground, puffing out its fur and arching its back. It made a loud "Dook" noise at its enemy. Forest stepped away from the spectacle, disgusted by what he saw, but the pig-man had seen him. Rising nearly to the cavern's height, the hair on its head falling to its waist and dirt covering the rest of its body like a second skin, it grabbed a spear that lay nearby. It crouched; growling with teeth bared and eyes flared. The stench from its meal stank, and Forest wondered why he hadn't sensed it earlier.

Then it attacked.

Forest shattered the rotting spear with one strike of his nunchuka, and with a side-kick he landed the large foe onto the dirt floor. The rest of the group stood behind him, unable to help in the narrow corridor. The vagabond felt their eyes on him as he advanced. Borysko watched with anticipation. Dedrik looked stern, and Old Man ... appeared only curious. Kasmira covered her eyes as the ferret perched on her shoulder. Forest turned his attention back on his opponent, cursed, and knocked him out cold. The vagabond again turned to look at his party, and saw Kasmira holding her eyes shut.

"Kill 'im!" Borysko shouted.

Forest looked at the large Umbrian, sighed, closed and opened his eyes. He looked at Kasmira, who had slowly begun to open her eyes, and then he continued to walk down the cavern. He left the creature alone, and refused to look back. When he heard the Umbrian plunge a knife deep into the beast's throat he pretended not to hear. He moved into a large opening in the cavern.

Kasmira touched his shoulder, and Mask ran down her arm to climb back into his hood. He turned to see the woman smiling at him, and saw by her misty eyes that she appreciated his letting the monster live. She appreciated his mercy. She mouthed the words "thank you," and he closed his eyes again, only for a moment, and shrank from her. Then he moved into the opening. Kasmira's hand snapped from his shoulder, and again he turned. He thought of something to say, and nearly said it, but Old Man interrupted by pushing through the ranks to take the lead.

Old Man cleared his throat to get their attention. The sound of his raspy voice echoed throughout the room. "We should stop here to rest. In case of trouble, we shall have watches. Borysko, you shall watch first. Then Kasmira second. Forest, you will be next, followed by Dedrik. For the last, Selandria the adventuress."

"And what of you, Old Man?" Borysko asked.

"I shall be too busy sleeping to watch!"

Kimbra never figured she'd have found herself sleeping on a cold, hard dirt floor. She looked about herself, at her exciting new surroundings, and forgot her discomfort. Instead she concentrated on the wonderful adventure she now tasted. She thought of her brother, Terrell, and wondered where he might be, but she was more curious if her father missed her as much as he did him.

Possibly, but she doubted it.

Forest shivered from the chill air but let the cold ward off his despondence. Cold, but not alone. Mask lay beside him curled on its back. Forest grabbed his worn blanket and tried spreading it over himself and the weasel. He wondered what hellish nightmare awaited him this night as he looked about his surroundings, especially at his companions. Perhaps, for this one night, his nightmares might forget him. Perhaps tonight he would succumb to a sleep deep enough to stave them off.

Possibly, but he doubted it.

Forest felt a hand gently waking him. He opened his eyes, looked at Kasmira, and grumbled in recognition. "I'm awake," he said. But again slumber took hold, and Kasmira had to shake him harder.

"I'm up, I'm up!" Forest grumbled louder, this time sitting upright. He shook Mask, but the ferret just scurried beneath his blanket and fell back asleep.

Forest reached for his nunchuka, rested them on his lap, and peeked out the corner of his eye. Kasmira was staring at him. She lay flat on the ground, propped up on one elbow. Her long red hair was draped over her shoulder, and her green eyes sparkled in the torch light. Her scarlet lips looked pensive and her high cheek bones had blossomed a light cherry. At first his heart fluctuated, then his breathing labored, and finally his cold body perspired. He looked away, and fixated on a spot far into the dark cavern. She still stared at him.

"Where did you train, Forest?" Her voice sounded nervous, and he wondered what she might be up to.

"The Coastal Mountains." He looked directly at her, his two silvery eyes a glowing challenge.

"I heard the Krim 'Tiak had slaughtered the Easterners. They laid waste to that land. No survivors are ever left by the Krim 'Tiak that aren't taken as slaves."

"No deserters either, yet you trust Dedrik."

"You have a retort for everything, don't you?" Her tone sounded colder than the air around them.

"I know the difference between right and wrong."

"Do you? Is that why you didn't kill that orc back there?"

Forest didn't respond. Again he fixated on the spot in the cavern.

"No one here wishes to pass judgment on you," she told him.

"That's why Dedrik challenged me to a duel? To show me his non-judgmental side?"

"How dare you! Dedrik suffers from a temperament disease called 'battle fever.'"

"We all suffer something, don't we?"

"Two years ago when I first met him, he would not have even challenged you. His sword would have been drawn and in you before you took a second breath!"

"So I'm supposed to think him a saint?"

"I will point out, that had you not complied with his challenge, Dedrik's temper would have subsided and passed."

"So now the blame has shifted from the disease to me?"

"I'm not saying that! What I tell you is that you judge the evil in others, yet refuse to acknowledge your own!"

"Your watch is over, Kasmira. Go find sleep." Forest stayed fixated on his spot on the cavern wall, and refused to look at her. She sighed and turned her back to him.

Forest pressed his palm against the cold, stone floor. The Creation seemed far from here, like it survived in these depths only in memory. There was nothing natural about the cylindrical tunnel, the eerie moss nor the constant sound of metal pounding metal like the beat of the cavern's heart. Where was this Krim 'Tiak taking them, and why did he need this company? He watched Dedrik sleep, curled in a corner with a grey blanket drawn over him for warmth. His breath exited his lips in puffs of frost, cold like the lies he spun.

When his shift ended Forest prodded Dedrik with his nunchuka. The two met eye to eye in the torchlight, and Forest silently cursed Old Man for bringing him on this quest. Dedrik sat up. Forest lay back, but kept a discreet watch over the Krim 'Tiak. Sleep didn't offer his fatigued body rejuvenation. The only thing that offered him fuel to go on was the vengeance that coursed heavily through his veins. Sleep had become nothing more than an unyielding enemy; the nightmares that gripped him as its first wave of attack.

Dedrik stared back. "If you have something to say, then say it."

Forest remained silent.

"I truly wish you could forgive me. My earlier outburst was wrong. Is, wrong."

"I will not forgive one of the Krim 'Tiak."

"Then don't. Forgive me, Forest. *Forgive me!*"

"I would sooner kill you then forgive you."

"Then do it damn you! If your retribution demands my life as payment, then do it!"

Forest stood. He hadn't noticed the rest of the party waking. He armed himself with his nunchuka, but said nothing more as Dedrik stood before him.

"Do it, Forest! End my life or run! Find your retribution or scamper away like you did when my people laid waste your land!"

Forest shook. He hadn't noticed the party gathering around them. Even Mask watched the spectacle. Dedrik released his sword from his belt. It fell to the ground with a clang. Then he fell to his knees and spread his arms wide.

Whispering, he commanded, "Do it!"

Forest felt the grip on his nunchuka loosen until he could hold the weapon no more. A battalion of tears suddenly besieged his eyes, and weeping Forest fell to his knees. "I cannot! Damn you! *I cannot kill!*"

Dedrik wrapped his arms gently around him, and pulled him close. He, too, wept. The Fallen replied harshly, "No, Forest. Damn those who gave you this desire. Damn them!"

Forest wept in Dedrik's arms, and Kasmira rushed to embrace him. Mask scampered to the vagabond's shoulder, wiping away the tears with its furry nose. Even Borysko, and the princess disguised as Selandria, hugged him leaving only Old Man who watched from a dark corner. He recalled a lesson told by a dear friend long ago, one who had taught him that there was no honor in fighting. He whispered, "To kill with honor, Forest, is to never have killed at all!"

Soon after Kimbra's watch began the time had come to resume the trek. They all took out stone bread and dried fruits for meals, helpless to the silence that held them captive. Forest still wished he had never come on this journey; more so after last night's nightmare. An affright, he knew as he avoided everyone's gaze, as real as that of the moment.

Forest didn't wait for everyone to finish eating. He took the lead, and marched from the vast opening back into the corridor. Again, Kasmira fell in behind as did Borysko with Selandria. Old Man walked the flank, and behind him was Dedrik the fallen. But Forest paid them no heed. He felt immensely uncomfortable after his confession, and wondered why everyone seemed so understanding. He had only confessed under duress, and certainly not because he had accepted Dedrik! And yet, Forest thought as he discreetly looked back, this Krim 'Tiak was one of the most honorable people he'd ever met.

Dedrik caught Forest looking back at him. He had hoped that after last night the walls of judgment might have started to crumble, but he knew Forest had built his walls thick. So thick that it would take much more than the battering ram of a single confession to tear them down. Times like this Dedrik cursed himself for ever being born a Krim 'Tiak, but more so he cursed himself for not having found the All sooner.

But if not for living as a Krim 'Tiak, he never would have learned the truth behind the Prophecy. The Krim 'Tiak would have followed their god of Death, given Him the Chosen One as His fresh body, and founded their Leader unopposed. At least with his knowledge, knowledge that haunted him, he could fight back against the Evil to come. But whenever Dedrik met his people's victims face to face, he could not help cursing his lesson. Looking at the vagabond Dedrik silently prayed that through him he might find forgiveness.

And that's when he noticed something....

Dedrik frantically recalled a passage in the prophecy, "...this Chosen One shall fall from a place on high; unable to take the life of mortal man."

Forest reached out with his left hand to grab a stalagmite for support in the treacherous cavern, and on his palm, through a large hole in his glove, Dedrik saw a birthmark. Crimson red; formless, yet so loud in color that he wondered how he could have missed it. More passages entered Dedrik's thoughts: "*The Chosen One wears a glove to cover an ugly red birthmark on his palm,*" and "*I know the mark of the Chosen One. The red scorch on your left palm.*" How much more of the prophecy, he wondered, did Forest fit? Had Old Man delivered them the Chosen One unwittingly, or was the elder more than just a player in the All's plan? The party stopped in front of a corridor that split in three. Dedrik looked at Old Man and whispered to himself, "Is there knowledge in your experience so divine that you believe it is your duty to guide the destiny of the All?"

"Dedrik!" Forest called. "What now?"

"It doesn't matter who travels down what path." Dedrik walked to the lead. "According to the prophecy, all passages lead to dead ends. Only the Chosen One can find the right one."

Forest sighed, long and loud. "Reason commands that if we pair up one of us has to find this Eye."

"Fair enough," Dedrik responded. "Forest, why don't you travel with me? If you're comfortable with that."

Forest mumbled, "If I don't you'll just ask me to kill you again. Since I can't, guess I'm stuck."

"No!" Old Man shouted. "I mean, t'would be wiser to pair a warrior with someone who has no ability. For protection, of course."

"So comes the wisdom of age." Dedrik glared at the elder. "Kasmira," Dedrik turned to her and bowed. "Would you accompany me?"

"T'would be my honor to do so." She curtsied.

Old Man pushed her aside, as if her presence were not important. He leaned into Dedrik's ear and whispered, "Let the young ones travel with each other. They won't enjoy traveling with us old fogies."

Dedrik looked into his eyes. He stared deeply enough to see past the age and into his youth. Old Man had more of a reason than he let on, but out of respect he would never pressure him out with it. The formation would be as the senior saw fit.

Old Man turned back to the party and stood between Kasmira and Dedrik. "I will travel with Dedrik. Pray that the All frees me from my magic."

"And who do I go with?" asked Borysko.

Old Man looked at Kasmira and Forest thoughtfully; a tear that built in his aged eyes betrayed a recollection of his past. "Borysko, take Selandria with you. Take her and feel most at ease, for she is her own god!"

As the party split their separate ways, no one but Dedrik had noticed the exchange of looks between Selandria and Old Man. Indeed, he wondered what knowledge this senior had of the All's plan.

Forest walked silently beside Kasmira, preferring to keep his thoughts for himself. He wished desperately to keep the silence between them, and, to help, he averted her gaze, knowing that she watched him. She breathed loudly in the deafening silence. Breathed and fidgeted.

"Why do you have such a chip on your shoulder?" she asked.

Forest looked at her, then stared into the silence and said nothing.

"I once thought my life's perils had given me justification for anger as well."

Forest stopped walking. He closed his eyes, leaned against the cavern wall, and breathed long, labored breaths. He held the stale air in his lungs a moment, released it, and held his breath. When he opened his eyes he looked first at the ferret on his shoulder and then at Kasmira.

"I apologize for my outburst last night. I have spent a long time without friendship, and am not at all certain how to accept one."

"But you and Selandria are friends."

Forest smiled. He stared, and then whispered, "Never truly friends."

"Is that your fear? That once we no longer find it convenient our friendship will be gone?"

"I fear nothing. I know that when our friendship begins it will have to end. That is my reality."

"A self-made reality that is. Friendship is more than a fleeting thing, can you not see that?"

"It is easier to understand damnation than acceptance. I am a warrior who cannot murder, how can you accept that weakness in me?"

Kasmira met his eyes and was taken aback by their melancholy. "I am an adventuress who does not wish to murder, nor see it done by others. I accept you because of your gift."

"Gift?"

"It is in our Law not to murder."

"And what of when Borysko slayed the creature? Or is it only murder when a human is killed?"

"There is a difference between man and beast, just as there is one between murder and killing."

Forest smirked though no joy emanated from his gesture. "I can do neither. I cannot tell the difference between man and beast, nor can I tell the difference between killing and murder."

"I have always found the boundaries confusing, and do believe the world would do well with your curse."

"It is that curse that killed my village."

"The Krim 'Tiak laid waste your land, not you. Can you not understand that?"

"I understand death. I have been sentenced to it seven times in my life."

"Seven times? Perhaps I should be afraid, walking with a living corpse." She smiled. "We best continue."

The two weary adventurers approached a mouth in the cavern. Forest held his arm out to keep Kasmira behind him, and then crept around a large stalagmite nearly as high as him. Trepidation nipped at his heart, more so when he noticed that the jettisons of rock made the opening appear like an angry snarl. Forest wondered what evil could live beyond such a nightmarish entryway, and listened. Metal banged on metal, a blacksmith's fire exploded and whips cracked.

He peeked beyond the tooth, saw he was atop a ledge, and peered into a large pit below. Inside were men, women and elder children constructing weapons of war. The men, bound to their ovens by thick chains, worked the fires. The women took away the finished weapons and polished them nearly as bright as the chains that bound their ankles to the nearby men. The elder children did not have chains, for their job was to take the finished death instruments to the rail cars. Dark green humanoid pigs, much like the one encountered near the entryway, snapped whips to remind the slaves who their masters were.

And on every slave master's breastplate shone the Krim 'Tiak's symbol.

As Kasmira crept beside Forest he whispered, "And you wonder why I desire to kill."

"A slave camp run by orcs. We had no idea the Krim 'Tiak were crafting so many tools for war."

Forest half-smiled and let a long breath escape. "I wonder what else Dedrik has chosen not to tell us?"

"He has not been a Krim 'Tiak for nearly a decade." Kasmira checked her temper, and then whispered, "I would sooner offer him my trust than I would you!"

Forest's eyes grew misty. At first he tried to meet her hard stare, but found he could only do so indirectly. "Perhaps, for now, we should concentrate on finding your artifact."

"If our sources are correct the slave foreman wears it around his neck."

Forest scanned the room. "That must be him over there, on the other side. The big ugly one standing alone, overlooking everyone with crossed arms."

"Big ugly one? You may as well say 'Look at that tree' when we are in the woodlands."

Forest smiled at her attempt at humor.

"I see him." Kasmira turned serious. "He's high on a platform. I'd say a dozen or so feet beneath us."

"I don't see a key around his neck."

"Neither do I. Any ideas how to get to him?"

"Aye, but none that involves a partner."

"And what am I to do, wait here for your return? Perhaps I should cook you a meal?"

"I can stick him with a sleeping drug, and crawl along that ledge. You said yourself that you possess no skills."

"For war, but I do for stealth. What do you intend to do once you're over him?"

Forest didn't answer at first. Then: "What's your plan?"

"You hit the slave master with a sleeping drug, and I'll sneak along the ledge. Should your animal permit, I will lower him over with my rope to get the key. Just like fishing."

"You don't need to fish. Just lower Mask to the ground. He'll know what to do."

"How?"

"He has been listening ... Mask isn't daft."

The ferret leapt onto Kasmira's shoulder, letting out a firm "Dook!" The red-haired beauty smiled at the animal, then brushed the vagabond's cheek and started along the ledge. Forest watched her and took out his blowgun.

He waited until Kasmira was on the ledge above the slave master, then with painstaking aim he blew his shot; uncertain if it hit or not. A few seconds later the orc fell, without anyone's notice. Forest's heart beat fast as Kasmira let down her rope, with Mask at its end. The weasel ran to the key, took it between its teeth and looked at Kasmira as if to signal her. She raised the animal back to the ledge and slipped the key into her belt-purse. Forest kept his eyes on the orcs in the pit to ensure no one took notice of her, but with so many, should they take notice, he would not have much of a chance against them.

And then, as if reading his thoughts, an orc noticed Kasmira as she made her way back.

Forest quickly shot his second dart, knocking the orc unconscious. But when another yelled, "Grik kaf!" it pointed at him!

Forest scrambled to grab several egg sized bombs from his pack. But as archers lined up to shoot one noticed Kasmira and aimed at her. The arrow released, slamming into her shoulder. She screamed but did not lose her balance. The orc readied another, and Forest watched helplessly. This one would surely bring her down.

Mask suddenly leapt into the pit, landing on the orc's face. Biting deep and clawing hard the ferret forced the archer to abandon his weapon. The pig-man grabbed the assailant, threw it to the ground and stomped on its back.

"No!" Forest screamed and leapt to the animal's aid. But Kasmira stood in his way, having finished her climb back.

"We must go!" she yelled.

"Not without Mask! You dropped him!"

She spun him to meet her eye to eye. "The animal leapt to save me!"

"'The animal'? He is my brother in the Creation! I must go to his aid!"

"Then you will die, and Mask will have sacrificed his life in vain!"

Arrows flew all around them. Forest grit his teeth. He looked down at the pit, and saw mask lying motionless on the ground. "Accurse this world," he whispered and tossed the bombs into the pit. The orc archers lined up to shoot again, but when the bombs hit the hard cavern floor they exploded into a peppery smoke that created a wall. Those nearest it fell to the ground, screamed and held their eyes. Forest threw his remaining two, grabbed Kasmira's arm and yelled, "Don't breathe that smoke!"

Together they fled the cavern.

They burst through to the outside in what seemed like only a few moments. Full daylight bore down on them, blinding them briefly, and Forest barely made out Dedrik, Kimbra and Borysko. He fell to his knees, panting to regain his breath.

"Where—where is Old Man?"

"Left on another quest, he will meet us back in town." Dedrik, already mounted, rode to Forest with two steeds. "He will meet us in the town tomorrow evening."

"No matter!" Forest yelled. "We - we better - better hurry! The orcs can't be far behind!"

"Then, you found the Eye?"

Forest scrambled to get onto his horse. "Aye! Didn't you hear me? The orcs are coming!"

Kasmira took supplies from her pack to tend her arm. As Borysko dismounted to help her, he said "Relax. Orcs can't come out in the full heat of daylight. Should they choose to, they'll be blind as bats."

Once Kasmira was bandaged the party rode toward the town, Forest following once more in the rear. The adventure now ended, he wondered what value it held in his battle against the Krim 'Tiak. *At least,* he thought as he looked at Kimbra, *I won't have the princess slowing me down any longer.*

Dedrik broke riding formation and chose to ride the flank beside Forest. "Perhaps, for the duration of our acquaintance, I shall ride beside you."

The vagabond glared at him, sighed and closed his eyes tight. When he opened them he said, "Let me apologize. For misjudging you."

"Only if you let me accept that apology." Dedrik smiled.

Forest smiled back, but caught himself and frowned. "Now what will you do?"

"I shall explain when we are at the tavern."

"From what you've told me, I gather you'll wait for the Chosen One to seek you out."

"Perhaps he already has."

Dedrik and Forest stared hard at one another. Forest wondered if he'd apologized too soon.

"What do you mean by that?" he asked.

Dedrik looked pensive. "Nothing. Nothing at all."

Chapter Fourteen

Terrell walked beside Lightning without uttering a word nor meeting with the steed's gaze. He sliced his way through thick elfin woods, studying the path he made as if it were the thing that preoccupied his thoughts. But it wasn't. The Umbrian war, Karel, the statue of Fri' La, and even Terrell the Prince held his thoughts captive. As he cut through a particularly tough branch he wondered how the Umbrian's fellowship could have come to mean so much so fast.

Terrell sighed.

Lightning rested his muzzle on the Wild's shoulder, and they stopped.

Terrell said, "'ow is it that you know my thoughts, often before I do?"

The mustang rubbed his nose against the human's cheek.

"'T'would be mockery should I deny my pain to you, but betrayal if I speak it." He turned his back on his friend. "I fear I am no longer wild."

Terrell glanced back and pivoted so he could stroke the steed's long mane. He avoided the animal's ebony gaze, and jingled the coins in the pouch that Karel had given him.

"What can I do to cure such confusion in my soul?" He looked up to meet Lightning's gaze. "Would you wait for me? This place where my madness has led me is no place for a wild beast." Terrell started to cut a path, but stopped to add: "When I learn that it is also no place for a wild man, I shall return."

Getting past the elfin guards was as easy as surrendering a few gold coins. Terrell walked cautiously into the civilized elfin town. The streets were littered with merchants and shops. Amidst that commerce acrobats and puppeteers put on shows, each display that much louder than the other. The Wild remembered little of what townships were like and wondered where he should go. His eyes darted from person to person, from display to display, and from shingle to shingle. The pictures carved into the wooden shingles looked strange, and the lettering beneath more so. He recalled from his schooling that some elves spoke Hauldinian as well as their own native tongue, and his inability to read either saddened him. Terrell looked back into the woods, and thought about his companion. Lightning had become the best friend anyone could ever have. He wondered what he hoped to find here. Several large men wearing battle dress stood beneath a shingle with a carving of wolves drinking. The picture made Terrell curious and he pushed his way past them. He hardly took notice of the emblem on their breastplates of a shrouded fellow brandishing a sickle.

Inside, Terrell nearly choked on the heavy tobacco-laced air. He pushed his way through the crowd, and wondered again what had ever made him think to leave the wild. To leave Lightning. But, as people bought hot meals, his own empty stomach prayed for nourishment. He found an empty table at which to sit, hunched his nose to ward off the sickly scent of smoke, and looked at the empty mugs littered about his table. Terrell stretched out his forearm and pushed them away, deciding to make his stay as short as possible.

"What's your pleasure?" a voice sang loudly over the noisy tavern.

Terrell brushed his long, matted mane towards the back of his head and looked at what he thought must be heaven. The woman who stood before him smiled porcelain under full red lips, and tossed shoulder-length brunette hair back with a flick of her head. Terrell met her eyes without meaning to, and nearly lost himself in their golden spirits. He dashed his vision to the table, only to find his sight locked on her bare belly. Embarrassment burned him as he stared at the table, yet not before his eyes ran down her slender legs. Terrell had never seen such a low cut tunic before and found that he couldn't speak.

I fought the Krim 'Tiak! he thought, unable to defeat Fear who now bound him fast. *I led a people unknown to me into battle!* Terrell held his attention away from the group of Grim Reapers who had taken the table nearest him. He didn't even notice the one who glared at him.

The waitress repeated her question.

Terrell swallowed hard, tried to divert her eyes, and hoped she wouldn't notice that his hands shook. He dug deep into his belt purse, stumbled on the coins within it, and, after grabbing a small handful, he dropped them onto the table. "I know not. I … am uncertain … 'ow much coinage be this?"

The woman's eyes widened. She gasped, gathered the coins, and put them back into his hands. When she closed his fingers tight Terrell blushed from her soft touch on his rough skin.

"This is enough to get you killed!" she told him.

Her outburst made him feel foolish and miss the familiarity of freedom. "Can I buy a meal?"

The uneven wooden planks that made up the table before him was what he concentrated on, but still the woman's eyes bore into him. His hands continued to shake against his will.

"Why not get ripped on ale?" she asked.

Ripped? What is that? Terrell looked into her eyes and she smiled. "Yea, then. But can I still buy meat?"

"Aye." Her smile widened.

"Beef?" Terrell's voice was weak.

"The best there be! And you can call me Kyrie. I hate 'hey you's!'"

Just then an elder sat at the table and broke her spell. He stroked his long, grey beard and smiled wide. "A double helping of haggis instead, Kyrie!"

"No haggis!" Terrell said.

"You aren't a vegetarian?" Old Man asked, putting on a face as if he might be sick.

"Nay. I want beef."

"Good choice Sir! A double helping of beef it is, and two mugs of boiler makers!"

Terrell enjoyed this thing called "ripped." He held one of many glasses that rested on the table, all the while trying to look about the world around him. How much more pleasant things had become, how much less loathsome did civilization seem when ripped. Even this elder didn't seem as brass, or as dull. And Old Man had spoken long, on seemingly meaningful things.

"Terrell, there is a Movement among us. A Movement of people that are as misunderstood, as they often misunderstand."

Terrell looked across the table. At least that's what he thought he was doing. "Old Man, speak Hauldinian. What be this moving thing you keep speaking of?"

"The *Movement*. Not a thing, but a who. Perhaps, a whom." Old Man chuckled and waived his arm for another ale.

Terrell nodded. "That I know of. 'Tis a thing crazy people believe."

"A thing crazy people believe?"

"T'is a thing wars 'ave been waged for. A thing which people 'ave died for."

"If you were to compete against a man at archery, and he kicked your heel each time you shot, would you say that the game of archery was a thing which corrupted men?"

"That would be absurd and 'ardly the same thing."

"It is exactly the same. If a man does not follow the rules of archery, you would not call that man an archer. So why then, if people do not follow the rules of the All, do you credit them as a part of the Movement?"

Terrell did not answer.

"I will tell you. Man fears the Movement. Through fear he condemns it. The All teaches a message of accountability, and those who live outside it must be questioned. The questions should not fall on Him."

"On who?"

"Or, perhaps whom?" Old man took a swig of his brew, and again waved for the barmaid. "Terrell. Young Terrell the Wild! Do not call the Movement crazy for following a message of good. Instead, perhaps, call your world evil for refusing to follow it."

"I 'ave not been a part of society for a long time. I do not know what this world follows."

"Do you not know that Evil has made Its prophecy? Are you unaware that Mankind has chosen to follow his own savior?"

"And why would man do that?"

"For fear of not being a god. For fear of not being the one to whom he shall answer."

Terrell looked at him and shrugged.

"The All is a father, and humanity is His children. In the End humanity will have to answer for their actions and be accountable for what he has done. To avoid judgment, humanity first decided to make the Creation his god. But the Creation dies, and can be manipulated. Surely gods do not die, nor can they be manipulated. Then mankind decided there was no god! No one to answer to! And he was alone, and afraid. So man made himself a god, and hoisted himself above everything."

"And now man has made his chosen?"

"Indeed, man has. But this chosen can not save man."

"Why?"

"Because man is not a god."

"Why tell me this?"

"Because the Movement has the Chosen One's artifacts. And this I need you to remember: We will head to the city of Peacehaven, perhaps even stop by the Great Oak. This will not be for many weeks."

"If man's chosen one can not save us, whose can?"

"The All's can, will, and has."

Terrell raised a palm to beckon the elder to stop. But he didn't. He rambled on, and on, and on. The Wild sighed. *At least,* he thought, *I have the drink.* He decided that the civilized world did have its good side. Three Kyrie's walked to the table that Terrell was using to hold himself up. She set down six more drinks, three in front of one man and three before the other. The Wild held his three with half of his six hands. Never had he experienced a world quite like this, and after taking stock of his surroundings he leaned to grab his companion. Terrell stared at him and tried to concentrate on his face. "Dis is amazemen'!"

The elder swallowed his final drop of ale. He looked sad as he savored the burning liquid. Terrell raised his arm and yelled for another. The elder looked at him and smiled. "Much of life is amazing." A tear broke free, and rolled down his wrinkled face.

Terrell, much too intoxicated to care, paid no heed to his companion's melancholy. For companionship he relied more on the drink before him, of which his glass was now empty. He wondered where Kyrie had disappeared to ... some time had passed since his last order, and sleep had started creeping in. Another drink should wake him, he figured.

A loud raucous brought much of the tavern to an eerie silence. Terrell spun in his chair, much faster than he should have, and craned his neck to witness the commotion. When the world stopped spinning a blood-rush boiled in the Wild's veins which woke him. One of the Grim Reapers was holding Kyrie captive while several others lay motionless scattered about the floor. Kyrie held no hopes for aid, and Terrell knew he had to pull himself together.

The Wild grabbed his head firmly with both hands. He rose, struggled to focus on single objects, and tried not to rock. He stumbled towards Kyrie's captor and allowed her cries for help to give him drive. After what seemed like the longest trek in his life, Terrell found himself face to face with the enemy. He fought the need for sleep, struggled to bring the triplets before him back into one, and as gruff laughter rang inside his mind the Wild no longer enjoyed his lost grip on reality.

The Grim Reaper let Kyrie free, only to fling her to a companion. He rose, pushed Terrell hard in the chest and bellowed, "You dare challenge me, boy?"

Terrell nodded ... hoping he did so at the right triplet.

The Wild did not feel the next few moments. He thought he remembered a fist flying, but in all honesty all he felt was his body fail and suddenly he fell to the ground. He wondered if the Grim Reaper had been responsible, or the booze?

The taste of blood dripping from his head into his mouth answered that.

The world about him became drenched in the man's gruff laughter. Terrell looked at his enemy, and turned red. The Grim Reaper massaged his cut knuckles. "Want another go?"

Even before Terrell rose, the battle fever had embraced his drunken stupor. No more did he see triplets when he looked at his adversary. No more was he lost to the power of sleep. All that remained was a crimson version of his enemy. The Wild sturdied himself, grabbed the Grim Reaper by the throat, and kicked out his kneecaps. The surprise in this man's eyes was evident to all.

The tavern fell silent.

The elder left, sadly, unable to watch.

But most importantly, Terrell thought, there was no more damned laughter.

When Terrell woke from his heavy slumber, he thought he'd surely found death. An unyielding hammer pounded against his skull, his stomach turned yet growled, and his mouth felt like a dessert cat's. He opened one eye a crack so only a touch of sunlight would enter, but there was no light. He opened his second eye, sat up and licked his mouth with his tongue of sand. Terrell hoped he had equally hurt whatever had left him in such a terrible daze.

The Wild didn't recognize his surroundings. He lay on a bed of hay in a loft. A few feet from him a ladder descended to where horses could be heard, and blackbirds cawed from rafters. The Wild thought hard, grimaced at the shards of pain, and wished an end to this sickness. A ray of dim sunlight broke the darkness through a cracked shutter in the ceiling, shining into a corner where his belongings had been tucked away. Terrell noticed he was bare, save for an elfin blanket that covered him.

They had my sword! he thought, recalling pieces from the night before.

Someone ascended the ladder. With the first creak Terrell realized he had woken in a barn's loft, and wished he held his sword for safety. But reason told him that if his captors had wanted him dead they would have killed him when he was unconscious. Terrell left his sword alone.

What happened after that last drink? Which one was the last? Terrell tried calming himself as the cold Hand of the Unknown grabbed him. The steps grew louder as the person drew closer, and just as Terrell was certain he'd never leave this moment ... Kyrie appeared. He looked into her eyes and felt Fear's grip subside. She smiled.

"You're white as an Umbrian."

Terrell tried speaking, but tripped over his thoughts. He examined her, curious why his heart pounded so frantically. In a dark whisper he forced out, "Yea?"

Kyrie smiled more brightly than that single ray of sun as she climbed into the loft. She balanced a tray adorned with two bowls, which she placed next to him.

"I imagine you must be quite ill."

It was then that Kyrie looked so deeply into his eyes that Terrell knew she shared his nervousness. His bottom lip trembled and, though he looked at his belongings often, he didn't wish to depart. But how right would it be for someone of the wild, a prince who had given up his throne, to befriend an elf of a warring kingdom? Did she even want to offer him friendship? If she did, Terrell knew, she would open themselves to scrutiny by her people. Did she care as little as he of what society thought?

Terrell averted her steady gaze, but when he met her eyes, an embrace not enjoyed long, he knew she shared his thoughts. He brought his palms up against his ears, looked at her pleadingly in hopes that his gesture might take the attention from his emotions. Kyrie advanced nearer, took one of his large hands into hers, and again their eyes met. His hand shook in her gentle grasp. She smiled and handed him a water-skin along with a bag of white powder.

"Eat the magic powder, and wash it down with water." Kyrie stared deeply into his eyes. "It'll ease your sickness."

"Th-thank you," Terrell answered, averting her eyes. He swallowed the foul tasting powder, gagged and added: "I should depart."

"You fought quite admirably last night."

Terrell gave her a questioning look.

"You know, if you can fight like that when you're sober, we could use you in the tavern. You know. To take care of trouble."

Terrell gradually stopped quivering, and the red in his eyes lightened to pink. He grinned, but gave no answer.

"You could live in the loft and...." Kyrie stopped when he raised his hand.

"I would need to say farewell to my companion."

"You mean that old man?"

"Nay. Lightning. 'e is a horse."

Kyrie turned her head to examine him from the corners of her narrow eyes. Her smile parted, and beneath her lips the white of her teeth showed. She looked down into the barn below at an empty stall.

"Nay, Kyrie. Lightning and I met as the untamable. We 'ave never lived as master and beast. In man's eyes we both 'ave been beasts." Terrell looked deeply into her soul and took her hands into his. "We fought side by side for our freedom, and though I may now give mine up, my companion could not."

Terrell rose, a little unsteadily on his feet, and Kyrie stared at him with a wide smile. He walked around her and started down the ladder. His only hope was that he wasn't making a mistake.

The wolf preyed on a familiar, yet strange scent. He had never scavenged through this part of the thick woods before, and with a yip he tried to contain his glee. He sniffed the air, the ground, and then advanced one paw after the next, each step a conscious move. He tried to determine what the scent could be. Three moons had passed since he'd estranged from his pack and now, with the sun high above, it would only be a matter of time until he saw his fourth. All his life he preyed primarily on mice, but today he hunted for sport.

Today he hunted a Man.

"That's madness Yip," his brothers had told him when he had first proposed the idea to the elders.

"What a challenge it would be, to hunt a man!" Yip had growled back.

Yip peered around a tree's trunk and found his prey. It smelled like no Man, but it walked on hind legs and wore one of those long, silver branches on its side. Yip knew he must stay wary of the branch, for when wielded by Men they were sharp as teeth. And Deliverers of Death.

Yip crouched, growled, and staved his desire to howl.

He leapt, taking his victim by surprise, and offered the Man no time to grab his silver shaft. Yip would be on its throat long before it could defend itself. The wolf, howling in mid-flight, knew it had won its greatest desire. To have killed a man. When he told this to his elders they would see which one of them was mad!

A hard force suddenly slammed into his side moments before he would have landed. He fell to the ground, heard several bones crack as he tried rising, and saw a raven colored stallion brandishing a white mane raise its hooves over him. Yip closed his eyes, and a thunderous whinny echoed – then stopped short.

Darkness besieged the wolf's consciousness. No sound. No pain. Then light, and, before darkness, Yip saw the man walk to the stallion and stroke its white mane. The wolf realized why this Man had smelled so odd; it was no creature of civilization, but a beast of the wild not unlike himself.

Then Yip died, knowing that it had never had the chance to fulfill his one desire. To hunt a Man.

"Thank you, old friend," Terrell whispered. "Whatever would I do without you?"

The Wild walked a few paces from Lighting and hovered over the creature that had attacked. How could he betray the trust he and Lightning shared, how could he turn his back on the only friend that had ever understood him? *When I found myself completely alone, you came to me.* Guilt crept into Terrell's wild heart, giving strength to a void that had already lent an unbearable shame. How could he say good-bye? Terrell turned to his old friend. A bright ray of sun broke through the dark woods and basked over Lightning's white mane. Walking to his friend Terrell wondered if the mustang sensed the love he had found for Kyrie. And if so, did Lightning understand? For certainly the Wild did not.

Lightning gave a quiet whinny, and in that sound was the answer. Regret consumed them, spreading from one to the other. Lightning had read him. Lightning knew his human had been tamed. The stallion gently rubbed his nose across the Wild's cheek, and in return Terrell stroked his white mane.

Lightning nudged him in the chest, gently at first, harder the second time. The stallion reared onto its hind legs and let out a loud cry, suddenly felling into a gallop and running from the woods. Terrell stared through the darkness after him, feeling blessed to have found a friend so understanding.

"Farewell, my friend. May you never be tamed. May your heart stay free, at any cost."

Chapter Fifteen

As night fell upon the Forbidden Lands, it did so not as a feather caressing the air but as an iron trap snapping shut. The sun which fell and the moon that rose were its spring, the stars that pierced the hazy ether its teeth and the mist that settled upon the ground was the manifestation of anguish from the world it caught. The inhabitants of this cursed place, those who looked upon Death as a way of life, took the darkness as a sign of blessing. Their worship began with the ending of light and the desert came alive with shouts of malevolent praise.

But not all in this land rejoiced. Hidden within a tavern, gathered around a long table, the Movement waited in silence for Old Man to return. Upon the table mead and beef had been laid out, but not one in this group partook in them. They sat and stared at a sword and golden key that rested innocently before them. Their adventure in the cavern was a success, but it was that journey which now lay before them that staved their revelry.

The hinges on the door squeaked, but no one turned to face it. The door clicked as it shut, and whomever it was that had entered walked to the head of the table. "Have I walked into a funeral?" Old Man asked as he poured himself a drink.

"Nay, elder." Dedrik rose and spread his arms to show his welcome. He then addressed the others: "We now have Koontah and one of the Eyes in our possession. My kind will come seeking us to take them back, let us seek refuge with the elves. Who will accompany me to the Elfin Lands?"

Borysko stood first. "I go!"

Then Kasmira said, "As will I."

"I will not," Forest said. He met with everyone's gaze, paused and answered: "My village may still be in the Krim 'Tiak's hands, but they once named me 'Marcus the Avenger'. It is a title I must earn."

"We understand, Forest," Dedrik said. "But should you ever desire to join our fight, know that you are always welcome."

Forest smiled his thanks knowing that the only people in the whole of Nalor willing to make a stand against the Krim 'Tiak sat here in this room. A part of him, this he knew, wished he could be a part of them. But he had to help Tully. Kasmira stared at him, her eyes glistening from candlelight and the edges of her lips quivering. Forest wondered why, and wanted to redirect the attention away from himself. He looked at Kimbra.

"You will also have to make do without Old Man ... and Selandria the Adventuress."

Borysko stood, slammed a fist on the table and bellowed, "Eh! I think that's her decision to make!"

"That, it is," Old Man interrupted, stood and moved between the two warriors. He stared hard at them. "Sit and be at peace with both of you!"

Borysko sat without taking his glare from Forest.

Kimbra said, "Thank you! I do think that I can speak for myself."

Old Man smiled and chuckled. "Indeed you can. But, before making your decision, perhaps you might consider what your ... *father*, would say of it."

Kimbra shirked from his words.

He stared at her hard. She shirked deeper from that stare, and coddled close to Borysko. Forest knew, that Kimbra knew, that Old Man, knew. Both her and Forest realized that he had known her identity all along. *How long did he know?* they wondered. Kimbra looked to Forest, her eyes pleading. The stare equaled the look of innocence she had given him when they had first met in Hauldine's park. But this time Forest did not fall for it. He glared back and saw by her eyes that she had realized that he, also, knew. Kimbra cuddled closer to Borysko to try and escape both Old Man and Forest.

"'ow could you know what my father might say of my choices?"

Old Man smiled. He removed his glare from her, and turned it to the half-full pitcher of mead that sat on the table. He looked at his own half full glass, thought a moment, and grabbed the pitcher to put a head on his ale. "I recall the day your father lost his son, and his wife before that. His sorrow went unprecedented." Old Man turned his attention back to Kimbra. "I am certain it would be no different with the loss of you."

"Bearer of false-witness!" Kimbra shouted. But she sounded afraid of his words.

Forest's eyes narrowed as he looked at the elder. "You knew all along, didn't you?"

Old Man rose, a little off balance, with ale in hand. He held the table to steady himself, looked at the quarter-filled pitcher and at Dedrik (who rose to refill the pitcher) and then took out a wooden pipe. He reached into a pocket and searched. He came out empty-handed. He searched another pocket and then another. Finally, searching his last pocket, he smiled and chuckled.

"I have run dry of tobacco."

Borysko threw a pouch on the table. "Tell us what you're getting at!"

Old Man packed his pipe full, lit the drug and breathed the heavy smoke deeply. He closed his eyes, savored the flavor a moment and sat again. Dedrik returned with a full pitcher and poured Old Man his fourth ale.

"Kimbra, your father lost a great deal when your mother died. You children lost even more. But, when your father lost Terrell, he thought he'd never recover. To lose you, he would surely lose his life."

They all stared at her. Every single one. Except for Forest, who stared at Old Man. The elder sat, sipped his ale and looked back at the Creationist. He winked a bright emerald eye.

"I just wanted to find adventure," Kimbra finally said.

"Adventure at what cost?" Forest said. He decided to forget about Old Man for the moment. "If Sir Theomund had caught up to us, mine and Dedrik's quest would both have ended. Only because Old Man had to resort to his magic did we escape. You are the cause of this Faith Man's failure in his god! Is that your desire?"

Old Man's eyes grew wide. "Failure is such a harsh word Forest..."

"It has nothing to do with you!" Kimbra shouted. "Any of you! What right do you have to tell me what I do is wrong? Just because it is not right for you doesn't mean it isn't for me!"

Old Man finished his ale and cleared his throat. Dedrik took the pitcher he had just bought and went to pour him another, but Old Man waved his hand to tell him no. Then he thought and took the container to pour one himself. He said: "This is your decision, Kimbra the Princess ... and Forest, we will speak on your choice of the word 'failure' later."

Kimbra crossed her arms and pouted. "All right. I'll go home."

That evening, Forest sat alone in the tavern. The group continued their celebration upstairs, but he could not bear to join them. Every time he thought he had life by the reins, it would buck and dance until the situation no longer resembled the one he had figured out. He found himself in one of those times now.

He wondered to where the joy he had found with the thought of going home had gone, and how far he would have to travel to regain it. Loneliness, that thing he had once thought conquered, had only hid itself within his heart. And upon its escape so his heart had burst, leaving him to know that only by going home could he return that destruction to a whole. But if it were true that his village was now a Krim 'Tiak slave-camp, then he had no more home to which he could return.

"More goat's milk, or would yea be 'aving a man's drink?" a voice said, breaking through the trance in which Forest had found himself.

Forest looked away from his table and at the obese barmaid. Beneath a flat nose a light shadow covered her upper lip, as it also did a wart on her lower chin. She crossed her arms at her chest (yet still above her breasts), and though she stood at quite a distance her stomach brushed the table. Dark eyebrows sat high upon her forehead, and beneath them were eyes as icy as the first fall of snow. Forest declined the offer. He did not believe in the consumption of alcohol, partly because the Creation forbade it, but mostly because of what he saw it do to those around him. The woman stormed into the back room, shouting as she pushed clientele out of her way. Forest stared at the glass of goat's milk before him and considered taking another sip. The liquid was quite warm and tasted much like tobacco smoke. Forest shuddered, and chose against drinking it.

Someone sat at his table. His thoughts came to an abrupt halt. Forest looked away from his mug to see Kasmira, her friendly eyes brightened her wide smile.

"Why are you here alone?" she asked.

Forest furrowed his brow. "I've spent so much of my life alone I didn't see the harm in one more night."

"Perhaps, that is partly my fault. I have not offered you much of a chance."

He looked at her; his eyebrows fell low and his lips pursed tight. She stared at the table and not at him, though she smiled her sparkling emerald eyes betrayed in them sorrow. Forest let her continue.

"When I joined the Movement, I gave up my old way of life. Yet, often, parts of that life tempt me to regress back. Mistrust, even hatred, was a large part of that life."

"And yet you give your trust to Dedrik and Old Man."

"Give?" She looked at him, and her narrow eyes grew wide. "I give them nothing! I offer only what they have worked to earn."

"'Tis not such a terrible thing to make people earn your trust."

"So long as the tasks are not excuses for an empty promise."

Forest took a long sip of his milk without thinking. He cringed, slammed the glass down and fought the urge to spit it out. He swallowed. "Does it matter? I am leaving for my village. Tonight."

"Then you believe your people are victors? That your friend still lives?"

"I must! Should it have been Tully in my place he would have taken the risk. After my cowardice, I have only my life to offer them."

Kasmira reached across the table and took his hands into hers. "If I offered you my trust, would you value our friendship as dearly?"

"Perhaps. If I should know the value of such a barter."

"Fair enough. I was born a slave in Protecteur. In my sixth summer my owner sold me into the sex trade to be used by men whose wives were with child. This went on until I lived to a half score of summers, when I became with child. After the birth my baby was taken from me. I was then to be sacrificed to Fehr 'Le for cleansing. Old Man saved my life."

"What became of your child?"

"I don't know. If it was a girl ... she is a slave in my place. If it was a boy, he would be a warrior."

"Then you have never seen your child?"

"Never."

"And yet you wish to save Nalor from its damnation?"

"Nay. I wish to help deliver the people for the End. I have found much love for this world."

"And every day I find that much less."

She held his hands tighter. "But you have found so much."

"I have found nothing."

Kasmira smiled, though a tear left her misty eyes. "Look inside your traveling pack. Dedrik has given you a parting gift."

Forest reached inside his pack, felt the gift and battled a doomed war with a defensive barrier. He took the gift out, an elfin map it was, and let Kasmira's hand go to unfold it. On it were detailed directions leading from the Coastal Mountains to the Elfin Kingdom.

"Why would you give me this?" the barrier inside Forest asked.

"So you can find us. Join us."

"Yet you know my purpose is to help my village restore itself!"

"You saw the slave camp."

"Damn you!" Forest rose. He flushed a bright crimson. "Accurse this whole world!"

Kasmira fell silent. Another tear escaped her, and silently she whispered, "Forest, please don't ... we only want to be there for you. To comfort you."

"Comfort? You mock me! You pity me!" Forest suppressed the voice who begged him to reconsider his harsh words. He slung his traveling pack over his shoulder and turned to leave.

Kasmira broke into tears. "Please look at me." She rose and ran after him. He stopped. She rested her hand on his shoulder and whispered, "Don't leave like this."

In her whisper Forest sensed sorrow. He knew how difficult it had been for her to open up to him so freely. But he left, though it made his heart break to do so, without saying fare thee well.

Kasmira collapsed into a chair and wept. Dedrik emerged from a shadow to join her.

"I overheard. I did not wish to interrupt."

Kasmira wiped away her tears and painted on a smile that quivered. "Not all hope is lost."

Dedrik took her hands in his and reached out to her. "We can not force our friendship upon him, Kasmira." Dedrik looked out the tavern's open door, into the night where Forest had left. He whispered, "I wish I could have been with him in his trials. Even after my own Hell, I found it in me to accept love. I wish I could know what could make a man curse even that part of the world which loves him."

"Dedrik," Kasmira cried. "He took the map! He took the map!"

Chapter Sixteen

Forest never stopped to rest on his trek home. He wanted out of the Forbidden Lands, away from Death, and away from his thoughts. Throughout the night he had pondered long and hard on what Old Man and Kasmira had told him. Mostly, he had considered what he might do should he discover that their warnings were truth. The letter sent by Tully was a definite forgery, as no one among his peoples had the knowledge to write. What then did he hope to gain by returning home?

The narrow paths that twisted up the mountain slopes now lay in view. The Avenger stopped and stared into the sunrise, into the crimson tarp that it shed over Nalor. He recalled the last time he had seen so much red, the last time he had been home. Forest knew what he wished to deliver to his people: Salvation! But what salvation could be found in a man who cannot murder?

A pressure suddenly burst in Forest's chest and spread throughout his body like fire. He collapsed, landed hard on the ground and held his pounding chest. His legs burned, and closing his eyes he meditated; concentrated on calming his pounding heart, evening his breaths, and relaxing his muscles. When he next opened his eyes, he saw his surroundings for what they were. The barren shrubbery, the petrified woodland and vultures circling high above. Death had replaced the lush vegetation and the sweet song of birds.

"They've killed the Creation," he whispered, seeing that his world now resembled the Forbidden Lands.

Forest rose to his feet and continued his ascent up the slope. He avoided the open pathways, and when he passed an area where a battle had been fought, he saw bones of warriors piled high. He now knew for certain that the Krim 'Tiak had been victorious; if his people had triumphed custom commanded them to dig graves for the dead. Be them friend or foe.

He sought out a place where he and Tully had once hid whenever they'd got into trouble, and there he lay amidst the dying shrubbery. He felt like the innocent child who hid from his Master's repercussion, and a tear nearly formed in his eye. But anger barred it from leaving. He and Tully had found themselves in trouble many times, and now childhood seemed so far away. Yet he still felt like a child. *Am I now a man*, he wondered. Had life offered him that choice? For his village, for Tully, for his Master, he had to be! Their only defense, their only avenger against the Krim 'Tiak, lived in a man without the will for murder. Their hope for honor lay in a hammer without a head.

Forest stared into the heavens and prayed that Tully was still alive. He was no longer able to fight sleep, and succumbing to it he dreamt on his last thought.

When Forest woke, twilight had long since passed and now night captured the world. He waited for his eyes to focus in the dark, and gathering his senses he began his journey to the village. He took paths that only he and Tully had known about; paths that brought back an eerie familiarity that he couldn't shake. When he neared the top, he noticed that orc slave masters were now posted strategically around the village, ordered about by Krim 'Tiak soldiers. Forest wished for the days back when the only purpose for his hideouts had been to avoid a spanking. As a child he had never imagined his life in such peril, and he wondered why the Krim 'Tiak wanted him so badly. Was it so terrible that their reputations be tarnished from one escaped boy?

When the village came into view Forest first noticed that all the mud huts had been torn down and replaced with stone slave cells. He examined these prisons further, saw bars over the windows, and iron doors with padlocks to prevent escape. He wondered if the Krim 'Tiak had moved Tully, or if he was even alive at all. The gravity of this deceit fell on him as a heavy, unwanted burden.

The only path that seemed at all logical was a roundabout one that had brought him behind an area where Tully's hut had once been. Forest took a deep breath, wiped sweat from his brow, and crept to the stone cell. What would he do if Tully no longer lived in this place? Had the Krim 'Tiak scrambled the residents as well as replacing their homes? Once more, Forest checked to ensure that no one had spotted him, and then he slowly crept underneath the barred window.

"Psst! Tully? You there?"

"Who's that?" The loud voice sounded familiar.

"Shush! It's me! Marcus!"

For a moment only silence. Then: "Aye, and I am the lost heir to Hauldine! Be off with you!"

Forest squeezed his right arm through the bars and opened his fist. "Look at my palm!"

Tully grabbed his hand. Forest held tight. For the first time in a whole year he felt the rebirth of all their unspoken vows. With hushed enthusiasm, and the sound of renewed strength, Forest heard Tully exclaim, "It is you! How did you know to come?"

"I got a message. Signed by you ... In my excitement I forgot that you can neither read nor write."

"The Krim 'Tiak are searching for you, Marcus! Things have really changed. Something terrible is happening to the world outside the Creation! We witnessed their deity destroy our god! The Krim 'Tiak are too powerful. There is nothing anyone can do."

"There is always hope Tully! Hold fast to that!" Forest thought hard. "I met followers of another god. A Nameless One who also wages war on Death. His people offer help in our cause."

"Who be this god?"

"I don't know him, Tully. But he is our last refuge. Our only hope."

They held each other's hand tighter. Neither wished to let go ever again. When next Tully spoke Forest felt the sadness in his hushed voice.

"You renew my strength by coming to my aid. Go find this god. See if He will help us."

Forest let Tully's hand loose, and slipped his own out from the bars. He turned from the window to resume his quest, stopped, and looked up into the starry sky above. Then he walked back to the window. "One more thing. I go by a new name now. I call myself Forest."

As the friends said a final farewell, both recalled a time, not so long ago, when they had vowed never to leave each other's side. Adventurous childhood dreams. Always knowing they could count on one another. Neither had ever thought, for even a moment, that those dreams might one day become reality. Forest took one last look at the stone cell before going on his way. He also took one last look at the guards posted around the village. He wondered what hope lay in this god of Old Man's; in this Creator who would deliver them from their peril.

Forest took the same paths down the mountain as he had taken up. He studied the map that Dedrik had given him, curious if he would still be welcome after such a terrible farewell. Forest closed his eyes to ward off his anger, and wrestled with the sadness brought by seeing his village in slavery.

The sun dawned over the death of Creation. That Death gave Forest a strong desire to leave his land, and his attention was preoccupied with the map. He hadn't noticed a Krim 'Tiak soldier posted near him.

"Who goes there?" the sentry bellowed.

Forest froze, map in hand. He wondered how many more might come should the sentry call. The soldier walked into the barren woods toward him. Forest remained still but ready, uncertain what he should do. The enemy drew his sword.

"Why are you away from the camp?"

Forest knew that any more hesitation would cost him his life. He jumped in a flying circle kick, struck the sentry in the brow, and felled him to the ground. Forest drew his nunchuka. The sentry flipped to his feet with sword in hand prepared for battle. Forest blocked his adversary's blows with the chain on his nunchuka, never giving it a second thought to how many blows his tool had taken until the sword cut the chain in two. Only by forming an "X" shape with the sticks had he stopped the blade from killing him. Forest ignored his urge to panic, dodged the thrusts, and found the chance to jump kick the sentry to knock him out cold.

Forest took the sword. He stood over the seemingly lifeless figure, wondered if he should test his curse and thought about Dedrik. "Damn those who gave you this desire!" he had told him. For the first time, Forest felt no shame for not finding it in him to kill. He felt no shame, because he knew someone out there had respect for his curse.

Forest took some rope from his pack and tied the soldier, gagged him with a rag and hid the body under what shrubbery he could find.

Chapter Seventeen

Yellow, brown, orange and red covered the horizon above as dusk painted the sky. A wind, accompanied by leaves whose rustle sounded like tiny hands clapping, whistled through the grass. Color exploded throughout the woods as autumn painted the world without abandon. For any traveler it was the most beautiful sight in all of Nalor.

Blood. It was everywhere. On her hands, clothes and face. None of it was hers, but that brought her no comfort. No matter where she looked, the grass, trees, thickets, crimson soaked her world. As the breeze blew by her, Kasmira wept. The wound Dedrik had taken when the Krim 'Tiak fell upon them would not heal, at least not with conventional means.

"Forgive me," Kasmira whispered to the Heavens as she began a chant taught to her as a babe. Dedrik placed a finger on her lips, grimaced and smiled.

"No more, Betrayed. We have forsaken the All enough on this quest, it is time to leave the magic behind."

"But you will die."

"Then my service is ended ... at least it is so on this world. 'Tis better that I go to that other world with the All by my side, then to stay on this one by forsaking Him." He paused to wipe a tear from Kasmira's eye. "You should be jealous of me."

"You can't leave me alone."

"Let 'im die in peace, woman!" Borysko shouted from beneath the shade of a nearby tree. He cleaned his blood-stained sword.

"Have you no compassion?" She cried back at him.

Dedrik stroked her cheek, and took great effort to smile. "Be understanding,

Kasmira. He does follow the All, but only with an ember of faith. Don't turn on him and extinguish it. Love him as you love me, as you love the All, and turn his ember into an inferno!"

"You can't die, Dedrik. Who will find the Chosen One?"

Dedrik smiled, and his eyes reflected a Gateway to that other Dimension. He would soon leave, a tear escaped his eyes. Sadly he smiled.

"Beautiful Kasmira. I am but a man. The Movement does not need me. Tell me that it will be carried on. Tell me...."

"I will offer you that oath," a voice said, though it belonged to neither Kasmira nor Borysko. "Your life will not be one lived in vain."

Kasmira turned from Dedrik to look past the Umbrian, who snored from beneath his tree, and saw a silhouette approaching from the setting sun. A bright myriad of sunlight surrounded it, making the figure appear as if it had descended from Heaven. When it stepped into the shadows, leaving the brilliance of dusk behind, they saw the vagabond who carried beneath his heavy brow hope. Hope washed away by the sight of Dedrik. Forest knelt beside the Fallen, and cupped his hands over Kasmira's. He closed his eyes and breathed deep. When he opened them their silver burned with anger. "What happened?"

"The Krim 'Tiak attacked us." Kasmira choked on her words. "Dedrik took an arrow meant for me."

"Forest," Dedrik choked, "take up the quest for the Chosen One. Old Man brought you to us for a reason ... You must be very blessed, to have garnered such attention by the All."

"Don't speak." Forest watched helplessly as Dedrik's eyes closed. "I'll get herb for healing."

Kasmira began to shake. "Forest."

"I can aid you."

"Forest."

"I can save you."

Kasmira reached out and held the vagabond close. "Why have you returned? We did not part on the best of terms."

Forest rose, silent. He closed his eyes and breathed the scent of the elfin woods, remembering how sweet the fragrance of the Coastal Mountains had once been. Then, opening his eyes, he looked at Kasmira. "I saw the heart of the god I follow, the Creation, destroyed. The Krim 'Tiak killed It ... I do not know your god, but if He is against Death, then I offer Him my allegiance."

"To avenge your god?"

Forest thought a moment. He considered it. Vengeance had been a driving factor since the day Death had enslaved his village. Did vengeance still drive him? Or had it now become something more? Forest's brow furrowed, his eyes glossed over, and he inhaled deeply. He sighed, again remembering the magnificence of his village, and the love he had shared among his friends. Before answering, he held Kasmira's hands.

"Vengeance no longer has a part in this. I ask to join you, so we can set things right!" Forest let her hands go and knelt. He began to dig a grave.

Kasmira smiled. "Then you are closer to the All than you might believe."

Borysko took the lead when the trio resumed their trek. Forest took the flank, and tried to make a spiritual connection with Nature. But the Creation did not reach out to him, and instead memories of the dead vegetation around his village saturated his thoughts. The heart of his god had died, and if Its heart could so easily be destroyed then what of Its limbs?

A faint sound of a twig snapping reached Forest's ears. He stopped. It wasn't Nature Who called out to him. Nor was it his god crying out for forgiveness for leading him to follow an unknown Spirit. Forest listened harder, and tried ascertaining where from the noise had come.

He realized too late.

Two elfin warriors stepped into view as if manifesting from the trees themselves. There were more who watched. Forest relaxed, folded his arms and did not move. Elves were bigots against humans, and he had no wish to give them reason to become hostile. But it wasn't him in the lead.

An elf looked the trio over and said, "Nik Tah!"

Borysko grasped his hammer, but did not draw the weapon. "Speak Hauldinian!"

"Name your business." The elf sounded cold.

"To see your leader."

Forest watched as the elf and Borysko glared at one another. The elf demanded, "Turn away, or we will kill you."

Borysko drew his weapon. Forest rushed to step between the North Umbrian and the elf. "Don't you ever think before you act?"

Forest turned to the confident warriors, and lifted his arms with open palms to show submission.

"We seek an audience with your Chieftain. In the name of the All's servant, Dedrik the Fallen."

The two warriors nodded and turned away, heading toward the village.

Forest wasn't certain if they'd been given permission to follow, but he hoped they had and did.

Pillars as high as the tips of trees, positioned twenty-five paces apart, circled the perimeter of Le' Nok. Connecting each tower was a wall, honed smooth save for arrow slits, where warriors paced. In the center of the fortress two giant gates, each adorned with a carving of an elfin warrior, held out those whom the elves wished ... or, so Forest wondered, did they hold in whom they wished?

The two warrior guides stood before the gates and shouted to the elves on the wall above. Forest knew that both his companions were staring at him, uncertain if what they did was wise. Elves did not mind those who came with gold, so long as they did not mind parting with their wealth. But what would they do with three humans who wanted allegiance to a Nameless god; especially when that pledge meant denouncing their riches? Forest sighed.

The gates opened enough for the two warriors, and before they closed the trio followed. Inside they found a city made of colorful buildings, paved streets lined with golden statues, and all sorts of beings from human to Grothian selling wares. Some sold spices, others sold clothes. And that was when Forest noticed the one certainty of why they would never obtain the elves support. Outside of a purple building that brandished a shingle with two wolves drinking, Krim 'Tiak auctioned off humans for slavery. Blood boiled in the vagabond's veins, and when he looked at his companions he saw that they hadn't noticed. They were too busy watching after their two guides, who had scurried through the crowded streets.

The elfin warriors led the trio into a majestic hut in the bazaar's center. The ground was carpeted in camel fur, and along the walls tapestries hung depicting elves in various deeds. Merchants, wars, and what appeared to be slavery. Golden idols sat below each tapestry, each one an exact replica of an elderly elf that sat on a golden throne. A feathered head dress sat atop his head and his garb was crafted from the finest silk. Soldiers surrounded him, each one armed with a large sword. The elder rubbed his chin with a jeweled hand.

"Who might you be?"

Forest stepped forward. He thought he should bow, but knowing that the elves had sold their souls to the Krim 'Tiak he found that he could not.

"My name is Forest of the Coastal Mountains."

"And what would give you the audacity to come into my presence, and not kneel?"

"Many years past you were served by a human called Dedrik the Fallen."

"I hold much respect for that human. Do you bring me news of him?"

"Yes I do. News of his death! Death, by the hands of the Krim 'Tiak."

"Why should this concern me?"

Forest turned to look at Kasmira. She was staring back at him, uncertain where he was headed. He turned back to the elfin king. "Because he died in your woodland. He wished to come to you, to ask for your refuge against his people, but now I come in his place."

"You come to enlist my aid." The elfin king rose from his throne. He walked to a small silver chest that sat atop a table, sifted his heavily jeweled hand through coins that were filled to the chest's top, and picked out one. He held the piece up, examined it, and smiled. The elfin king then walked slowly to stand before Forest, holding the coin between them.

"You insinuate it is my fault of Dedrik's death."

"I insinuate nothing."

"Forest, we all follow gods. Mine is here before me. There is nothing that can destroy this god, but many things that will lend it strength."

"And I say your god is greed, and one day you will see it destroy you."

"I would not say such a thing of your god! Does the Coastal Mountains not worship Nature? Where was your god when Dedrik met his death?"

Forest again turned to look at Kasmira. She stared at him as though she now understood why he had been whipped so many times. He ignored her and turned back to the king. "I have seen my god destroyed by Death, as Death will one day destroy you. I now follow another god, One that Dedrik introduced me to. We do not need your help. But one day, you will need ours!"

The king met Forest eye to eye. In his cold stare Forest sensed that he had pushed him to his limit.

"You are an insolent boy. For my respect of Dedrik I will not kill you, but by morning I expect you will be long gone. Or the Krim 'Tiak will be a worry of yours no longer!"

Forest turned from the king, escorted his companions out, and closed his eyes tight.

"We needed there help!" Borysko screamed, towering over Forest. The city guards around them chuckled, and the passers-by scurried to pass.

Howling air carried dust into Forest's eyes as they narrowed. He crossed his arms. "And how would you propose we convince a husband to leave his wife?"

Chest to chest the two men squared off until the Umbrian looked away. "Bah! I'll go get a room in the inn. We'll think of a plan tomorrow."

Forest watched Borysko disappear into the crowd. He turned to Kasmira, she stared at him with wide eyes that shimmered with sadness.

"And what of you?" he asked. "Do you think me a fool as well?"

A wind swept through the streets, blowing Kasmira's long hair over her face. She stepped toward him, brushing her hair back, and placed a hand on his shoulder. She whispered, "I do not think you a fool."

Forest pushed her hand from his shoulder and glared. Through gritted teeth he snarled, "Then perhaps you are the fool."

He turned and stormed a few paces, his shoulders tense. But he stopped. His heart pounded and his hands shook. Turning back he whispered, "Kasmira, I'm sorry."

She raised her palms to stop him. Slowly she shook her head from side to side, and then she, too, disappeared into the crowd. Forest watched her leave, and wondered how it was that before they met he could go at life alone without dismay, but now he could not imagine a moment without her. He breathed the brisk evening air deeply, and wandered through the maze-like streets. He walked past displays and performers, through shops and temples, yet saw none of them. The sun had long set by the time he did notice his surroundings, and when he glanced at the overcast sky he sighed. His thoughts returned like a clap of thunder.

The clopping of hard-soled shoes against the cobblestone echoed in his ears, the only noise louder was the merchants who bartered for the most profit. Multitudes of people still loitered the streets. Their greed knew no time, and Forest wondered how Wealth could prosper under the tyranny of Death. He wondered how death would treat that god, when it had killed his own. He stopped, and looked up at the first star that peeked through the clouds. He closed his eyes. "What am I to do then?" An idea came to mind: Sir Theomund! If they were to appeal their plight to Hauldine, Sir Theomund could help them convince the king to give them refuge. And with Borysko's royalty, they could be certain of an audience.

Shouts from a nearby tavern stole Forest's attention. He looked back to Nalor, and moved aside as a large wild-looking man threw two drunken adventurers out from a building. He stood by the doorway waiting for them to leave. They did. Forest met that man's gaze, neither backing down, but the wild man shook his head and returned inside. Forest looked up at the shingle above the door, and saw that he had come to the Drunken Wolves Tavern.

The smoky tavern boiled with noise, beginning in a low hum to crescendo into a terrible revelry. Kasmira sat alone amidst the crowd, looking out of place. Forest, as he stood in the doorway, stared and wished he hadn't snapped at her. A gust of cool night air brushed past him, reminding him of the god he once followed. Had that gust meant to encourage him in, or had it rose as a beckons to leave? Or had it come only as a rise of wind, the moving of dead air. A group of angry men cursed him for letting in the cold, and closing the door he wondered if he could accept another god.

He pushed his way through the crowded tavern to make his way to Kasmira's table. He approached from behind, without saying a word, and meandered around the small wooden table to a stool. Kasmira did not look at him. He closed his eyes and sighed, mentally creating a barrier between them, and life. When he opened his eyes, he leaned on the table. It creaked.

"Mind if I sit?"

Kasmira looked up, surprised as though she hadn't noticed him. She had been crying, but smiled and nodded without uttering a word. He sat, uncomfortably, and wished he'd never paid heed to the beckoning wind.

"Are you all right?" he asked.

"Certainly. But I need a friend to ease my sadness."

Forest frowned. He was silent. Then: "I'm sorry. Sometimes words slip before I think."

"When Dedrik came to us, he was the same. You two are a lot alike."

"He must have been a good man for you to miss him so much."

"The best. Besides Old Man, Dedrik was the only man I ever trusted. Ever cared for."

"Then tell me what it would take for another to earn that trust?"

Another tear emerged from her eye. Kasmira quickly looked at the wooden table, and her smile disappeared. Through the heavy smoke she shook, and Forest wondered if she had been shaking the whole time. Her delicate porcelain hands rested in tight fists in front of her, and, feeling as though he were a spectator, the vagabond reached out and took them. He held tightly, for his own security as well as hers, knowing he had at last done the right thing.

They both sighed.

Chapter Eighteen

Alviss had wanted to rest after his tiresome journey to Peacehaven, but he had arrived just in time for his meeting. Thankfully he had managed to avoid any perils during his trip to the castle's Great Hall, but he wondered what danger now awaited him at his destination. At a long dining table, so also sat three other youths. None of them spoke, and for that Alviss had been grateful. But the silence had encouraged his curiosity of what the Sun had in store for him, and he looked about to ease his curiosity.

He had a glass made from the finest crystal before him filled with wine. Alviss had drunk none of it. The other three drank much of the wine that had been brought to them, and only the one who donned South Umbrian garb ate the feast set before them. After the Umbrian had begun his fifth plate, he had nearly finished the last of the beef and venison. That left only fruits and vegetables for the others. Umbrians never ate vegetables; except for stewed broccoli it seemed. On that the Umbrian had gorged much.

Alviss didn't wish to take the chance of starting a conversation. He looked away from the Umbrian to the empty seat at the head of the table. He wondered for whom they all waited, but mostly he wondered why. His life with his Master, though filled with hardship, had at least offered familiarity. A quality he had never truly appreciated until now. Suddenly he wished he had said farewell to his Master. Suddenly he realized how much more a father his Master had been than a mentor.

Alviss tried to forget the life he had fled. He looked away from the vacant seat to examine the room again, and noticed eight portraits on the surrounding walls. They were so life-like that they sent chills cascading through his spine. They were interpretations, ideas of heroes from a legend of long ago, one forgotten by most. Alviss took much comfort in those portraits. Especially one of a young warrior, perhaps his own age, who brandished the crest of a yin-yang on his bowl-shaped helmet. Alviss knew this legend well. The man was called Forester Renrock, fabled to have been the Prophet whose line would make men gods. But Forester had succumbed to a false god, one who abhorred Pride. The legend had always intrigued Alviss, for he loved stories of parallel, fantastic worlds, especially one where warriors befriended wizards. This legend, though meant to show the importance of pride, had always been a favorite. Alviss had taken it as one of heroism, choosing to interpret it with his own ending rather than accepting the one of betrayal to the Life Force.

The portrait portrayed Forester's pride well. Alviss studied the surreal features, and noticed something odd. Perhaps he had only noticed it out of a wish to, but locked deep within the painted eyes was a heavy burden of sorrow. Sorrow that lent the question, "Why?"

After what seemed an eternity of listening to the appalling sounds of the South Umbrian munch and gulp, a figure entered the Great Hall. Alviss took his attention from the portrait, and offered it to the man. When he came into the candlelight it became distinguishable as an elderly, frail looking gent who donned a ghostly white beard and eyes that resembled a python's; their icy ebony pools hidden deep beneath wire framed spectacles. When he walked, he did so slowly and with obvious effort. Several attendants aided him.

The aged man took his seat, captured everyone's attention, and held it as a child who held the first tadpole it had ever caught. The elder sent shivers up Alviss' spine, more so when the South Umbrian ceased feasting to look upon this strange man. The elder waived his bony hand and sent his attendants scampering away, then he waved it again, accompanied by strange, arcane words, and a brilliant flash imbued from his spirit. His strength returned to its youth.

When the elder.spoke, his deep voice bellowed as if he were speaking into a canyon. "Many centuries have passed since I last tread the soils of this corrupt world. I see many changes in its faces, but few in its souls." The elder paused and looked at the South Umbrian, the elf, the Grothian, and lastly at Alviss. A light burned in this man's eyes, one which indicated he had seen something unnoticed the first time. He took a deep breath, and Alviss prepared for a long speech. But again the elder paused. The bearded fellow released the air from his lungs, looked back to the young wizard, and then at Forester Renrock's portrait. With another deep breath, one he held, he stared at Alviss. This time with eyes that burned.

140

"I am called Geldin the Wise. I am the one who summoned you all to this destiny. A destiny that will leave Nalor in the same fate as the fabled Earth." Chills rushed into Alviss' spine with the emphasis placed on the word "fabled." Geldin continued: "To stop Earth's Fate from happening on Nalor, to renew hope for all races to live as one, Nalor must be saved. Saved, by its misfits."

They all shrank from his gaze. *"Learn a lesson from us? Is the world so doomed that its salvation lay in me?"* Alviss thought.

"I speak the truth to you, young Alviss," Geldin said as though he could hear thoughts. "Salvation does depend on you. But this destiny comes as your choice. The Wise shall not force it upon you."

Geldin paused, and examined the youths before him with devilish pleasure. A devilish pleasure that turned to displeasure when brought upon the wizard from Protecteur. The elder looked from portrait to boy, and from boy to portrait.

"Dis crazy!" the South Umbrian shouted. "I be Ardal, and I be no misfit! I quest wit' no one!"

Alviss hated to stereotype, but he couldn't help but notice how clearly the South Umbrian showed in this man. Right from his massive muscles and tall stature to the tip of his ignorance.

The Wise calmly implored, "Tell us why, young Ardal."

"Well, the complexity of traversing on a quest to save the world stacks the odds highly against us. Let's take all the variables into account, shall we?" Ardal stopped, and everyone's jaw dropped. Then he added nervously, "Uhh ... Duh! I ain't goin'!"

Alviss picked up his jaw and noticed how somberly the South Umbrian wore his war hammer. A genius in the mind of an Umbrian, North or Southern, indeed would constitute a misfit bent for ridicule.

The hooded elf stood as if to steal the attention, surveyed his surroundings from beneath his mahogany hood, and guffawed. "As well, I shan't quest with these obvious aberrations." The voice sang as a gentle song, like a soprano from young Hauldinian males. But where would a Hauldinian have garnered an elfin military cloak? The man withdrew his hood, rather *her* hood, dismissing all questions. She said: "I have disgraced my people enough without traveling with humans."

Tales of this beautiful warrioress' prowess had reached even the ears of those in Protecteur, although no one had believed them. They were only rumors of an elfin female born void of magic, the first female elf born without spell. She had not only turned to, but had mastered, the sword. "Aloysia of the Sword," she had earned the name. Greatest warrior in all the Elfin Kingdom.

Alviss knew the reason for the bulky hooded cloak: a disguise to obscure her appearance, a hope of hiding her womanhood. For only a moment, then a longer time after that, Alviss met her silvery stare with his own. In her eyes he sensed the strong contempt elves held for humans, but he also sensed a contempt for her own race as well. She needed this quest, needed to teach her people to embrace her difference. Lastly he sensed fear, one common to his own heart. A fear that things may worsen should they dare to speak out.

After all, if their own people shunned them, how could they expect a world to not?

The third stranger stood. "Myself, I shalt not quest with these three. Though, I am at least willing to admit my uniqueness. A uniqueness you all so belligerently call 'misfit.'"

The accent in his voice made it difficult to understand him. Alviss had heard that accent once before, while on a journey to find a rare herb in Mount Groth. By the youth's narrow eyes and long, sharp nose he knew this third stranger was at least part Grothian, but even though he donned a baggy cloak all could tell he had no wings. The Grothian continued:

"My name is Kolenka. Kolenka the wingless. I am undoubtedly the most shunned of all." Kolenka sighed. "My wingspan, the blanket of skin that normally spans from the tip of our fingers to the bottom of our ankles, is non-existent. Because Evolution saw in me to make me more human than Grothian my people ridicule me. I, out of all of us, have the greatest reason to deny this fool's quest!".

"Fool's quest?" Geldin reiterated. His brow furrowed, and he looked to every one of the youths. He stopped only when he had reached Alviss. "And what of you, young wizard? Do you, as well, share their sentiments?"

The elder's gaze penetrated his emotional barrier with an ember of hope. The Wise again looked at the portrait to boy, and Alviss wondered what Geldin could possibly see. Alviss stood, took a deep breath for courage, and said, "My sentiments ... are somewhat..." he paused, intimidated by the glares. But thinking of his village's prejudice, and of Wyborn with Andras, he spoke with conviction. "I do not, at all, share your sentiments.

"I do not believe that Kolenka has the best reason of all to deny this 'fool's quest'. We all have been shunned with equal suffering! For all of you, misery has come in the form of ridicule. Regardless of how much or how little, our anguish is all equal. We relate it to what we know, and by that we cannot lessen our pain just because someone else's appears worse. Even my pain, next to yours, is not any worse.

"Your people would never harm one of their own, for none of your people fear you. Mine do fear me. Out of that they wish to destroy my kind. But because they need us they do not. But they do test us. Violently, until my kind reaches a position of power. I am a wizard. One from Protecteur. Because my knowledge is magic, I have been shunned by a mother I never knew, by friends I never had, and by strangers I never befriended."

Alviss tried to bring his breathing under control. He stared the Grothian in the eyes and breathed deeply to finish: "Out of all of us, I have the most reason ... to accept this fool's quest. Not because the pain I suffer is worst, but because it appears, that out of all of us, I am the most tired of being alone."

The room fell silent. Alviss wondered if his speech had hit its mark, or if it had escaped them. He took his seat and looked at Geldin, seeing in him the most astonishment. Aloysia rose.

"Tell us of this fool's quest, so that we might begin."

Alviss looked at the others. They all nodded in agreement. Again, as Alviss looked at Geldin, he saw the elder look from the portrait to him, from him to the portrait.

And again Alviss sensed his displeasure.

Chapter Nineteen

Alviss walked about Peacehaven's capital city. The evening was still quite young, and he wished to enjoy the feeling of elation he had acquired since his meeting. He thought hard about the other three misfits with whom he would be traveling, and pondered over what Geldin had said to them.

"You will journey to the Mount Armageddon," Geldin had said. "There, you will wait for the Chosen One to arrive."

"But what are we to do?" Alviss asked.

Geldin had smiled then, and as Alviss walked about the city streets he recalled the serpentine appearance in the man's grin. The Wise had then said: "The Movement will try and stop the Chosen One from fighting Evil."

"Sir?" Alviss again interrupted. "I notice that none of us believe in the same god. Kolenka is an Evolutionist, Aloysia worships wealth, and Ardal prays to the elements. As for me, the Sun is my deity."

"Your point, young Alviss?" Was it hate he had felt as Geldin looked from portrait back to him?

"Who chose this Chosen One?"

"Alviss, surely you are intelligent enough to know that so many theories of gods can mean but one thing. It does not matter who or what you worship, for the Life Force is in all things. Perhaps there is even a god inside of you."

"I guess it's not important."

"What is his destiny?" This time, Aloysia had inquired.

"To send Evil back to the Abyss of Damnation." Geldin's voice had become low, and fearsome.

Alviss hadn't been able to shake his foreboding feeling after that. Even on his lonely walk through the crowded cobblestone street shivers cascaded over his spine. He thought about what they might encounter when faced with the Abyss of Damnation, or The Movement. He thought about this so much that he took no notice of the people about him. They were all dressed in costume, and celebrated beneath a splendor of decorations that hung above the shop-lined road. Alviss narrowly avoided a crowd of young children who ran past him, and took refuge in having his thoughts interrupted. For the first time he wondered what they rejoiced.

Many people in Nalor took Peacehaven as a model society, thinking that the Chosen One would most assuredly come from its descent. But Alviss was not among them. He watched with repulsion as the people sniffed the abundant Pollen, and wondered if peace could be achieved without intoxication.

Again losing himself in deep thought, he wandered around the narrow cobblestone streets. Only when he had nearly bumped into a group of teens did he snap from his trance. They gave him quite a scare. Alviss looked up from the cobblestones and saw four youths about his age; three large boys and a slender red-haired girl who smiled sweetly. Their colors were Protecteurian, and their giddy expressions meant they had reveled freely in the celebrations. By their dilated pupils it was safe to assume that they had taken part in the Peacehaven Pollen. Now Alviss knew which celebration he had found himself amidst.

Before Peacehaven had discovered the pollen, elves had attacked in an effort to seize control. Protecteur had then offered Her allegiance, without request or demand for payment. Today had marked the anniversary of the victory over the elves.

Again Alviss had lost himself in a deep trance. He returned his stare to the street and attempted to walk on. For courage he touched the bag of magic components he had strapped to his side, but no longer felt like, "Alviss the Great Questron," but again regressed into "Alviss the Worthless Wizard." At least he knew that if anything should happen, he had enough magic to feign power. He could conjure a minor spell and ... probably fail and embarrass himself.

Alviss had nearly walked past them when the female grasped his shoulder.

He wondered what to do. Glancing over his trembling shoulder he saw the three boys standing at a distance. Only the girl was near. Her beauty offered his fears comfort, her narrow, dark eyes twinkled in the dusk. She smiled, tempting him to turn and face her, reminding him of how much he cared for Andras.

"We would meet you well. I am called Dala." Her voice borne a friendly quality, and Alviss turned to face her.

"I am called Alviss. Alviss the Wizard." Again he could look at nothing but the cobblestones. "I am in a terrible hurry."

"Hurry?" Dala laughed. "There is no work during celebrations! Tell me wizard. Does your garb indicate Manhood?"

Alviss wished he hadn't been so conspicuous. But completing the Ritual had meant he had let the boy in him die and the man in him live. He could be proud of that. He wished he could be proud of that.

"You are correct." As the words escaped his throat they nearly choked him.

The girl again laughed. "You need not feel shame." She took her finger beneath his chin and directed his gaze to meet hers. "Not all in Protecteur abuse wizards! My friends and I would feel honored should you choose to accompany us."

Surprise replaced his fear. Had Peacehaven finally offered him a place where he could find friendship? Alviss smiled, unable to abate the joy inside him, and hadn't noticed the smiles on the three large boys.

The three evil, familiar, smiles.

"He is amongst them?" a cold voice asked from the dark chamber.

Geldin walked completely into the private chamber before he turned to the voice. His brow furrowed, and the elder sighed. He turned to shut the door, and secured the lock. He walked to a chair in the room and sat, breathed hard, and finally lit a candle to ignite the room. Geldin looked hard at the voice which had spoken to him.

"Why don't you just run into the Great Hall and see for yourself?"

"Geldin, don't take such liberty with me." The voice walked from the shadows. It was Kol the mad. "I am not nearly as patient as Death."

Geldin's spell casting finger twitched. "Nor do I wish to answer to Death when he asks why the misfits discovered His plan. If you had spoken any louder, they would have heard you."

Didzyn lumbered from the darkness. He had a bone stripped of meat in his mouth and saliva dripped freely from his maw.

"He is with them." Geldin answered.

"Good." Kol took out his pipe, lit the tobacco, and puffed generously. "That is very good."

Geldin breathed hard when the smoke from the pipe reached him. "Must you do that?"

The mad chuckled. "It doesn't bother Didzyn."

Didzyn growled. "Yes, it does."

Kol knocked the pipe against the stone wall. "Fine. When the misfits leave, I'll smoke in the next room. Now, you get back to your guests and send them on their journey."

Geldin waved his hands to ward off the remaining smoke. "He worries me. I saw a look in his eyes, one that I have seen before."

"Where?"

"From the first Chosen One. From Forester Renrock."

Kol laughed loudly. "That is good. That is very good."

Chapter Twenty

The sun had barely risen into the navy blue sky when Alviss, trying to ignore the pain from his swollen eye, strapped a full riding pack to his horse. He was consumed with familiar emotions; ones that added extra, unwanted baggage. Feelings that made him wonder how he could have fallen for the same old trap: Friendship. What does this world know of it? The only true friendship he had ever known was Andras,' and now she belongs to someone else. Now she belongs to Wyborn.

When Alviss finished packing, he reminded himself that, once the Chosen One set up his reign, he would be rewarded greatly. As dawn's warm rays absorbed into his spirit he mounted his steed, leading the horse in a prance through the empty cobblestone streets toward where his group had agreed to meet. The wizard tried to ignore the celebration's remnants that still adorned the buildings. The sun had climbed high into the Peacehaven sky, casting out night's shadows, winning the war of Light over Darkness. Birds sang their morning song, as if to show him a beauty that he had never before noticed. Alviss wished he had his one true love to share such beauty.

"Where ya bin?" Ardal shouted, breaking his train of thought. "Are you quite aware of the duration of time ... I mean ... Duh! We bin waitin' an hour!"

Aloysia rode her steed between them. The hood on her emerald cloak was lowered and her long, silvery hair blew freely. "We have only been waiting a few minutes, Ardal." Then she turned her icy stare on him. "But do not think to keep us waiting again!"

Alviss didn't know what to say. But Kolenka rode, beginning the quest with or without the others and Ardal followed with Aloysia behind. Alviss sighed loudly, fell in last, and wished his hopes didn't rest on such rootless ground.

The misfits journeyed silently through the course of the day. Alviss looked over the formless land, and tried to stave off the pain in his torso and thighs by occupying his thoughts with scenery. But Peacehaven's prairies offered little of interest. Not even a groundhog. He sighed, and dared to look at his three companions. Alviss felt foolish for thinking they might become friends. Even as the yellow sun climbed to its peak, not one word had been spoken between them. It wasn't until it had begun its gradual descent into the west, when Ardal's stomach gave out a loud growl, that words were used.

"Let's eat! It already past noon."

"Not yet." Aloysia glared at her human companion. Her eyes made Alviss believe she had disagreed only for the sake of disagreeing. Then she said: "We'll eat when we pass the Elfin Borders."

"That a few hours away."

"You can wait, Ardal." She glared at him.

"Maybe elf body can live wit' no food, but Umbrian body need to eat!"

"I said you can wait."

"Give me a reason!"

"Because now is not a good time." She glared harder.

"You're just arguing for the sake of argument!" Ardal turned red. "If you have facts to base your opinions on, I'd be glad to thwart them! I'm hungry, as I am certain everyone else is too, so let's eat!"

"Not yet I said!" Aloysia glared even harder.

Ardal's face tightened, his hands shook, and Kolenka backed away to stand with Alviss. The Umbrian coolly placed his hand over his battle-axe's hilt.

"I not ask permission, elf," he said coldly.

"Nor did I command. Nor, should your request be an ordinance, shall I comply, human." Aloysia did no more than face her horse to his; the hilt on her sword and the bow on her back lay untouched.

Alviss wished he could stop this foolishness. But if the elf and Umbrian were determined to kill one another, what could he do? The Grothian beside him watched with arms crossed. The wizard knew it lay on his shoulders to stop them. But how?

Time for thought had exhausted itself as Ardal raised his battle-axe and charged. In that same second Aloysia drew, cocked, and fired two arrows all in one motion. The first slammed through Ardal's wrist. The Umbrian ignored the pain and continued his charge. The second arrow, aimed for his heart, flew fast. Alviss panicked and threw his fire spell between them, without taking into account how much component he used. The spell went mad with a wall of fire exploding between them.

The arrow aimed for the Umbrian's heart became singed in mid-flight as it passed through the fire-wall. Ashes struck the Umbrian harmlessly, but the flame frightened the horses. They reared and bucked until their riders fell off.

Alviss landed on the hard road, hurt from his fall. When he rose he met with his companion's angry eyes. He ignored them until he managed to bring his inferno to resemble a campsite flame, hoping they hadn't noticed him shaking.

"Why don't we have lunch?" he said. "After all, we already have a fire."

The group stared at him unmoved. Only Ardal reached into his pack and broke out rations. "Told you the others were hungry."

Once again, words became a thing unused.

A shingle outside squeaked on two rusted hinges as the night air tossed it back and forth. To the travelers that entered through the door below, it seemed like a hand bidding them welcome. And many came; all with nothing in common save for the gold in their belts-purses. Of that the proprietors could be certain, as that was why the elves had allowed them access into Le' Nok.

Terrell leaned against the doorframe, first looking up at the shingle and then at the brilliant ether. The elfin city was lit too brightly for any stars to stare upon it, and that seemed just. Any society that focused so heavily on what man made deserved to be ignored by the gods above. Terrell sighed.

A bard who told tales by rhyme and lyre held fast to the attentions of the drunken crowd. When the storyteller had first come, and whether it had been weeks or days Terrell could no longer tell, the Wild had been thankful. Intoxicated merchants had little cause for trouble when entertained, but much need for adventure when bored. And those who had chosen to challenge this new guard during his first few nights had done two things: they helped to spread the word that the Drunken Wolves Tavern was not the place to be rowdy, and also spread the word that the Drunken Wolves Tavern was the place to be rowdy. Meaningless battles these were.

Terrell recalled the combat in North Umbria, how thrilling it had been to lead those people to freedom. Fighting an army to save your life was honorable, but fighting as a means to earn food was not. Especially when nature provided food for free. Why am I here? He no longer felt like "The Wild." He turned to face the smoky tavern, glanced at Kyrie who waited happily on her customers, and savored her for a moment. She brought happiness into his heart; reminded him why he stayed. Over the past few weeks, certainly more so during the nights, Terrell had fallen deeper in love with her. But still he questioned, often, if love had been worth the price of freedom.

Terrell needed refuge from his mind. He turned from watching Kyrie, and examined the odd assortment of characters that she served. An Umbrian, female elf, wizard and what appeared to be a Grothian. Terrell had witnessed many strange things since his coming to civilization, but none stranger than this. What would rally such an assortment of cultures? Greed. He watched this band, sensed their strong distaste for one another, and allowed their distaste to return his hatred of civilization. He wondered what vile profit would come about by their union.

Kyrie cried out! The Wild snapped his attention away from the odd characters, scanned the room and found five adventurers in a circle. One held Kyrie captive in the middle. They pushed her back and forth to one another, pinching and touching her, ignoring her pleas. The bard kept on with his tale, the patrons continued with their own business. No one cared what might happen to the serving girl.

Terrell moved quickly, but the wizard rose and told the men to stop. Terrell paused, unaccustomed to such bravado, but when a large mustached one broke the wizard's jaw he hurried in. Seizing the element of surprise, he grabbed the man's arm and threw him into his friends. The circle was broken. Kyrie quickly left the prison, and the men rose to face the Wild. But ... they also faced the South Umbrian, elf and Grothian.

The trouble showed themselves out.

Alviss lay on the tavern's floor. He raised his vision, saw the barmaid handing him her towel, took the rag and used it to wipe away blood from his wound. His cheeks turned hot, and he wished the barmaid wasn't staring at him.

"Are you all right?" she asked.

Though difficult to do, Alviss recited a spell to begin healing his wound. One of the few incantations he had mastered.

"Hardly a new wound. More like an old one resurfaced."

The barmaid smiled, and reached out to stroke his long braided hair. "Well,

I thank you, my hero. I am called Kyrie."

She did just as Andras would have done. But she was not her. She was only a painful reminder of how much he needed her. A reminder of how much his heart ached to hear her voice.

"You all right?" a gruff voice called from above.

Alviss looked up to meet the Wild's stern face. He tried to speak, but a lump suddenly bound his throat. He nodded. The Wild frowned.

"Not you," he knelt and looked into Kyrie's eyes with such passion that his love could not go unnoticed. Alviss rose, and decided it best to just leave them alone. Kyrie grabbed his arm. He stopped.

"Wait. Let me introduce you."

Alviss again met the Wild's dark, sunken gaze as the large man said, "No need," before returning to his post.

"I'm sorry about that." Kyrie offered him her hand. Alviss took it and was led to a table away from his companions.

Terrell stood by the tavern's door. He wondered what had made him act so rude. The wizard had, after all, tried to aid Kyrie. But such self sacrifice just seemed strange. Perhaps these past few weeks of living in society had begun a transformation, made him a part of the product from which he had once set out to flee. Had he now become Terrell the Tamed? Nay! It did not matter that the man wore wizard garb, but rather it was what he had seen in the man's eyes. A spark that seemed strangely familiar.

Kyrie finished apologizing for him and left the wizard alone. Terrell was curious that he didn't return to his companions, but chose instead to remain in solitude. Terrell swallowed his pride, swallowed it in a refusal to become a part of the society in which he now lived, and walked to the table. He took the seat across from him, and cleared his throat.

"Kyrie need not apologize for my imprudence. I pray you will meet me well enough to accept my own words."

The wizard smiled, and cringed at the pain from his wound. The effort seemed strange. "Of course."

"Might I inquire why you would travel with such unlikely companions?"

The wizard fidgeted. His smile disappeared. Then he looked at Kyrie, and back at the Wild. He breathed deep as though for courage and smiled; again cringing at the pain.

"We are on a quest."

"And what might that be?"

"We seek the Chosen One. The One who will Deliver us from our peril and make us gods."

Terrell checked a laugh. He recalled his conversation with an old man about a Chosen One, and a Moving Thing ... Terrell almost said something about it but, he suddenly knew what it was that had seemed so familiar. Lightning. This boy and the stallion shared the same empty gaze, a gaze that made the Wild yearn once more for freedom. Terrell looked at Kyrie as she waited on tables. She took the time to smile at him. He loved her, but not even that had had the strength to tame him.

Alviss had slept soundly for the first time in his life inside Terrell's loft. The brisk winds had howled throughout the night, and the shelter was welcome. With morning the air had calmed, and the chill bore a friendliness to it. Alviss rubbed his eyes, saddled his horse for the journey, and tried to shake his desire to go back to sleep. His other companions, not quite as thankful for the shelter as he, kept silent and to themselves. Alviss sighed. He didn't look forward to the rest of the journey at all.

The clouds retreated from the cobalt sky, and across the horizon the sun peeked over the elfin woods to cover Nalor with an amber blanket. The moon still loomed over them like a giant scarlet eye, and the night wind calmed into a breeze. Taking a deep breath Alviss fell in love with the woodland's scent, but seeing that his party waited for him to saddle-up he climbed onto his steed wishing he could have had more than Hope as a companion. But he had accepted solitude long ago. No way would he feel sorry for himself now. Or rather, anymore.

Alviss kicked his horse in the ribs to start it into a gallop, but immediately he pulled on the reigns to make it stop. The Wild stood before him, dressed and packed for travel. Alviss again rubbed his eyes to wake himself from his dream-like state, but when his eyes cleared he still saw the Wild before him. His expression looked dark and stern, and judging by his heavy breathing he contemplated something difficult. He looked behind himself at Kyrie's home where she slept unaware of his actions.

Alviss stared at him curiously. He knew the love shared between this man and Kyrie; knew it because he had once treasured it. But the love between himself and Andras had come to an end because a tradition had made it so. Because his people followed a way of life that permitted the strong to own the weak. Alviss would have done anything to bring that tradition to an end, and that included traveling across the globe with misfits who hated each other. Alviss could not understand one who would forsake true love without boundaries.

The Wild's eyes suddenly grew dark, and his brow fell on him heavily. "Wizard, I do not appreciate your stare. If we are to become companions, you must learn to trust me enough to speak your mind."

Alviss was hesitant to answer. He greatly desired such an open invitation to friendship, but, knowing the love shared between the Wild and Kyrie, he didn't want to see him make an irreconcilable mistake.

"You are more than welcome to journey with us. But, should you not say farewell, you may find yourself unwelcome here ... should you choose to return."

"Thank you for your advice. But should I see Kyrie's face once more, should I feel the love shed by 'er tears, my 'eart would not let me go."

"Then why?"

"Because my soul won't let me stay. I know I will lose love. But freedom for the soul must be gained ... at any cost."

The group had already started the journey. Alviss glanced at Kyrie's home and thought of his own broken heart. How could any man who knew such love not hold it? Would the Wild find happiness in freedom, or come to regret having walked away from this woman? As if he read the wizard's thoughts Terrell said, "There is an emptiness in my soul that I cannot fulfill. Kyrie holds a special place, but there is something bigger that I need. I just do not know what."

He turned and began the journey. Alviss sighed, kicked his horse in the ribs, and fell in beside his new companion. Glad for his friendship, but sorrowful for the union he deserted.

The day matured like a full-bloomed flower. A rose it was, with petals as red as the affections of a pure heart, yet as dangerous as the thorns on its stem. *Peace*, Alviss thought. *I have found peace.* They had left the dense elfin woodlands behind long ago, and now faced rolling hills. Alviss had fallen in love with the blossom-carpet laid out before him, and the elfin hills' scent tickled his nose. High above them birds circled and sang sweet melodies into his ears.

Alviss sighed, and wished he could have had Andras with him to share the incredible feeling of ... freedom. That thorn on his flower stung painfully.

The Wild lumbered beside him. The others in his group had made no efforts toward friendship, and after the incident between Aloysia and Ardal the wizard knew it was best to leave things be. They looked at them often enough, angered by the Wild's silent company. He walked tirelessly in refusal to ride a tamed beast. His actions, though noble in spirit, slowed them considerably. Alviss didn't mind, but he knew the others did.

The Wild looked tentatively about the rolling plains each time they reached a hillcrest. He listened to the gentle breeze as though it whispered an answer to a puzzle. The Wild looked as though that puzzle wrestled him like a great beast, and made him not at all as happy as freedom was supposed to. The Wild sighed, almost a growl, and released the air as though he were spitting it out.

"Wizard, why is it you stare at me like I am a circus side-show?"

Alviss snapped his vision forward. He didn't know how to respond. The Wild had sounded serious, but hardly angry. At least, Alviss hoped he wasn't angry.

"Uhm...."

"Alviss!" Ardal stopped his horse and rode between the wizard and the Wild. "We'll be in Sharp Tooth soon. Be wary whilst in those depths, for though the danger may not appear evident..." Even the Wild stared at the Umbrian in bewilderment. "...Er, Alviss! 'Urry up!"

"Strange companions you choose, Wizard."

Ardal had taken the Wild's mind from his question. Alviss sighed in relief. From now on, he vowed, he would look only to the road ahead.

Smoke dominated the tavern's air. An obese man with a hairy stomach threw out drunkards into the streets. Women sold their wares, and adventurer's lustfully bought them. Not at all unlike any other tavern in Nalor, Alviss decided. He pushed aside the metal mug before him. The Wild had drunk half his third mug, and pushed the wizard's back to him. Alviss wished the others would have joined them, but other than sharing accommodations to save silver they had decided it best to go their separate ways. His group had been quite angry with their slow progress, and had made certain that Alviss knew the cause was the Wild. But it was not the Wild they had blamed, and this Alviss had seen in all their eyes. They had blamed him. The sorcerer looked beside himself again, at his companion who had barely finished his third ale when he had started another.

"You're doing it again, Wizard."

"Doing what?"

"Staring at me like a circus side-show." The Wild finished his drink, and poured himself another.

"How can you stomach that?"

The Wild looked deep into the heart of the busy tavern's heavy, smoke laden air. His face grew dark and stern. "'ow can you stomach this world without it?"

"I'm sorry."

"Do not apologize, friend. Your concern is not at all unjust. Why don't you tell me more of your beloved Andras?"

"There is no more I can tell. She belongs to Wyborn. Only if I can find the Chosen One do I hope to find the strength to save her."

"Chosen One." Terrell looked ashamed, like he had been hiding something. "I 'ad met an old man who spoke of your Chosen One. I recall, sort of, him speaking of the Movement. Be they your allies?"

"They are our enemies. They are in a race with us to get to the Chosen One."

The Wild thought hard. "This elder told me they 'ad the artifacts. They would be 'eading toward a great oak ... but that was long ago."

"Perhaps that is where we should go."

He smiled. They looked directly at one another. The fallen heir stood, took his traveling pack in one hand and grasped Alviss's shoulder with his other. "No. Not 'we,' Wizard. I must leave you."

Alviss shrank from his friend's deep, emotionless voice. "Why?"

The Wild turned, and stared out the door. He closed his eyes, breathed deeply and felt the wind that blew into the tavern like a beckons to freedom. The Wild smiled with that scent.

"Wizard, you are more than I can ever be. You are meant to rule, to lead, to teach Nalor to embrace one another. Start first with your companions. If anyone can make your foolish dream come alive, it is only you."

"You don't have to leave."

"Fix this cursed society, Wizard." And with that said he left.

Alviss stood outside the door to his lodgings, uncertain if he wished to enter. He stood outside the door, grasped the cold metal handle, and wondered why the Sun forsook him time and time again. What had he done to deserve such a life of punishment? Alviss gently traced his finger around the metal handle, mimicking the tear that had traced its way down his cheek. He pushed the key into the lock and turned it slowly until he heard it click. Then, depressing the handle's button, Alviss opened the door only enough to let himself in.

He closed the door and turned to face the dark room. The moon cascaded his companions in an eerie shade of blue light from an open window. He stared at them, watched them sleep, and saw two empty cots beside Aloysia. One for him and one for the Wild. Alviss sank deeply into an abyss of despondence. He walked to the cot beside Aloysia, undressed to his undergarments, and tried not to wake anyone. As he crawled beneath his blanket and closed his eyes tight Aloysia rustled. He knew she was awake.

"Why is it that you return alone? Does the Wild not wish to travel amongst such misfits?"

"Rest easy, elf. The Wild felt badly for his hindrance, and chose to be on his way. Now, we can all be miserable."

A heavy silence followed his outburst. Alviss opened his eyes, and turned his head to see her sitting upright in her cot.

"Alviss, accept my apology. I know you valued the Wild's friendship, and my outburst was unwarranted. Perhaps you might think this meaningless, but I would offer you my friendship, in place of your loss."

Alviss didn't know what to say. She had spoken gently, and from the moonlight he could see compassion in her eyes. She extended him her hand. Alviss sat upright and took her in an embrace.

"I thank you Aloysia. I will cherish your friendship."

Kolenka rose from his cot behind them. "Perhaps it is time we all stopped acting as though we are at war." He walked to them and joined their embrace. They heard Ardal rise.

"I would most cherish the opportunity to be myself. It would be most refreshing to fully explore what boundaries my mind can overcome."

As they looked at the Umbrian, they listened to him ramble on, and on, and on....

Some things, the misfits knew, would take time getting accustomed to.

Chapter Twenty-one

Kimbra ran a hard-bristled brush through her matted hair; adventuring certainly hadn't shown any kindness to her raven tresses. This task would have been much easier with a servant, but her father had forbid her to call on any help. But no matter what punishment he might yet concoct, nothing would make her regret what she had done. Kimbra looked into the mirror, deep into the reflection that stared back, and noticed a definite difference in her. Her eyes looked wiser, older, and no matter how long her father may have harped on about the damage to her karma, the princess knew her adventure had strengthened it.

"And just where, young lady, did you disappear to?" her father had said, frowning hard from his throne above.

When she returned the other day, she hadn't at all known how she would go about explaining her absence. Old Man had told her to try honesty, and though she had insisted on confronting her father alone he had insisted on accompanying her. So the two of them had stood before the King, side by side in the Great Hall, neither saying a word. Her father had looked very angry, as had Sir Theomund. Even the Royal Spiritual Advisers looked grave as they whispered advice. Kimbra wished she could have known what the Cards and Crystals had told them. Recalling how uncomfortable it had felt to have her father treat her like a commoner, she also recalled how odd it was when Old Man had spoken.

"Your Highness, if I may...."

"No, you may not! Don't you know enough to kneel before a king?"

Kimbra saw a strange, defiant look in Old Man. Then the surprise: "You know I will never bow to any man, Osryd. I did not bow to your father or to his before him. I understand your desire to drive fear into your insolent daughter, but do not try it with me."

Kimbra stared at the King, she was certain he'd demand the elder's head. Instead, his demeanor lightened, and his voice softened.

"My apologies. You have provided my kingdom with much help. Hauldine owes you much." Then to her: "But you, young lady, gave me quite a scare! Off to your quarters with you to meditate on what you've done! Think on the loss of your karma that this little escapade will cost you. Old Man and I have much to discuss."

So very odd that her father knew the coot. So much odder that Old Man could speak to him as though they were both commoners. The princess had turned to leave then, but not before noticing that Sir Theomund refused to look at her. He was angry, but given time he'd forgive her. But her father was another story.

Yet now, two days later, she sat alone in her room, finally having combed the last knot from her raven hair. No one had come to speak with her, even during meal times no one acknowledged her. Kimbra wondered if they would ever forgive her.

A knock sounded from the door to her chamber. The princess turned from her mirror and, calling them in, a servant girl entered. Kimbra looked directly into her wide, nervous eyes, smiled and rose to meet the young girl.

"Be at ease, servant." Kimbra gently caressed her chin.

"My apologies, your highness. I bring news that Borysko of Northern Umbria is here to see the King. Your immediate presence has been requested in the Great Hall."

Kimbra smiled and rushed from the room.

Forest did not like being escorted by so many guards as if he were a slave. But this was the only way they could accompany the Chieftain of North Umbria in his audience. Kimbra sat by her father, donning her best attire. On her left was an empty chair, beside which stood Sir Athelbeorn and Sir Theomund in full battle dress. Soldiers surrounded the pathway that led to the king.

Every one, except the King, looked at Forest in shock.

"Borysko," his Majesty sounded hopeful, "what brings you to my kingdom?"

"The audience is not mine. I ask it for Forest of the Coastal Mountains."

Forest stepped forward and bowed. Sir Theomund whispered something to his lord, whose brow grew dark. Forest wondered if he'd made a mistake. He had known all along that Hauldine might sentence him back to apprenticeship ... or worse, the whipping. But the vagabond held his head high, and kept his hopes strong. For Dedrik. His friend.

"Your Majesty, I have journeyed from kingdom to kingdom seeking my destiny. Always it eluded me. What I learned was that destiny must find you. I come to ask that you give us refuge."

"Young lad, I have been told that you are a member of the protégé program. Your destiny is to finish your sentence."

"Nay. It is to stop the Chosen One!"

"Stop the Chosen One? The One who will crown me god over Nalor?"

Forest closed his eyes and breathed hard. When he again looked upon the king he said, "This is not a war of swords, but one of spirits. I tell you that it is the All who will be the only god victorious in the end! It will be Him who gives us freedom."

"Freedom? At any cost?" King Osryd rose and walked to him. "My son said that to me, the day before he betrayed me. If I can not trust my own children, then do not expect that I will take your word as honor." He turned, and Forest's face burned. King Osryd walked to his throne, and without facing the room he spoke loudly. "My laws are here to protect my people. Should I bend one, then I place them all into question." He sat and met Forest's dark stare head on. They looked like two warring cobras waiting to strike. "I do not follow a god because I am one! And as such it is in my will that you serve your rehabilitation."

Forest's hands shook. His breathing labored. His brow fell hard. He glared directly at Sir Theomund. "Then I will run again! Would you track me, then try and kill me?"

Sir Theomund shrank from him, but the king turned a fierce shade of crimson and rose.

"Should that be your desire, you shall receive your one hundred whipping!"

They found themselves in stalemate. Forest stared at Sir Theomund, recalling his master's words: *Dreams are hope.* "And what of nightmares?" he whispered.

The guards surrounded him. They shackled him. Forest flushed with despair, and offered no resistance. He had no more wish to go on with this charade. He had had enough of life, friendships, love, compassion ... pity! No longer could he bring himself to go on in a world that condemned one another. Not for anyone. He sank to the ground and realized, not even for

Tully.

"I will honor my sentence." Forest said through grit teeth, felling the room into silence. "One hundred whipping with a poison laced whip. If there be an All and He desires me to live, then I shall. But if you be a god then we are already doomed."

Borysko looked at the king, as had Sir Theomund, Kimbra and Kasmira. They waited for his response, though they knew he had no other option left open to him. And none could blame him.

"So be it. Guards, take him away to the prison. At dawn, he dies."

That night Forest sat in a cold, dark cell, staring out a barred window at an uncaring sky. The stars stared brightly back as did the moon, both igniting Nature's map as if to light the way home. A path, Forest knew, he could never take again.

"Accurse this world! Accurse it to the Abyss of Damnation!"

Forest wrapped his fingers tightly around the bars, uncertain if the voice that echoed in the dark was truly his own. He slid his hands down the cold bars, stopping only when they found a vine that had grown up the cell.

"Is the Creation truly dead? Or was it just a god made from human desire?"

Forest turned his back on the vine. He slid down the side of his cell, until he landed on the dirt floor. He pressed his palms against the ground, feeling the dry mud between his fingers. And that was all he felt. Curling into a tight ball, he shivered. He closed his eyes and prepared for sleep, no longer certain if he was awake, knowing that when he succumbed to slumber nightmares would besiege him. But he no longer knew how to distinguish when the nightmares began and when they ended. Tonight, unlike any before it, his dreams had died.

And come sunrise his soul would join them.

King Osryd sat in his chambers alone, save for a jug of wine. His head thumped and spun, and he knew he had already indulged in far too much. But his thoughts, at least in relation to his sight, were still clear. King Osryd stared at the heavy violet drapes that hung over his window in hopes they might steady his vision. He rose from his seat, braced his palms against his chamber walls to steady himself, and stumbled. He slowly made his way to the window. When he secured his balance, Osryd thrust open the heavy curtain to reveal a clear night sky.

"Young vagabond, why do I see in you my son. And now why do I feel that I must lose him a second time?"

Resting his bulky body against the window ledge, his eyes followed a trail that had been left behind by a shooting star across the black ether.

"Was Terrell right? Am I just a man?"

The rooster's call brought with it a familiar scene. Forest stood by the executioner's pole, and guards strapped his wrists to its top. He looked into the crowd to where Borysko, Sir Theomund, and Kasmira all watched. Even Old Man had returned. Just in time to see him die. Sir Theomund watched stoically, but turned his head whenever Forest tried to meet his stare. A large crowd gathered, each one coming to watch entertainment. Perhaps, it is not such a terrible thing to die.

The whip cracked above him. He waited for its descent, stood proud and vowed that if this was his time to die he would do so in defiance of those who had wished to break him. Surely, he could find honor in that!

Forest flinched from the first strike.

Flinched, but did not shriek.

He would give them no satisfaction in seeing his pain. Only in watching him die, an empty sacrifice so they would learn.

The lashes counted ten ... twelve ... the pain rose steadily. He ignored the warm sensation his blood brought throughout his back. He also ignored the taste of bile that mixed with the saliva in his mouth. He closed his eyes, and ignored the pounding in his temples. Forest refused to fall.

The lashes counted thirty ... thirty-one ... Forest opened his eyes. A tunnel appeared ahead of him, and at its end was a brilliant white light. A voice beckoned him to enter. The warm air welcomed him, and the pain hurt him no more. He wondered why the poison had acted so quickly, and why he could no longer defy it. His spirit floated toward the light, and he barely heard the crowd cheer as his body fell.

The lashes reached forty ... forty-one ... From amidst the brilliant white light Forest heard the execution still being carried out. He wondered how he could have survived so long in such a cruel world. He basked in the white light's love, and wished he could have found death sooner. Then, above the lash's sounds, he thought he heard someone sobbing. A woman.

Then a voice, faintly familiar.

And he recalled the voice. It was a man named Borysko to whom it belonged.

A man who hated him.

"He's fallen! Stop the whipping!"

Forest, confused at the compassion from the Umbrian, heard the woman yell: "Please Forest! Don't give up!" Kasmira she was called.

He stopped floating toward the white light. He wondered what to do. Go forward and die, or live and ... what?

Then a hand pulled him away from the light, the warmth, the love itself.

"You do not belong there!" the Voice said.

Forest turned and stared into horrible crimson eyes!

Kasmira fell to her knees, sobbed, and prayed fervently to the All. She begged Him for Forest's life, pleaded his execution end in vain. But, as the lashes neared eighty, she knew that her god had made His decision. He had made His decision long ago.

Old Man knelt beside her, and gently caressed her back. "Have you lost faith so easily?"

"No." She sobbed harder. "The All knows what is best."

"Then wipe away those tears, Kasmira. Wipe them away, and look!"

Kasmira lifted her head. The executioner called out ninety lashes.

Forest opened his eyes.

The executioner called out ninety-five.

Forest stood.

The executioner called out one hundred.

Forest survived.

Kasmira looked into the heavens and cried out in thanks to the All.

Forest also looked up into the heavens. Eyes wide, and breaths heavy.

Pain. Forest lay against a fallen oak, and his body screamed: "Pain!" Closing his eyes he cleared his mind of the fog born from both poison and Death. He thought on his vision. The White Light, the Dark Voice. Those crimson eyes had bore into him with such evil. They were so cold. Yet that brilliant White Light so far down the tunnel had beckoned with such warmth. Such peace. Forest opened his eyes and looked at the myriad of colors on the autumn leaves. The Creation was preparing for sleep. Or was it obeying the Law of a higher god?

Forest closed his eyes again. He meditated on his first execution in Hauldine when he had thought his god had abandoned him. Or that it had simply never existed. A leaf landed on his forehead, waking him from his thoughts. He took that leaf into his hands, held it before him and examined it closely. Then, crumpling it, he watched as the wind carried away the dust. Could a god turn to dust?

Footsteps crunched through the dry, fallen leaves. He did not stir as the person approached, for he knew that whomever it was they did not come to enslave him. Forest knew, even before the voice had sung, whom it was that had come.

"Kimbra said I might find you here." Kasmira sat beside him, holding out herb to show that she had brought him recourse from pain.

Forest met her misty eyes. He reached out and caressed her scarlet cheeks, knowing she had wept for him. Her sorrow of his near death had equaled her sorrow of Dedrik's. Forest felt his face draw tight and his vision stray into the distance.

"Shouldn't you be figuring out our next move?" he asked.

"Old Man seems to think we should journey to Peacehaven." She started to cry. "I thought I lost you."

He met her scarlet-rimmed eyes, and reached out to wipe away a fallen tear. His body shook. He was uncertain why he had reached out to her. But pulling her close he wrapped his arms around her. It felt good to embrace her.

"I don't know why I say the things I do. Fear, perhaps."

"What are you afraid of?"

"That you will learn something of me that will drive you away. For good."

"Then hide nothing more from me, give that fear to me."

"I cannot give that fear to you, but I can," Forest paused. Taking a step back from her he smiled. "I emerged to stare at a crossroads in my life."

"Tell me what you see down each path?"

"At the first one's start, I see myself with revenge. And at its end, I still see only revenge."

"And the other?"

"At the beginning, I see the All."

"And at its end?"

Forest pulled her close. "I see no end. I want this God in my life, I want you in my life."

As the setting sun bid adieu to a world on the brink of war they kissed.

Kasmira praised the All for His blessing.

Forest pleaded with the All to come into his heart.

Chapter Twenty-two

Terrell stood high atop a mountain crag. He looked down at the valley beneath him, and was alone. Every sun set and rise had made him miss Lightning and Kyrie, but he understood that to know freedom he had to love, and to know love he had to be free. And for him to appreciate either, he had to lose both. Terrell basked in the strong Protecteur winds and smiled at the faint scent of smoke from below. He knelt, stared hard at the village that lay in the dell's midst, and waited for the sun to begin its fall towards the horizon. Once again the Wild stood for freedom. And freedom for all it would be.

At any cost.

Terrell began his walk toward the village with only his sword by his side for aid. He thought on the story that Alviss had told him, of the woman called Andras whom he loved. More so, Terrell recalled the love borne so deeply within the wizard's spirit, and the despondence laden on his soul. "Wyborn" had been the name given as the man who dared demand enslavement. The one who had taken away her choice to love Alviss freely.

Terrell neared the village and noticed a group of young warriors. As well, he noticed a group of elders working nearby. The young men saw him approach, as did the elders. Both stopped what they were doing to come together and meet the stranger on the open road. The Wild let them come to him. He considered drawing his sword, but did not. He scanned the people and tried to determine which might by Wyborn. He saw one who matched the description, charred face and all.

"I come to champion Wyborn!"

"Then you come in vain," their chieftain answered.

"I come on behalf of Alviss the Great Wizard to champion Wyborn for the 'and of Andras."

The chieftain smiled. The others laughed. The one Terrell thought might be Wyborn looked to the leader. He nodded. The charred faced man walked close to the Wild. They stood at about the same size as each met the other with a fierce glare. Terrell's blood boiled for battle, his mouth tasted bile, and it was all he could do to stop himself from attacking.

Even more maddening was that Wyborn did the same.

"Andras is mine. I won her at the Choosing."

"If she be a slave to you, then I will champion for 'er freedom."

"You will champion for nothing. Andras is mine and I have wed and bed her!"

Terrell drew his sword. "Andras will be free! Free to make 'er own choice." Then, nearly in a whisper: "At any cost."

The men behind Wyborn drew their weapons. Wyborn laughed. "You and what army will set her free?"

"You may feel cowardice against my challenge, but I feel none 'gainst yours! Numbers do not scare me."

"Should I remember I will have Andras inscribe that upon your grave marker."

Only the howling wind dared come between them, its yell telling Terrell that enough words had been spoken. Now had come the time for action. Freedom for all, at any cost.

Terrell advanced. Then stopped. He heard a whinny behind him. The Wild glanced over his shoulder, scanned the horizon and thought his senses had turned mad. All he saw were the mountains, and nothing more. He turned back to Wyborn, again advanced, but this time he not only heard a whinny but also the bellows of North Umbrian war horns! Terrell scanned the mountains. This time he saw men dressed for war standing on the slopes.

The fallen heir also saw, running toward him, Lighting and Karel.

He turned back to Wyborn.

"Look about you, Slave Master! Look about you and choose what will be written on your grave marker!"

Wyborn drew his sword and attacked. Terrell met trained skill with honed experience. They clashed high and low, steel meeting flesh hungrily. All about them, the North Umbrian army met the small Protecteurian village. The surprise of sudden war flashed across Wyborn's face, and seizing the moment Terrell thrust his sword hilt into his adversary's nose, kicked his ankles hard, and knocked him to the ground. The Wild pressed his sword tip against Wyborn's throat, and glared into his frightened eyes.

"Such an easy thing for the strong to triumph over the weak. Isn't it?"

"Kill me if you will."

"So much bravado. Nay, Wyborn. You will live. You will live to know that this victory belongs to Alviss the Wizard." Terrell turned to Lightning. "Trusted friend, let us go and set a slave free!"

Andras scrubbed the floor, unaware that war was waged so close by. The brush in her hand felt heavy, much the way that shackles might feel. The corrosive soap that ate away at the muddy floor stank, and filled the home with a scent that had become to her that of captivity. On the walls around her hung tapestries depicting her people's history of male dominance over their women. "Their" women. The tapestries portrayed their prejudice towards those who were weaker. Even toward the wizards, wizards such as Alviss.

Andras stifled a tear. She dipped her brush back into the cold, soapy water and recoiled at its nip on her tender skin. She thought about Alviss, wondered how he might be. She spoke a prayer for him, and hoped he at least might have found an end to misery. As she took the brush from the soapy bucket and slapped it upon the wooden floor, the door opened.

Someone walked around the room until he had come to stand before her. Andras continued to clean. Tears rolled down her cheeks and into the bucket. She held her legs together tightly.

The man knelt, breathed steadily and powerfully, and spoke: "You are the one called Andras the Chosen?"

"I am."

The man placed a gentle hand on hers. Andras stopped cleaning. She looked up, met the iron gaze and wondered who this might be. He stared at her through dark sunken eyes that looked like a beast's ebony pools, and though his smile met her with kindness, his unkempt beard masked that kindness like the night storm did a full moon. She wondered what he intended to do.

"I am called Terrell the Wild. I am champion for Alviss the Wizard."

Andras broke into a fit of sobs and threw her arms around the stranger. "Is he here?"

"Nay. But should you so desire, I shall take you with me to find 'im."

"I desire! By the Sun, I desire!"

Terrell left the house with Andras, where Karel waited outside with Lightning.

"How did you know to come?" Terrell asked.

"After you left, the Krim 'Tiak were met with reinforcements. Some of us escaped, but most were taken as slaves. Many were sacrificed. We wandered the world looking for you. Your beast found us, and brought us to you. You have a strange kinship with one another."

"Strange?" Terrell walked to face Lightning. Shame fell over him and he was unable to meet the beast's eyes. "I wish this whole world could find in it, such strangeness."

As Alviss rode between Aloysia and Kolenka, he no longer felt trepidation to the quest ahead. With their differences set aside, they were able to concentrate on the task at hand; that is, to protect the Chosen One from the Movement so he can prepare man's way to become a god. Unencumbered by personal chaos ... except ... he still had not said anything about the Movement's acquisition of the tools. He wondered what the others would think should he suggest confronting their enemy.

Then, as if to respond to his questioning, Ardal said, "You know, we could be of much greater service to the Chosen One."

"How is that?" Kolenka's intrigue hadn't sounded feigned.

"Well, rather than wait for the Chosen One at the Abyss of Damnation, why don't we first gather his tools."

"Perhaps *she* already has *her* tools!" Aloysia commented.

Ardal ignored her. He said to Kolenka: "Who's to say the Movement isn't doing just that?"

Aloysia stared at Ardal. Then she said: "Because only the Chosen One can enter the Gate to Earth! Only she can enter to get the Eye."

Ardal stopped his mount. "Either way, the Chosen One needs all the artifacts. How will ... *he* acquire them from the Movement without us?"

Aloysia stopped her steed. She turned it to face Ardal. "I'm sure that *she* has a plan. Saving the world does, after all, take some thought."

Ardal turned red. When he spoke he did so softly. "Our job is to wait by the Abyss of Damnation until the Movement tries to interfere. Then we subdue them, and let the Chosen One complete *his* task."

"All except the his part, yea."

"Again the confrontation. So be it. Let's confront one another. The original Chosen One, Forester Renrock, was a man. Therefore, it stands to reason, that the next Chosen One will also be male."

"You ignore the fact that Renrock succumbed to the Nameless God. Do you think the Life Force will slip twice?"

"If the Chosen One were a woman, only a tirade of gossip would get accomplished!" The Umbrian brandished his hammer. "The Chosen One needs to do more than just talk about what should be done!"

"What are you implying?"

Alviss saw where this conversation was headed. Quickly riding between them he waved his arms to silence them. "Friends! I thought we were going to put our differences aside!"

"Out of the way, wizard," the two replied in unison.

"Nay! And if this bickering continues, I shall be forced to throw another mishap fire spell! Do you remember the last time I tried that?"

Kolenka dismounted. "No way am I ending up on my butt."

Suddenly they all laughed, and like a cool breeze bringing rapture to a hot summer day, the joke relieved the tension between them.

"I apologize, Ardal," the elf said.

"Perhaps if we concentrate less on the Chosen One's gender, we can concentrate more on how to help ... this non gender-specific person."

"When I consider it, perhaps it is best to confront the Movement now, and not later."

Chapter Twenty-three

As Forest rode with his allies over the Peacehaven prairies thoughts of Tully and his village burdened him. He now accepted that the simple life he had once led would never return, it had died in the flames that consumed his village. No longer did the memories of his past, his master and childhood, seem his own. It was as if someone had magically implanted them into his mind for cruel torture. He was quite uncertain who "Marcus" had ever been.

Forest looked past his grim thoughts to see Peacehaven's capital close in the horizon. As well, he saw a single tree that lay alone on a high hill crest. He wondered how the strange looking tree could have garnered his attention, just then realizing how engrossed in his thoughts he had become.

He rode next to the lone tree, stopped his steed and examined it. The oak stood as tall as three grown men standing feet on shoulders, and a berth enough to house at least a dozen as wide. As though it were a home, the oak brandished an odd metal door, and above it hung a shingle swinging in the breeze. On the shingle, strange words in a language ancient and forgotten had been written.

"What is this?" Forest asked.

Old Man rode the hill to stand beside him. "That, is legend personified."

Forest perked his eyebrows. "What legend?"

Kasmira fell in beside them and examined the strange placard. "It is said that this is the last Gate leading to the world called Earth. Only the Chosen One may enter."

Forest scoffed.

"This is where the second Eye is guarded. When the time comes for the Chosen One to open the Gates of Hell, he'll go through this way and retrieve the Eye."

"Seems logical to me that if you want to stop this Chosen One from opening Hell, one of us should get that key first."

"Only the Chosen One can open the door," Old Man said.

"Aye. And only the Chosen One could find the first Eye, remember? This is Man's Prophecy, not the All's. It is meaningless."

Old Man took out his pipe and searched his robe for his tobacco pouch. "Are you brave enough to risk it? Or are the words you speak just that, words? How much faith have you found in the All?"

Forest didn't know. But: "I would risk it."

Kasmira rode her steed between him and the Oak. "Only the Chosen One can open the door!"

"I have heard all I can take. 'Only the Chosen One!' Bah! Perhaps if we stopped putting faith in humanity and more into the god we follow, we'll have a better chance for success."

Old Man finally found his tobacco, took it out and started packing his pipe. "If you have so much faith in the All, perhaps you should quit scoffing and act." Lighting the pipe he looked at Kasmira. "And if you worry so greatly for him, perhaps you should go with him."

Kasmira glared hard at the elder. Forest dismounted and walked to the ancient oak. Grasping the handle he cringed at its hot touch. A strange fear passed into him from the handle, filling him with a terror he had never known. He wondered how wise his actions were, turned and saw Borysko watching. No way could he back out now.

"You coming Kasmira?" he asked.

Kasmira dismounted reluctantly, walked to the Oak and stood beside him. She also grabbed the handle. Forest saw the fear in her eyes, and hoped he masked his better. Placing his hand on hers, they opened the door together. Inside was a long tunnel, and at its end another door. The vagabond entered first with his partner following behind. When they came to the second door, he grabbed the handle and experienced the same hot sensation. He looked at Kasmira.

"How about we do this together?" he said.

She placed her hand over his, and again he felt her tremble. As the door opened, he was glad that if Death awaited them he would find it with her by his side. Forest thanked the All, without realizing he had done so, for bringing her into his life. Then, looking through the doorway into the world outside, he prayed for their deliverance.

A barren dessert lay before them like a soul longing for its rest. Wind, as putrid as the depth of a grave, drove sand swirling into miniature tornadoes, howling from within them as if they were snouts of wolves. The sun beat down as crimson as an angered demon, and it baked the world so hot that steam rose from the grainy surface. There were no lakes, no rivers, nor any streams. No trees, no grass, nor even cacti. Only a wail from a beast not far off indicated that this world was not void of life.

Forest released Kasmira's hand and stepped out into the sand, unaware that his feet sank several inches. "Everywhere I go, I see the Creation laid waste."

Kasmira left the Oak and stood beside him. Her nose cringed and her eyes darted everywhere. "It is said that the Earth followed itself as a god and was destroyed by its own evil."

As the hollow wail echoed, ever closer this time, Forest took his companion's hand and said, "If Hell is worse than this, evil is cursed beyond what man can understand."

He pointed toward what appeared to be a road of fused rocks, and as the sun descended they journeyed toward it. The crimson from the sun bled into the sky, creating an eerie night obscured only by a yellow moon and stars. In the horizon, where the road ended, a dome of white light hovered above the Earth.

Breaking away from the stars, specks of red, blue, yellow, and green spots scattered, shooting across the ether sometimes swooping close enough to the ground to display their broad, silver wings and pointed beaks. These birds roared rather than sang, and flew so fast they burned the air behind them with a trail of smoke.

Forest gave Kasmira's hand a squeeze and whispered, "Fright is only dangerous when it is not overcome."

She looked at him and smiled, but the ends of her lips quivered.

A man suddenly materialized a score of feet before them. He wore full metal battle dress, though its design was unfamiliar, and a long metal rod strapped to his back. He stepped toward them, drew his stick and pressed the side of his helmet. The visor disappeared to reveal his frown … and that it was a she.

"Who you be?" the stranger asked.

"I am called Forest of the Coastal Mountains. This is Kasmira the Betrayed."

The woman's eyes narrowed. "Huh? Stay silent man, I am speaking to your Controller."

"We seek the Eyes," Kasmira said.

"The Eyes? What's the matter? You two leave your holes before the radiation settled?"

"Radiation?" both Nalorians asked.

"I don't have the time," the stranger raised her stick and it glowed emerald. As one of the strange birds flew overhead it paused, hovered, and flashed a green light from its belly. When that ray disappeared, so also did the woman.

Forest drew his nunchuka and shrank back, holding Kasmira behind him. "We best not tarry," he whispered.

Night had fallen with an eerie red sky when Forest and Kasmira entered a city. The buildings were decrepit, shops had shingles with strange fires inside them, and people, dirty and broken, littered the streets. But it was the signs that captured Forest's attention; the strange lettering confused him. "XXX," "BOOZE CAN" and "PORNOGRAPHY." He didn't know what tongue this was; the woman they'd met earlier had spoken Hauldinian, as was a slogan painted crudely on a wall: BIG BROTHER HAS DIED. LONG LIVE BIG SISTER. SHE IS WATCHING YOU. The people were as decrepit as the buildings they stood outside of, all were male and all appeared ill. A large, dirty vagrant bumped into Forest and asked, "Want some hash?"

"I need information," he said and pushed Kasmira behind him to protect her.

The man smiled, displaying black gums and rotted teeth. "Nothin's free pal. Why not ask yer Controller for a coin."

Forest took out a silver mark from his own belt-purse, confused by the second reference to Kasmira as his "Controller" and examined the man's impoverished state. The Nalorian returned the coin to its place and produced his only gold sovereign. "I'm looking for something called an 'Eye'."

The man took the coin and his eyes grew wide as though all his prayers had been answered. "Never 'eard of yer Eye, but I know a man who would. 'e knows all, more than is healthy for our gender. 'is name is Indigo Anterion. Go to the Great Tower."

Kasmira pointed to a luminous building with a dome on its top. A soft, yellow light shone inside the pole-like structure, but unlike any fire on Nalor it never flickered. Another glow rode the shaft from its bottom to its top, then down again. The vagrant nodded. Kasmira grasped Forest's hand tightly; they looked at one another, and started walking to the strange building.

The structure had two front doors void of any handles. An old conundrum came to Forest's mind, "What if you were trapped in a room without windows or doors?" and he considered how much more frustrating it was to be trapped outside. They examined the entryway and the surrounding wall, but all they found was a black box that moved whenever they did. It made them nervous. Forest sighed and placed both palms against the door. He prayed for strength, this time to no god in particular, but when he pushed the doors swung easily.

Kasmira walked inside and knelt beside him. She offered him her hand and helped him up saying, "How many more strange phenomenon does this world hold?" They stood before a long hall, at the end of which was another set of double doors. Paintings lined the walls of women preaching on pulpits, burning books, and whipping the backs of naked men. The floor was covered by carpet, one red and the other a dull gray. Silver rods, pointing toward the red side, hung diagonally from the ceiling. A group of people waited at the double doors, three men on the gray carpet and three on the red. The ladies were dressed in bright, cheerful reds, yellows, and blues. Their clothes looked aristocratic, but not of a material that existed on Nalor. The men were clad in gray overalls of the same hue as the carpet. They kept their vision locked onto the floor.

A quiet bell rang, and the doors opened to reveal a tiny room. It was empty. The people stepped inside, and the doors closed. Forest made a move to step forward, but Kasmira stopped him. He looked at her.

She said, "The men and women on this world all walk on different sides. Men on gray, women on red. Perhaps we should do the same."

"Aye." Forest nodded and slowly stepped onto the gray carpet. When nothing happened Kasmira stepped onto the red side, and they walked to the double doors. The silver rods followed the vagabond. The bell chimed again, but as the doors opened the room was empty. Both Forest and Kasmira shrank back.

"Must be for executions," Forest said, spotting a stairwell. "Let's see where those lead."

The stairs went on until both Nalorians thought their legs might give out. At its top was another door, this one with a handle. Forest indicated to Kasmira to stay inside the stairwell by pointing to a space behind the door. He turned the knob, opened it, and stepped into the next room. The door swung shut quickly.

The room was filled with men sitting behind boxes that emitted a blue light. They tapped their desks, and had expressions similar to those of broken slaves. Women strolled around them, carrying clubs that hummed, glaring at each man as if to dare him to look back. When they spotted the vagabond shouts filled the room. Not one man looked away from his task to see what the commotion was about. Forest tried the door, but there was no handle on this side. Women surrounded him, a strange word brandishing their breasts: S-E-C-U-R-I-T-Y, and the clubs hummed louder than before. Forest crouched into a fighting stance and drew his nunchuka.

"I have no wish to hurt you," he said.

A woman with short hair said, "Hurt us? Please! Where is your Controller?"

"My what?"

A dark-haired one brushed at Forest's leg with her club, but he leapt over it and swung his weapon at her hand. When it connected with her flesh she yelped and dropped her baton. The rest closed in, but before a fight could erupt Kasmira stepped through the door.

"Hold it open!" Forest shouted, but the exit closed too fast.

The dark-haired one growled, "Keep him on a leash!"

Kasmira looked at Forest who shrugged. She said, "I-uh."

"What do you want?"

"We seek a man named Indigo Anterion," Kasmira said.

"He's not for sale."

Forest said, "We did not come to barter."

"I just wish to borrow him," Kasmira said quickly. She slapped Forest and added, "Don't speak unless I tell you to."

The leader smiled, pleased by the mark left on the man's cheek. "He's just a drone. He isn't skilled."

"I have work that must be done, and I will return him by the morrow. But what business be this yours? Bring me the man I asked for and get to work!"

The women scrambled back to their duties, and the dark-haired one bowed. After she had walked away Forest whispered, "I am a little confused."

"Speak not. At least for now," Kasmira replied as a short, pudgy man with fuzzy hair came to her.

"I am yours to command," he said.

"Then take us to your chariot and let us be off."

The man looked at her and grinned.

As another Great Bird roared through the sky, it left behind it a trail of green smoke. The yellow moon, as it hung to the left, reflected against the bird's body, caressing the desert below in a strange haze. Its eyes were large, black, and empty. They covered most of its beak and spanned as far as the slender wings that did not flap. But the strangest thing about the bird was that its stomach held three people.

Indigo sat at a console, strapped to a chair with cloth binds and metal buckles. With one hand he operated a stick that told the bird to go left or right, with his other he pushed a lever that made it go faster or slower. His legs moved as he pumped pedals, and every so often he'd depress tiny buttons that encased fires of many colors. Kasmira sat in a chair beside him, also strapped to it, and Forest lay in a bed tucked into the bird's rump.

Kasmira stared out through the eyes, speechless at how much this world resembled the Forbidden Lands. She was only vaguely aware that Indigo was staring at her.

"Looks as though your friend might be sick again." Indigo smiled, but Kasmira was silent. "Does this chariot suffice?"

"Aye, that it does."

He laughed. "It has been a long time since I last saw your kind."

"I do not know what you mean."

"Really? Then what was the name of the person who started the Equity War?" Indigo waited for a response, but when Kasmira did not offer one he said, "It's okay. I won't give you away."

"How did you know?"

"Your apprehension at being a Controller. I hate that term."

Kasmira gave him a look that said she was reading him like a complicated book. "You aren't like the other men. They seem...."

"Broken? That I'm not, but I'm also not a human." He paused, as if to take in her surprise. "Don't look so shocked. Don't you have other races in your world?"

"How do you know that I am from another world?"

"Because I am a Descender. My race began at the world's destruction, and will end at its inception. I know history from books, but I know the future from experience."

"World ends? You mean we lose?"

Indigo shrugged. "I don't know. I said my race began when this world ends. Whatever happens after, only God knows."

"How did this world come to know such destruction?"

"The Equity War. Women thought they should govern, men thought it should be them. After the War broke out people diversified into groups of color, sexual preference, economic situation ... bah. You name it."

"Obviously the women won."

"They seized control, but I would hardly call this world a victory. Women, men, color, sexual-preference, it isn't what's between our legs or carried in our skin that makes us evil. It's what's in our hearts."

"Where are you taking us?"

"To the rebels. They're a faction of religious kooks who survived, a group that follows the Life-Force. Their practices here are illegal, but I know of them. I've read their texts, and I know all about the Chosen One. I assume that's why you're here, I mean, if you just came to sight see tell me now."

"That is why we are here."

Even as his words trailed off, Kasmira felt herself growing numb.

Then all went dark.

When next Kasmira could see, her and Forest stood before a steep cliff's base. Forest grasped onto the rock, held his eyes closed and slowly inhaled the putrid air. He cringed, not from the rancid odor, nor from the queasiness that remained from the journey, but because he thought about the Coastal Mountains, the Creation, and his people. He recalled how his god coddled him as a babe, how It nurtured him, and how It had failed him in the end. When Forest exhaled he opened his eyes, and reflected at how much the barren mountain before him reminded him of home.

Here too, his god had died.

"Forest, there's an opening." Kasmira said, waking him from his thoughts. She grasped his hand and, accepting it, he followed her. They walked the length of a short tunnel until they faced a vast, lush dell. From where they stood they could see a village not far off, but a warrior stood between them and civilization. A warrior who looked like he might be from Nalor. He drew a savage-looking sword and said, "Who goes there?"

Forest turned to Kasmira and whispered, "Better let me handle things." Then to the warrior: "I am called Forest of the Coastal Mountains."

"What be your business."

"We seek the Eye."

The warrior glared at him with eyes as strong as an iron fist. Forest crossed his arms and glared back. Time passed like a babe learning to crawl.

The Earth-man said: "I'll get my queen."

He walked toward the village, and disappeared in a shimmer of light. A second later the light rose again, but it was not the warrior who had appeared. This time a young woman with hair as golden as the sun stepped out. Her body was covered with metal plates, as well as with skins from strange beasts. She frowned, and then looked at Kasmira with a smile.

"I am called Tirrace. I lead these people on Earth. I am told you seek the Eye."

"That is correct. We meet you well, friend," Forest answered.

"Friend? You are presumptuous. If you are with the Controllers, then you are no friend."

"I assure you that I follow no Controller."

"Then you will prove your value."

Forest chuckled, looked at the ground and whispered, "Go into the tree ... Get the Eye ... It all sounded so simple." Then to Tirrace: "And what be my test?"

"Show me your left palm."

Forest removed his glove and held up his left, unblemished, palm.

"Now show me your right."

After fitting his left hand back into his glove, Forest removed his right one and held up that palm. On it was his crimson birthmark. Tirrace looked confused.

"Step forward. Hold your palm before me."

The vagabond walked to her and held out his hand. Tirrace reached into her belt purse and took out a golden key, identical to the one Mask had died for, placed it squarely on his birthmark, and waited.

"What's supposed to happen?" Forest asked.

Tirrace snapped away the golden key and stepped away. She held out her hands and a brilliant, shimmering light shrouded her. The glow was so bright that both Nalorians had to look away. When the brilliance dimmed, they opened their eyes to face an army.

Forest drew his nunchuka.

"You will die for this treachery!" Tirrace shouted.

Forest stepped back to stay between Kasmira and the army, but his companion stepped around him to face their enemy.

"You haven't tested me!" she yelled.

Tirrace held up her hand to calm her army. "Indeed I have not. Show me your left palm."

Kasmira removed her glove and brandished her unblemished left palm.

"Now, show me your right."

A tear came to Kasmira's eyes. She removed her right-hand glove and brandished a palm with a crimson birthmark identical to her companion's.

Forest fell back in shock. Tirrace smiled and raised her hands in victory.

"Step forward and bear for me your birthmark."

Kasmira obeyed. Tirrace placed the golden key upon her palm. The mass of people gathered to witness as the mark slowly changed until it no longer resembled a plain circle, but a crimson yin-yang.

Tirrace took away the key, and Kasmira's mark once again became a simple crimson circle.

Kasmira fell to the ground and wept.

Forest had no idea what to do. He walked to her, knelt beside her, and finally held her.

"I had no idea you carried such a burden."

"Then perhaps now you can understand why it is that I need the All so desperately."

"He will take away your burden?"

Kasmira looked at him with eyes like red discs. "He will help me to carry it. Should Death steal my flesh, my spirit will always belong to the All."

Forest held her close. He felt Tirrace also join their embrace. She said, "Chosen One fear not. Take the Eyes and Koontah the sword, and claim your kingdom as a god!"

Forest rose and wished he could speak out. He wished he could call against humanity for erecting their own image in place of the All. He wished he could warn them, tell them of his own god, the Creation, which had died.

But he could not.

He could not because he still did not know what it meant to believe.

At first only silence. And then he said: "We best be off. We have a long journey."

The shimmering light again appeared. Tirrace said, "You may take our Gate, Chosen One."

Forest's brow fell heavy, and he closed his eyes. He did nothing but breathe, and when he opened his eyes he asked, "Where will it take us?"

"To the same Gate that brought you to Earth."

"And I say you meet Death Himself before you get the artifacts!" Borysko stood his ground with battle-axe drawn and ready. He kept Old Man behind him to protect him from the use of his sorcery.

"I don't recall requesting the Chosen One's artifacts. I recall demanding! And considering our numbers, I'd say you're outmatched!"

An elf, Grothian, and wizard all stood poised for battle behind a young

South Umbrian. If Borysko had cared, he might have acknowledged them as a challenge. But his body shook, his blood boiled, and his vision had turned everything crimson. Borysko didn't even notice the door in the tree swing wide. Forest stepped out with Kasmira behind him.

"Perhaps we should even the odds," Forest said, drawing his nunchuka.

"Perhaps we should."

The voice hadn't come from Borysko, or from Forest. Nor had it come from the misfits, nor from Kasmira. Old Man, too, wondered where from the voice had come. A tall, muscular man donning furs of wild beasts stepped up as if from the grasslands itself. Behind him stood a small army of men.

Only the young wizard had run to the strange man. "Wild!" He called him.

"Wizard!" The Wild met his friend in an embrace as he motioned Karel to come by his side. "Karel, take my friend to our guest."

"Aye, Chieftain."

Borysko ran forward to grab Karel by his shoulders. In Umbrian he said, "Chieftain? What treachery is this? I am Chieftain!"

Karel met Borysko's stare with a cold one of equal measure. "And where was our Chieftain when the Krim 'Tiak enslaved half his people?"

"Called on a sojourn by the Nameless God."

"Then decide, Borysko, whether you lead North Umbria or follow this Nameless God."

Borysko let Karel go. He turned his back to the man. The Movement had no idea what had been said between them, but when Borysko looked at Kasmira, Old Man and Forest, he knew they understood the choice placed upon his shoulders. For perhaps the first time since he had shed his swaddling cloth, a tear fell from his eye.

Borysko walked to stand among the Movement. Then he faced Karel once more. In Hauldinian he answered: "My soul belongs to the All. Yours can too, Karel."

Karel hadn't understood the Hauldinian tongue, but he knew its meaning. "I belong, as does North Umbria, to Terrell the Wild." Then he led Alviss away.

Alviss followed the stranger through the Umbrian ranks until they reached a clearing. They stood before a tent. Alviss looked at the Umbrian, wishing he had learned to speak their language. But seeing the Umbrian point at the tent, he gathered he was to go inside. The wizard walked to the tent alone. His hands shook, and he wondered if he should ready a spell. But he didn't.

He trusted The Wild. Trusted him enough to know that no harm would befall him. Standing motionless he grabbed the soft flap of animal skin that acted as a doorway, and slowly opened it. He peered inside and waited for his eyes to adjust to the darkness.

Then he saw her.

Andras had been sitting with her back to the door. Her long, golden locks lay on her as a shawl, and as she turned her head they fell over her shoulders.

Alviss' heart stopped, and then it fluctuated madly.

She rose and smiled; her full reddish lips looked as they had the day they had said fare thee well. Her eyes sparkled when she looked at him.

Alviss tried to speak, but could not.

Andras walked to him, and placed her arms around his shoulders. He closed his eyes and smelled the faint scent of jasmine.

When he opened his eyes, she was still there. He embraced her and wept. "I thought I'd lost you."

"As did I." She, too, wept.

"The Wild brought you to me, didn't he?"

"But do you still want me?"

They broke their embrace only slightly, enough to feel the kindness of each other's lips. "Aye!" was all Alviss could say. At long last in his young life he had no wish to be anyone but himself.

The Movement sat among themselves as the North Umbrian army left with the Chosen One's artifacts.

"What are we to do?" Kasmira asked.

A look passed between her and Forest that only Old Man noticed.

"If they get to Peacehaven, the Chosen One will have won."

Forest rose. He walked to a place where he could see that no one was left behind to spy on them. When he was satisfied, he returned to the group. "I have a plan."

"What?" asked Kasmira.

He met her eyes, and caressed her cheek. A pause, then he whispered, "We will deliver the Chosen One to them."

Chapter Twenty-four

The Umbrian horde stopped marching just a few miles outside Peacehaven's city gates. Alviss stood with Andras, hand in hand, both facing Terrell the Wild. Behind them, what had been left of North Umbria broke out encampments for the coming night. Stars had already broken out in glory, and a cool breeze basked them with a hint of the Peacehaven Flower. Alviss smiled ear to ear as he faced the Wild. He extended his hand.

"If I am made a ruler, I will make you my general."

The Wild smiled as he took the hand offered him. "That would please me ... provided I am allowed extended leaves."

"Then you are leaving immediately?"

"Not until dawn. Tonight, we will camp. Come sunrise, we march to take back North Umbria."

"I owe you everything," Alviss replied. He looked at Andras.

She smiled. "*We* owe you everything."

The Wild breathed heavily, turned from them, and held his head high. His long matted hair blew freely in the wind like a great storm. He walked a bit, with Lightning beside him, and stopped. He never turned, but he spoke: "You owe me nothing. Freedom belongs to us all, at any cost."

And then the Wild returned to his people.

Alviss and Andras both watched after him, thankful they had been so blessed as to have met him.

Then they left for Peacehaven's capital.

Geldin sat on his throne in the Great Hall. As he breathed he winced with pain, then exhaled, and closed his eyes to brunt the discomfort that accompanied the wheezing. He considered the act of breathing a moment, and began it all over again. Over, and over again. Geldin wondered when he could stop. He had been alive for so long now, sustaining what life he had with his magic. But age crept nearer him, ailing his health with every sin.

A servant entered. "They have returned, Wise."

Geldin's eyes grew narrow and white. A light enveloped his aged body, and he sat straight and tall.

"Send them in."

Alviss headed the misfits when they entered the Great Hall. A plush scarlet carpet formed a narrow path from the door to Geldin's throne, and alongside that path soldiers stood at attention, one arm grasped a halberd and the other in salute. Torches sat in golden sconces, separated by tapestries that hung between them. Alviss walked the carpet's length in awe. The others followed close on his heels, also feeling the awe. They only bared the Chosen One's tools, and yet Peacehaven treated them as if they were kings! They stopped before Geldin's throne, dropped to one knee, and held out their bounty.

"We bear the artifacts," Alviss boasted.

"And so you will have your just reward."

The voice hadn't come from Geldin. It had come from behind them, at the Great Hall's entranceway. Where the plush carpet began.

The misfits turned and saw a short hooded man riding a giant wolverine. He climbed off and walked the carpet's length, until he came face to face with Alviss.

"Who are you?" Alviss asked.

The hooded man removed his cowl, and stared into eyes that mirrored his own. "Don't you know me, boy?"

"No, I do not."

And then he did. He knew who stood before him. He discreetly readied a spell.

"You're my father."

Kol the mad broke into a cackle of laughter.

"Indeed I am! Seize them!"

The guards moved in quickly, but Alviss released his magic. A fog of smoke rose to blind everyone but the misfits. They broke into a run, but a blue light flashed and dissipated the chant.

Kol the mad stood with the fog in his hand. He transformed Alviss' spell into an amber rock, and threw the spell back at his son. When the rock hit him, he fell to the floor in shackles. The others stopped running.

"Run!" Alviss yelled to them.

They turned to run again with several soldiers in pursuit.

Kol the mad walked to his son. "You are adept with magic. A boy after my own heart."

"Am I the Chosen One?"

Kol burst into a fit of laughter.

Terrell the Wild felt his blood boil as never before. He stared hard at the misfits who had come running to him only moments ago, retelling to him a story of betrayal.

"And you just left the Wizard there to die?" Terrell had spoken Umbrian without knowing he had done so.

"Easy, Wild." Karel placed his hand on Terrell's tense shoulder. "Had they stayed to battle, they would've all died."

"You are right, Karel. I apologize. What are your plans then, Ardal?"

Ardal shrugged. "We don't know. We thought we were working for the good guys."

Terrell thought a moment. Then: "Perhaps we should trade sides. What of this 'Movement'?"

"They are evil," Ardal said plainly.

"So say the Wizard's captors! I say if they wage a war on Geldin, then we best speak with them."

"Who will go?"

Terrell thought. "Myself, Karel, and you, Ardal." Then, after a pause: "Aloysia, too. We will take her as well."

"Why not I?" Kolenka asked.

"The wingless Grothian will attract too much attention. And Andras, in case you wonder, bears no skills."

"I didn't wonder," she said.

"Good. We will leave right away."

An adventuring party's loud bellows drowned out most of the tavern's revelry. Forest left Old Man and Kasmira alone to seek out a table and lodgings with Borysko. He scanned the tavern to find the owner, but was so near the boastful adventurers he could do little else but listen. Had it not been for the life he had lived he just may have found the tales interesting.

"'Ear ya lookin' fer me." It was the owner, a stoutly, well fed gentlemen, perhaps in his late forties. The muscles around his face were quite animated, even when he wasn't speaking. He leaned over a pot on the floor and spit a wad of black saliva into it.

Borysko leaned over the counter. "We need rooms. One fer men, one fer de lady."

The stoutly owner looked through the smoke at Kasmira. An eyebrow lifted slightly, and the muscles around his mouth stopped moving. "I kin git ya a deal. Fer a 'tr-duction."

Borysko lashed out and grabbed the man with his strong grasp. The Umbrian's skin had turned a deep shade of red as he pulled the owner near. Then, in a voice that Forest had never heard before he said, "You will address de lady wit respect!"

"I'm sorry! I'll go git de keys to yer rooms!"

And then the owner left.

Forest looked at Borysko curiously. He didn't quite understand him, nor was he positive that he wished to. Most of the time he thought Borysko was arrogant, ignorant, and not at all the kind of person who would believe in the All. But then, in times like this, Borysko seemed almost human. The large Umbrian noticed his curiosity.

"What you lookin' at?" he asked.

"I'm trying to figure you out."

"Don't."

"I need to."

Borysko stared hard into his eyes. Then he said: "What for?"

"To know how you forsook your own gods to follow the All."

"'E called me. Same as 'E called you."

"And that's the whole reason?"

"Forest, you have seen this god do de same things as me. De Krim 'Tiak hate life, and love Death. In Protecteur, women be slaves. They sooner spit down man's bloody neck den give him love.

"This nameless god we follow, taught a Krim 'Tiak to love life. Dedrik had great love for life. Then this god taught a woman of Protecteur to love man. When Dedrik died, she wept. More when she thought she lost you."

Borysko turned his back on him, and started to walk away. After a few paces he stopped and turned. For the first time Forest saw true compassion in his eyes.

"You ask why I left my gods to follow de All? I think you should ask yourself why you have not."

And then Borysko walked to the table to sit with Kasmira and Old Man.

Forest stayed by the counter, contemplating his words.

"Need anything else?" The stoutly owner slapped two keys on the counter.

Forest took the keys, and closed his eyes. He breathed heavily for a moment, and then gradually drew his breaths more steadily. When he opened his eyes he said, "Yes. I need an answer."

And then he, too, walked through the crowded tavern to join Kasmira and Old Man.

Kol had been sitting with the boastful adventurer's party long before the Movement had arrived. He didn't like the stories the arrogant adventurer was telling, but honestly this was the only ... apparition he could remember. But, at long last, he found his opening.

He rose from his chair and left his spell. He wormed his way through the crowd until he stood behind Kasmira. Old Man's eyes grew wide, and his brow dropped into a crimson sunset.

"Be gone, vile creature!" he stood and shouted.

Kol laughed. "I am not a demon to be exorcized!"

Kasmira turned and shrieked. Kol said: "Glad to see I'm so well remembered."

Forest and Borysko looked at one another perplexed. Old Man bustled around the table to stand before Kol.

"You have no place here," Old Man growled.

"Then let me say my piece, and I will leave." Kol bowed.

Forest stood and held Kasmira's hand. "What's going on?"

Kol's eyes grew wide. He smiled. "Is this your new man? Hope she pleases you as much as she did me. I must have smiled for a week!"

Forest drew his nunchuka and moved to attack the vile man. Kol casually lifted his hand and threw a blue light that embraced his attacker. He fell to the ground screaming, and the whole tavern was brought to an unnatural silence.

All but the apparition of the adventurer and his companions.

Old Man moved to help Forest ... but what could he do?

Kol laughed. "Go ahead, Old Man. Use your magic!"

Old Man met Forest's pleading eyes. "Forgive me. But I cannot."

Forest yelped in pain. He closed his eyes and whispered, "There is nothing to forgive. You are a man of faith now."

Kasmira rose to face Kol. She stood a foot taller. "What is it you want?"

"I want you." Kol caressed her cheek and ribs. "Or, more accurately, I

189

want your body."

Borysko wrapped his hand around Kol's throat. "You die first!"

"Forgot the other one," Kol said, struggling for air. He waved his hand and had Borysko also lying helpless on the floor in a bluish prison.

Then he bowed to Kasmira. "You have yet to respond to my request. Perhaps if I sweeten the pot?"

"Sweeten the pot?" A tear left her eye.

Kol smirked. "Give yourself to me, and I will return to you ... your son."

Kasmira glared at him suspiciously, unable to speak.

"That's right Kasmira. Our son. I have him, and I will kill him."

"You want me to bed you?"

Kol rolled his head back in a fit of laughter. "No! Was that the reason for these theatrics? I don't want to bed you. Meet me on the city outskirts at midnight. We will make the exchange then."

"What do you want her for?" Old Man asked.

"Because she is the Chosen One." Kol turned to leave the tavern. At the door he stopped. "Almost forgot."

He snapped his fingers and released the spell on Forest and Borysko. They writhed in agony from the lingering pain.

And then Kol left.

Forest closed his eyes. He concentrated, putting the pain into the back of his memory. He breathed more easily now, steady after a time. When next he opened his eyes he was able to stand. Borysko still writhed on the floor, Kasmira was on her knees crying, and the elder consoled her. He saw Terrell coming to him. Forest grabbed a chair and collapsed into it, meeting the Wild's dark gaze.

"Are you to insure that we honor Kol's request?" Forest asked.

The Wild's brow grew dark, and his eyes sank to the table. He sat in the chair across from Forest, and placed his hands in a restless fist. "No. I am here to offer you my aid. We seem to have found a common goal."

"What would you care about Kasmira?"

"Nothing. My interest is with the Wizard."

Forest remembered Kol speaking about Kasmira's son. "All right. But we best not speak here."

The room inside the inn was crowded. Terrell, Ardal, Karel, and Aloysia sat on one side of the hearth and Forest, Old Man, Borysko and Kasmira sat on the other. Forest and the Wild had spent a long time in heated debate over how to rescue Alviss from the Krim 'Tiak's clutches, so much in fact that only two more time candles were left to burn before the exchange.

Kasmira rose to ignite the first of the two time candles. "We only have thirty minutes left." She warned.

Forest closed his eyes and breathed heavily. Then, opening them he said: "Whether you agree to it or not, my plan will still work best."

"It's as though we're giving up!" the Wild said again.

Forest felt Old Man's hand on his shoulder. He turned to him, and met with his compassionate gaze. "Are you aware of what will happen, should you execute your plan?"

Forest nodded and rose. "I am not afraid."

Kasmira walked from the time candles. She left the one she'd last lit at half point and wrapped her arms around her love, holding him tightly.

"What 'bout army?" Borysko glared across the fire at Karel.

The Wild stood between the two men. "I think Borysko should lead North Umbria."

"We follow you!" Karel stood.

The Wild stared at the man, embracing him spirit to spirit. "You never followed me. You followed an idea of me. You hoped I might be a god. If it be a god you seek, then you would do well to listen to this Nameless One Borysko follows. Borysko is, after all, your chieftain."

"And what of you?" Forest asked.

The Wild walked to the window. Kasmira strolled to light the final candle. Terrell sighed. "I will convince Hauldine to join us in battle."

"How will you do that?" Forest asked. "We tried and King Osryd."

"Because I am Terrell, the sole male heir to the throne of Hauldine. Or at least I once was."

"A god?" Aloysia asked.

"A man," the Wild responded in a hushed tone.

Old Man walked to the prince. "I will come with you. Together, we will beseech him."

"And what about the rest of us?" Ardal asked.

Old Man turned to him. "Make the exchange. And may the All bless us in it."

Chapter Twenty-five

Stars danced in the night sky as though for an orchestra. Below them, alone in the desolate city outskirts, Kol the mad rode his giant wolverine. Beside him Geldin stood with his robe blowing in the wind. Krim 'Tiak soldiers surrounded them. In their midst, Alviss lay on the ground, shackled and hurt.

"The Movement approaches," Kol said, pointing toward a small group in the distance.

"We could wipe them out now," Geldin said.

Didzyn growled. "Go back on our word and I will tear out your throat. We promised a fair exchange, not their suicide."

The Movement stopped. A young man carrying nunchuka stepped forward. "Send us Alviss!" he yelled.

"First, send us the Chosen One!"

A pause. Then: "We meet halfway!"

Kol climbed off Didzyn's back, and placed Alviss in his place. The two walked until they met Forest and Kasmira at half-point.

"Release the boy," Forest demanded.

"Not until Kasmira walks to Geldin."

"Why her?" Forest paused. Then he raised his right palm to show his birthmark. "I thought you wanted the Chosen One."

"What kind of trick is this?" Kol demanded.

"Give us the test." Forest hoped that Kol wouldn't notice that he held his breath.

"What test?"

Forest relaxed. "I fight Renrock style. Who, but the Chosen One, could do that? Send a Krim 'Tiak to fight me!'"

"And do you think you cannot be defeated in mortal combat?" Kol lifted an eyebrow.

"I can kill any man you send to me."

Kol laughed. "So be it then! But you will fight no man, you will fight Didzyn. Then Kasmira will be ours."

"But I am a man," Didzyn growled.

"You were never a man, Didzyn." Kol waved his hand and a blue light formed in a ball above his palm. "Nor shall you ever be! Go fight, or I will kill you now."

Didzyn glared through eyes as scarlet as a sun that only sets over the Forbidden Lands. "As my master wishes."

The giant beast and Forest left to square off. When they were far enough the beast circled his enemy hungrily.

"The prophecy says nothing of physical prowess," Didzyn said.

"Why didn't you give me away?"

"Perhaps I like the sport..." Didzyn leapt with claws bared. Forest ducked beneath the beast. He landed a kick in its chest. Didzyn fell to the ground, rolled back to his feet, and then leapt once again. This time it managed to strike Forest with a claw across the cheek. Forest struck with his nunchuka, striking it also in its cheek. Then Forest leapt onto the beast's back, wrapping the chain around its neck.

"Why don't you fight for real?" Forest asked.

"How do you know I do not?"

"Because I still live. I fight men, not beasts."

"I have been a beast of madness for all my life. I became this thing for reasons of power. Now all I wish is to find peace."

"I never met a beast like you."

"You and I are not completely unalike."

"I cannot murder!"

"This is not murder. This is compassion. Kill the beast, and the man in me shall live."

Forest felt a tear leave his eye. He pulled hard on the nunchuka's chain and snapped Didzyn's neck. As the body turned limp he climbed off.

"We have our Chosen One!" Kol yelled.

Forest returned to Kasmira. "Release Alviss first."

Kol snapped his fingers, and the shackles on Alviss disappeared. Then Kol said to Forest: "Now, you will come with me."

Forest turned to Kasmira. He held her close. She wept, and Forest wished he could ease her pain. But he knew that he already had.

"I love you," he whispered.

"And I, you."

"We will meet again, Kasmira. Do not weep for fear of us parting eternally."

Kasmira broke their embrace enough to meet his eyes. "I weep for every day that we will be apart."

They kissed.

"Let's go!" Kol demanded.

Forest left Kasmira, and gave himself up to the Krim 'Tiak.

Chapter Twenty-six

Forest refused to die. Throughout the journey the Krim 'Tiak had beaten him often, and each time he had refused to die. But now as he faced the two iron gates to Hell, embedded deep within Mount Armageddon, Forest knew that his captors had never intended to kill him.

His refusal to die, this time, had been in vain.

A geyser erupted near him. The steam scorched a soldier and sent him reeling with pain. The Krim Tiak's masses flooded the cavern like a parasite, and those who could not fit inside littered the slopes outside. Soldiers knelt with their heads down, except for the unholy attendants who had readied him for the ritual.

For the first time in his life, Forest admitted to himself that he was afraid.

A dark laughter resounded in the silence. Laughter challenged only by the eruption of geysers.

Forest knew the laugh belonged to Kol the mad. The father of Kasmira's child.

He hated the evil in that man.

Two unholy attendants left his side. They walked to the two iron doors, each holding a key. The Eyes. He watched with fear as they inserted their respective key into the keyholes in unison. Then, as one, they pried the doors apart.

Tormented screams from Hell's fiery depths displaced the silence, nearly bringing madness to his ears. Forest stared deep into the Abyss, bared the searing pain of the fire, and saw a man.

Death.

This time, Forest knew, he was no apparition. This time the Death who stared back at him was real.

Again, Kol the mad's laughter rose above the tormented screams.

Joined by Death's laughter.

The unholy attendants fell to their knees. Death came as near to Hell's Gates as he could.

"Welcome to Judgment, Forest."

"My Judgment is not with you. Mine will be with One who will judge even you."

"No one will judge me," Death yelled. "Come, Forest. Denounce the Movement and I will spare your soul."

Forest no longer shook with fear. He looked at the Evil masses about him, and no longer felt much of anything.

Except, perhaps, pity.

"No, Death. I joined the Movement and found the All. In my end you might take my body, but my soul belongs to the All."

"You will not survive this prison, boy. Prepare him!"

The unholy attendants strapped strange armor onto him. Strange armor that covered his entire body.

When they had finished, they walked him to the gateway.

Forest stood, stoically, saying a silent prayer.

Then he walked into the flames and met Death in Hell.

Pain.

Searing pain as never before.

First his memories shed from his mind, and then his thoughts.

Forest held his eyes closed. When he opened them he discovered that his soul had left his body.

His memories and thoughts returned to him.

And as they did, Death entered his physical form.

To walk from the flames.

"Where is your All now?"

A brilliant white light beamed from above, and everywhere. A portion of the Light entered Hell, and the flames retreated from it. Forest became basked in it, and the pain he felt was no more.

Then a voice: "Come from that eternity, Forest."

Forest rose. A man stood next to him, one imbued with brilliance and wearing a flowing white robe that moved as though it were alive.

Forest met his face and looked into the eyes of Dedrik the Fallen.

"Are you ... the All?" Forest stuttered.

"No, Forest." Dedrik smiled and embraced him. "I am a messenger. He sent me to retrieve you. Come and begin life, anew!"

Death shrank from the Light. "No! He belongs to me!"

Dedrik led Forest through a tunnel, but before they disappeared he said, "Nothing belongs to you."

"This world belongs to me!" Death yelled into the darkness as he drew Koontah. "This world belongs to me! Blood surges through these veins, and with it I shall wreak murder through this world! Murder by my hands."

Death leapt into a blinding circle, intending to bring the sword's blade onto an attendant's neck. But when the blade reached an inch from its victim, it stopped. Death was unable to complete the kill. Again he thrust the sword and failed. Time and time again, he could not murder. It was as though an invisible barrier had encased all Life.

"What trick is this?" Death yelled. "I cannot murder with this body!"

Kol the mad's eyes widened and his mouth fell open.

"Sir," It was a Krim 'Tiak captain. "The armies of North Umbria and Hauldine wait to attack."

Death ran to the cavern's entrance and stared down upon the armies. He saw Terrell the Wild and his father leading Hauldine with Old Man to advise them. Borysko and Ardal lead a united Umbria with Karel to advise them.

The Krim 'Tiak waited to see what Death would command.

"To war then!" It called, sending the demons marching down the slope.

Epilogue

Tully lay motionless in his dank cell, cringing from the Forever Sleep's icy touch on his soul. He had spent a decade at least in slavery. It had been more than half that time since he had last seen Marcus. A week ago, he had first felt the sickness upon him. The same sickness that had already taken half his camp. That which now threatened to take him.

The village had all but given up on Marcus the Avenger. All but Tully. He had never given up. He had, in fact, begun to pray to this god of which Marcus had spoken.

The god with no name.

The past half-decade had been lonely. But not nearly as lonely as the half-decade prior.

He had prayed to this Nameless God seldom at first. Then, gradually, he had spoken to Him until he did so at every available moment.

Now, closing his eyes, Tully prayed for the last time.

Then a voice: "Tully, open your eyes."

Tully obeyed the voice.

Marcus stood before him, clad in a long white robe. Around him was a showered bright light.

"Come brother. Let us both go to Him."

Tully rose and the sickness washed away. He never looked behind, but left his body to run into his friend's waiting arms.

Together, a gift from the All, they would be able to fight the war side by side.

* * * * *

Printed in the United States
1339900005B/301-348